Falling for Prince Charles

(A VERY DIFFERENT KIND OF ROMANCE)

LAUREN BARATZ-LOGSTED

DIVERSIONBOOKS

Also by Lauren Baratz-Logsted

The Sister's Club

Jane Taylor Novels
The Thin Pink Line
Crossing the Line

Johnny Smith Novels
The Bro-Magnet
Isn't is Bromantic?

Diversion Books
A Division of Diversion Publishing Corp.
443 Park Avenue South, Suite 1008
New York, New York 10016
www.DiversionBooks.com

For more information, email info@diversionbooks.com

First Diversion Books edition January 2016.
Print ISBN: 978-1-62681-723-4
eBook ISBN: 978-1-62681-722-7

For Laura Duane:
Thank you for bringing
Prince Charles to life.

1999

A Very Good Year, All Things Considered

… The daisy, by the shadow that it casts,
Protects the lingering dewdrop from the sun.

"To a Child" (Written in Her Album)
~ William Wordsworth

Part One
It's All Down the Drain

A fool must now and then be right, by chance.

"Conversation"
~ William Cowper

April, 1999

1

As Daisy Silverman squatted in front of the toilet bowl, first depressing the flush lever and then watching as the milky outgoing spiral removed the mildew and replaced it with fresh water, the thought occurred to her for at least the thousandth time that if the fickle hand of fate hadn't cast her as a cleaning lady, working in wealthy households and offices in Westport, Connecticut, she would have made a perfectly lovely Princess of Wales.

This was a fantasy that Daisy had entertained off and on since 1981, the same year that the late Princess Diana had first *become* Princess Diana. And to this day, eighteen years later, whenever she thought about it, Daisy still thought that she could have done the job better.

Oh, sure, Daisy had loved the late Princess, would have said that she loved her more than anybody. Well, even Daisy was aware enough not to say that; she did know that Diana's family and friends had surely loved her more. But Daisy could legitimately claim to love her easily as much as anybody who had never met her, and that was plenty. So if Daisy felt a little competitive with a dead princess that she had loved beyond reason, what matter that? After all, there were some compelling reasons for making a comparison between the two women.

Just like the woman who had possessed the most photographed profile in the world, Daisy had a genius for making the kind of seemingly interested, throwaway comment that left others feeling a little cheerier about their own lot in life. Although even Daisy had felt that the Princess had been pushing things a bit several years back, when she had blithely informed a widow on the dole with a flat full of small children, "Oh, yes, I just love those microwave pizzas too. Whenever the Heir and the Spare start to look a little peaked, I just nuke a couple of them in the palace micro, and we're all set to go skiing in Klosters or windsurfing on Necker."

Amazingly enough, however, the Dole Woman had failed to take offense at the patronizing lie but, rather, had caved as totally to those unbelievably blue eyes as had hundreds before her.

"Cor, tha' one's such a charmer, she is," the woman had reportedly told her neighbors after the Royal visit. "An' it's simply loverly to think tha' she's got the same problems we all do. I tol' 'er, I says, 'If that little 'un, 'Arry, gives you any troubles—cause tha' one do look like 'e'd be a caution, don't 'e?—you do what I does with me Darren: you thrash 'im one good with the fry pan. Works for me, it do. An' Darren don' seem any the worse for it.' Yeah. Tha's exactly wha' I tol' 'er, I did. An' wouldn'cha know it? She just kept smilin' away, that smile of 'ers just gettin' bigger an' bigger all the time."

Sharing the same birth week in 1961—the first of July for Diana, while Daisy's was a jingoistic Fourth—only added fuel to the mental fires that kept telling Daisy that the two of them had been separated at birth. It was just too bad that the separation had landed one of them in palaces, while the other was doomed to a life inhaling cleaning fluids.

Truth to tell, the Silvermans, all prototypical underachievers, had always been involved in the septic business. In fact, the claim could be defended that, at any given moment in recorded human history, there had been at least one Silverman somewhere on the face of the planet who was up to his or her elbows in some form of toilet water.

But while her late father, Herbert, had been the founding genius behind Silverman's Stupendous Septic Service—or SSSS, for short—Daisy's own misguidedly independent, septic-seeking running shoes had led her to become a lower-echelon employee of an enterprise called the Klean Kottage Klub. In a fast-moving society, where a need to make abbreviations for the sake of saving time was often of paramount importance, the resultant acronym of KKK often caused Daisy to experience the imaginary heat of flames on her face and to worry that she was somehow aiding an Aryan cause. Not to mention that the recent vast proliferation of businesses across the land exhibiting that worrisome triple K in the shingles hanging over their doors made her think that perhaps the Neo-Nazi movement in the country was even larger than anyone suspected.

Actually, though, when Daisy thought about incidents such as the one involving the Dole Woman, it reaffirmed the idea in her mind—similar to assembly-line workers at Chrysler assuming that they could market rings around Lee Iacocca—that, if given the opportunity, she could make a far better go of it than the Princess had done.

Following the shifting of the royal spotlight during the events of December of '92, Daisy's own sentiments concerning the Princess and her then-estranged husband had undergone a gradual but equally seismic shift of their own. Where previously she had been in a state of complete empathy with the world's favorite beleaguered blonde, the ensuing years had altered this somewhat. Gone was the image of the poor waif, tossed in a turbulent sea and borne along by unfriendly currents beyond her control.

Take all of the furor about Charles's purported dalliances, for just one example. Some people reacted to this as if it were in some way out of the ordinary, a big surprise, the stuff of scandals. And while Daisy, having been reared with as fine a sense of values as the next person, didn't condone wholesale infidelity, a large part of her had begun to wonder: Just what exactly did some people expect? After all, if you were willing to live in a country that still chose to refer to itself as a monarchy, it seemed unreasonable to demand that you be treated to a fair and equitable lifestyle. It seemed to Daisy that the British Monarchy was the ultimate pyramid corporation, and that all of Diana's problems had started with the erroneous assumption that she could blithely leapfrog her way to the pinnacle, when even peasants, even commoners, even Americans like Daisy knew that there was only ever one person at the top of any pyramid—and that in England, that person's name was Queen Elizabeth II.

For some reason that she couldn't quite put her finger on, over the years Charles and Diana had come to put Daisy in mind of Lucy and Ricky Ricardo. And while Daisy had always loved and even idolized Lucy's spunk, it had been Ricky whose plight had commandeered the lion's share of her sympathies.

It could be argued that Charles, unpopular as the concept might be, had performed a lot more graciously under circumstances that had afforded him a lot less choice. Daisy was constantly amazed when someone would comment on one of Charles's spoiled-seeming behaviors as if it were somehow surprising or proof of something. The only thing that really amazed her about him was that, with his upbringing, he did not run through life harum-scarum, waving a sword and demanding beheadings right and left.

And it must be perfectly awful to have to go through life with the belief that no one would ever like, let alone love, you if it weren't for the sheer accident of your birth. Which brought her back to—

"*Dai*-SEE!"

Just like those old black-and-white movies, Daisy thought, when Henry Aldrich's mother used to scream, "*Hen*-REE!"

Daisy was just giving the sunken tub a final swipe—preparing to engage in her all-time favorite fantasy where it was *her* winning smile that was making the masses feel temporarily more satisfied with their lot—when she heard the strident punches of Mrs. Reichert's voice shouting to her from the master bedroom. Straightening stiffly, Daisy caught sight of herself in the wall-to-wall mirrors.

The mirrors were of the expensive kind that only the truly wealthy could afford, the kind that took a good ten pounds off of a woman's figure without having to go on any punishing extensive stays at a spa. This had the unfortunate funhouse effect of making Daisy, whose height had never attained a full five feet or her weight triple digits, almost completely disappear. Still, she could just barely make out the salient features of the head that was perched atop the stick figure.

A practical wedge of a very impractical auburn shade of hair was her undoubted crowning glory; brown eyes, closer to brick than black, that some saw as warm and friendly while others viewed them as intelligent and frightening; a typical mouth, but a makeup-free complexion that was resultantly clean of blemish; and a nose, genetics' plaything, that could be termed "ethnic" at best, but not much worse.

"*Dai*-SEE!" the summons came again.

Daisy yanked open the door and a woman, for whom no amount of distorting mirrors could ever make appear slim, all but fell into the room. A relative newcomer to the KKK, Mrs. Reichert was as wide as Daisy was tall and only a hairsbreadth taller. A muumuu by any other name is still a muumuu, no matter how much money you've spent on it. And all of the money in the world couldn't keep a woman like Mrs. Reichert from committing the colossal fashion boner of wearing a twenty-seven-year-old's long blonde tresses attached to her own fifty-something body.

"Didn't you hear me calling you?"

"The water was running," Daisy quickly covered.

"Well, your boss is on the phone. Says she needs to talk to you."

Daisy formed a mental picture in her mind's eye of MindyLou McKenna, founder of the KKK, clutching the phone receiver, her blood-red nails manicured to talon-like perfection at Kuttingly Kute Kuticles. Only to herself did Daisy ever refer to her boss as the Bottom-Feeder.

Now she found herself wondering, with a nod and apologies to Dorothy Parker for wasting her wit on some presumably mundane thing, what fresh hell was this?

"I can't believe you people," Mrs. Reichert was panting with angry effort.

Daisy thought she might have missed something here.

"Don't you realize that this is my time? I'm paying your boss for you. From twelve until three you're supposed to belong to me. I would think that would mean no phone calls."

Daisy ignored the blatant images of slavery, choosing instead to focus on what she knew about Mrs. Reichert, with the hopes of finding just the right thing to say to make her feel better.

Mrs. Reichert was married to a cardio-thoracic surgeon, who spent what little time when he wasn't at the hospital hiding out at the golf course. What more did a person need to know about another person in order to sympathize?

Daisy hoped that she was sending a message of warmth through her eyes. "You seem to be having a particularly tough time with things today, Mrs. Reichert."

"What?"

Daisy bestowed on Mrs. Reichert's plump shoulder a reassuring caress. "It must be dreadful at times, having to go through life as not much more than a walking appendage to a much more valued human being."

"What's the matter with you? Are you nuts?" Mrs. Reichert shrugged the offending hand off of her shoulder, her expression one of unvarnished horror. "The last cleaning lady I had used to get high from sniffing the tile cleanser. I had to let her go."

Mrs. Reichert pushed her way further into the room and began inspecting things.

Daisy tried in vain to think of something to say that would perhaps strike more of a balance between sympathy and inoffensiveness.

"Just look at the rim on this toilet bowl! You call that clean? This isn't clean. You do it again right now. You can call your boss back after you're finished," Mrs. Reichert wound up, pushing her way back out through the bathroom door.

The Bottom-Feeder would not be amused.

So maybe Daisy wasn't always letter-perfect at saying the right thing. But she still believed that all that most people really wanted in this life was for another person to listen to them for just a little while. Even if there were those few exceptions who didn't know how to properly appreciate such a service.

She wished that she had the kind of life where there actually was time to listen to another human being and to have that person listen to her. But there were some days, like today, when it took forever just to make it out of the bathroom.

As she depressed the flush handle a second time, staring into the swirling toilet-bowl water, she commenced wondering idly what *they* were doing right at that moment.

2

One wouldn't imagine that the reputedly staid archetypal Briton would go in much for a thing like playing practical jokes on April Fool's Day. But one who wouldn't imagine such a thing would imagine quite wrong.

All over the kingdom, little boys were waking up their mums by screaming that there was snow on the ground; teenage girls were causing their fathers to choke on their muesli by claiming to be preggers; and, just miles from London, a man who was somewhere in the vicinity of fifty years of age awoke in a bedroom in one of his mother's digs to find a breakfast tray beside him with a note on it, informing him that his presence would not be required at the embassy party that evening.

The man's name was Charles. His mother's digs were surrounded by fortified walls and just happened to represent the largest inhabited castle in all of Europe, and commonly went by the name of Windsor.

Up to this point, the Prince had been lolling about under the sheets, having grown oddly lethargic of late. But at this unexpected turn of events, he leapt energetically from the bed and, pressing a button that was discreetly hidden next to it, summoned Sturgess. The valet-slash-bodyguard-slash-confidant appeared immediately before him as if transported by light.

Standing at attention in front of the Prince was a man who, while at the present wearing his metaphorical valet's hat, looked as though he himself had first conceived of spit and had, likewise, invented polish. A gentleman, probably in his late sixties, he was of average height, with a reliably strong body that only reflected the beginnings of a comfortable paunch around the midsection. Blue eyes that danced no more often than one would like, and a nose with a pronounced bump in the ridge—where it had been broken during a childhood spent boxing—were the dominating features in a face whose complexion was otherwise curiously devoid of any markings of the passage of time. His pate, with a few sparse remnants of gray hairs ringing the central expanse, gleamed with a bright reflectivity that was only equaled by the shine on his shoes.

"Good morning, Sir. I trust that you slept soundly last evening," Sturgess said, beginning his day's address to his boss in much the same way that he did every day. Any evidence of his native Highland Scot accent were absent at this time in the morning. Present instead were clipped consonants and vowels that were so pear-shaped that one was tempted to eat them.

Glancing pointedly at the button that had been used to summon him, he said, "Was there something special you wished for me to do for you this morning?" He waited expectantly, one might even say eagerly, for instruction.

With an awkward hurriedness, the Prince donned a plush blue bathrobe, transferring the sheet of paper that he was still clutching from hand to hand as he did so. He waved the page in front of Sturgess's face.

"This!" he cried excitedly, his expression that of a mad scientist in the throes of inventive rapture. "This, Sturgeon. Is it true that my presence will not be necessary at the embassy party for the Polodni States this evening?"

The grin on Sturgess's face fled like a world-class sprinter. "Oh, that. Sir."

"What do you mean by 'Oh, that,' Sturgeon?" The Prince's own hopeful smile was much more sluggish than Sturgess's across the finish line, but it got there all the same. "I do not like the sound of this 'Oh, that.'"

Sturgess cleared his throat. "I merely thought it might represent a welcome change this year in the old routine, Sir, if you quite follow me."

"I have not a clue as to where you are trying to lead me, Sturgeon. But I am beginning to suspect that it is to somewhere that I no longer wish to go."

"It is not so awful, really. It is simply that I figured, rather than making a fool out of you yet again this year, that it would be a novelty to try to paint a smile on your face, for at least a short time instead. Sir."

The Prince slowly lowered his body to the edge of the bed, that listless feeling flooding his limbs again, the page hanging limply from one hand. "You mean to tell me that this was all a practical joke?"

"I'm afraid so, Sir."

The paper, like a feather that had been detached from a bird shot while in the midst of soaring flight, floated gently to the floor.

"And that would mean that I do have to attend the embassy party given by the Polodni States this evening?"

"That too, Sir."

Charles allowed his body to fall back onto the bed sheets, arms fully extended, as if he were only marking time until the nails were pounded in.

"Aargh!" The Future King of England screamed.

"I had been just a trifle worried that this might be your reaction, Sir."

3

Daisy Silverman had once had a boyfriend who had been driven insane by the sound of her constantly running refrigerator. She herself had never even noticed the incessant hum until he had pointed it out to her, minutes prior to tossing all of his belongings into two bags and rushing screaming from the apartment, never to be seen again.

This experience had only served to reinforce one of her pet theories. Daisy believed that each human being had their own very individual thresholds of tolerance and pleasure.

The refrigerator had never plagued her because, as far as she was concerned, all forms of noise represented an almost universal good. Sound, to Daisy, meant that there was life. A foul smell, on the other hand, could be testimony to a high-fiber diet or just as easily mean that, somewhere, someone had died.

For Daisy, even a whiff of cabbage could spoil an otherwise perfect spring day. At the other end of the spectrum, there had been a number of men she had dated for a time that would normally have been rejected by her far sooner had they not given off an odor of fried onions and garlic, the scents of the Italian kitchen representing her version of olfactory nirvana.

In fact, her whole obsession with the aroma thing was all of a piece with her equal obsession with food. This was in no way surprising from a scientific standpoint, what with the nasal cavity residing in intimate biological proximity to the oral cavity. She knew that if you smelled something that you liked, that part of the enjoyment was that you were actually tasting it on the air. Of course, this likewise meant that if you were smelling shit, you were probably eating… best not to go there. Suffice it to say that Daisy often found herself being led around by her nose.

Which explained what she was doing waiting in line, yet again, to pay for her purchases at the not-so-convenient Quik-Cart, when she could have bought her diet soda and lotto ticket at the supermarket that was even closer to her apartment in Danbury, where things were run more efficiently and where the gouging did not cut quite so deep. As Daisy tugged at the brim of her baseball cap, she looked to the head of the line where the cashier was waiting on customers. And she acknowledged to herself that the reason that she kept returning to this grim little slice of consumer hell was all due to the Lotto Lady.

The Lotto Lady was like a human receptacle, a walking atomizer of every good thing that she had ever consumed or had a hand in preparing. On that particular night, a cloud of curry and chocolate suffused the air around her, reaching out to Daisy where she stood in line and making her wish that they had dined together. The larger supermarkets might have faster service, greater selection and lower prices, but those sterile environments had nothing on the aroma of the Lotto Lady.

The Lotto Lady, being every inch Daisy's equal in the vertically disadvantaged department, was clad in something deep purple and tweedy, and was the kind of woman who gave roly-poly a good name. A face with the textured character of a walnut betrayed a depth of experience far greater than what you would normally imagine based on a life lived mostly within the confines of a Cheez Doodle and Skoal emporium. Brown eyes looked out at the world from behind frameless half-glasses that were perched precariously on the tip of her nose, sometimes—especially with taller customers—creating the curious visual effect of a groundhog on February 2, peering up at the sky from out of his hole and trying to decide whether to cast his shadow or not. A large and extraordinarily loose Victorian bun crowned her, its topknot never quite successful in keeping the somewhat scraggly salt-and-pepper tendrils from escaping.

Time in the Quik-Cart never seemed to quite keep pace with that of the outside world—moving either slower or faster, as if it were its own dimension entirely—and Daisy found herself suddenly at the head of the line.

"Help you, dear?" The Lotto Lady gazed straight at her inquisitively. "Oops! Couldn't see your hair. Almost didn't recognize you under that cap." Her speech pattern, while reassuringly susurrant, possessed an economy that revealed a distinct prejudice against the usage of first-person pronouns.

In spite of a bone-weariness brought on by a long day in service to the Bottom-Feeder, Daisy was able to muster a warm smile of her own. "How are you this evening? I'll just take the soda and—"

"2-7-18-33-36-41," the Lotto Lady finished for her, punching the numbers into the ticketing machine.

"How did you know that?" Daisy asked, shocked.

"Wouldn't have to be a brain surgeon. You've asked for the same six numbers every week for the last three years."

"Yes, but you must wait on thousands of people buying numbers each week."

"Don't remember all of them," the Lotto Lady chuckled. "$3.06 for the soda and ticket. Just yours."

Daisy studied the eternally spinning hot dogs that were being heated under a glass enclosure set up on the counter. As usual, she found the experience mesmerizing. She would be willing to swear before a jury that they were the exact same six weenies that had been spinning for the last three years.

"Why only mine?" she asked, absentmindedly extending a five-dollar bill.

"Always the same. Only one." Pronouns of the second-person variety were not as common to her as they might be either. "Others get frustrated, change a number here, a number there. Three years. Only one, always faithful." She peered around the tiny shop as if she were casing the place for spies. For once, the place was empty of other customers. "Always wanted to know why. Why always the same?"

Daisy strained to tear herself away from the rotating weenies. She pocketed her change. "They were my father's numbers. It was what he left me in his will."

"Thought you said he was in the septic business. All those years of work." She shook her head, whether in dismay or disgust was anyone's guess. "And all he left you was six numbers?"

Daisy gave a nonjudgmental shrug.

"Thought those guys made decent money. What happened to it all?"

"Bad investment idea. You could say that his fortunes all went down the drain."

"And you still play his numbers every week?"

Daisy shrugged the shrug again.

"What's your name, honey?" the Lotto Lady asked, her tone growing confidential.

"Daisy," she replied, realizing that they had spoken at least once a week for the last three years without ever once having asked each other's names. "Yours?"

"Bonita." The Lotto Lady smiled, unveiling two rows of the tiniest teeth that Daisy could ever recall having seen on an adult before.

Bonita leaned across the counter, her face drawing close to Daisy's, as if for secrecy, even though the shop was still empty. "So, Miss Daisy, what would you do if you did win all of that money? Just for the fun of it, pretend you only have a minute to decide."

Daisy looked at the poster on the door. The week's jackpot was set at the minimum one million dollars. At $50,000 a year for twenty years—before taxes—the sum wouldn't exactly make her wealthy beyond her wildest dreams, but it would mean that she wouldn't have to look at another toilet bowl with a professional eye ever again if she didn't want to.

She didn't even need the whole minute. "I'd go to London." And then she paused for only the barest of fractions before impetuously adding, "And I'd take you with me."

The glare brought about by the marriage of fluorescent light and glass temporarily obscured brown eyes as the topknot bobbed approval. Bonita flashed another one of those childlike grins before uttering a rare, and therefore wonderful, personal pronoun:

"I'll hold you to it."

4

The King of Small Talk was working the room as only he knew how. Sturgess, now wearing the hat of royal bodyguard and detective, was trailing at an unobtrusive distance behind.

By that evening, the Prince had once again regained his famous urbane composure. Even as he shot his cuffs, adjusting the onyx and gold links, it was a mien that smacked of a palatial—and thus, suitably fashionable—ennui.

For one who had been brought up with the belief that the laws of primogeniture ensured that one day his hand would grasp a scepter and his face appear on a stamp, he liked to listen and was surprisingly good at it. As he engaged in the usual internal debate concerning whether it would be more time efficient to work the perimeters or to simply make an energetic beeline straight up the middle, he felt his innate good humor threatening to make a comeback and take on the interloping boredom.

"Sir!" The whinnying cry attacked from the left, tamping any good humor right back down again.

Charles sincerely hoped that it wasn't what he thought it was. Perhaps a horse was summoning a waiter. He strode on, determined to keep to his mission of working the edges without being sucked into the vortex.

"Yoo-hoo! Sir!" There it was again, only much closer this time, and threatening to overtake him.

The Prince slowly turned, with an outward smile and an inward sigh, prepared to face his doom. The visage that confronted him came as close to being that of an aging equine as any that he had ever seen on a *Homo sapiens* before.

He flashed a smile that he desperately hoped was benevolent enough to mask the fact that he hadn't the slightest idea what her name was. He wished that Sturgess were standing nearer so that he could ask him under his breath. But the bodyguard had become momentarily sidetracked by a tray of skewered chicken satay—a relatively minor failing in one who ordinarily served so well—and was thus unable to offer assistance. The Prince had been abandoned to his own recognizant devices.

Was this one, then, Miss Tryte-Smythe, Ms. Slyte-Knyte, or was it perhaps Mrs. Austin Spyte-Blythe? Charles wondered idly. They all looked so much alike, all with their steeplechase-worthy proboscises and their other pickled and preserved parts. It really was too tiresome trying to keep all of their names straight when they were all so bloody interchangeable. As if it mattered somehow in the slightest.

In fact, the Prince had never understood why one couldn't simply call them all Bootsie and have done with it. Charles chuckled to himself silently as he speculated as to what his mother would have to say about it, if word were to get around that he had begun doing *that*.

He tried to refocus his attention on the still nameless woman, who was turning out to be much more of a charger than the glue factory candidate he had originally taken her for. Maybe he shouldn't always be so quick to be judgmental. Perhaps she wanted to discuss something of value, like Balzac or the Baltic States, the current state of Parliament or Peshawar.

Now, then: What *was* she nattering on about?

"… so I thought to myself, who better to ask than Sir?"

"Pardon?" he enquired hopefully.

"About the fertilizer problem that I was just telling you about, Sir. I thought that, surely, a man of your expertise would be just the one to ask about my troublesome petunias. Who could possibly pretend to know more about fertilizer than you?"

He felt his hopes plummet. *Not more small talk!* his mind resisted. There were times when he swore that he would end up in Bedlam if he had to talk gardening with one more neophyte.

No, it wasn't that Charles minded listening so much. It was just that he felt that it would be nice if, only every now and then, people were to find something interesting or worthwhile to say.

And where the hell was Sturgess anyway? Nobody could possibly like satay that much.

5

Daisy had always deemed the "ee" sound, required at the end of her name, to be particularly reprehensible. In fact, she had always found it odious when that phoneme appeared at the end of any woman's name. She believed that it doomed a woman to a childish existence, one in which she was destined to never completely grow up; or, if she did manage to, it was preordained that the rest of the world should refuse to take her seriously. Men, on the other hand, could get away with the detested "ee"—provided that it wasn't affixed to Louie (as in "get the car") or Morty (as in "nu, so how big vas the gefilte fish that got avay?"). For most men, the "ee" suffix provided a welcome respite from self-absorption. And besides, from where Daisy was sitting, it looked as though the rest of the world—men in particular—already took men as a whole far too seriously anyway.

For herself, Daisy would have preferred it had she been given a more adult and, possibly, regal-sounding name, like Catherine or simply Jane. But, she reasoned, with a Morty-like shrug, it could have been worse.

Her father had once confessed that, during her mother's ninth month of pregnancy, they had gone out for a pre-celebratory dinner, assuming that it would be months following her arrival on the scene before they'd get another such chance. Daisy's mother had become typically tipsy on a single glass of wine.

They had still not come up with a name for the baby, and the giddy Rachel had suggested to the more sober Herbert that, if the child were a girl, they should call her Goldie Silverman.

Herbert, desperate that his child not bear a name that was in any way reminiscent of an Atlantic City pawn shop, had seized on the first thing that his eyes had fallen upon. Plucking a cheap flower from one of the equally cheap Chianti bottles that dotted each of the restaurant's dozen tables, he had declared imperiously: "Nein. Nyet. Nevermore. If our bundle of joy has an innie, we shall name her Daisy."

Still, it could have been a whole lot worse, and Daisy was accustomed to making do.

In light of the considerable disadvantages that Daisy associated with her given name, it was somewhat surprising then that her surname posed no similar problems for her. But she had always considered Silverman to be of a piece with herself, much as she did the gold Star of David that she wore on a slim chain around her neck, unconsciously fingering it with her left hand as she stood in her microscopic kitchen, inhaling and tasting the eggplant, garlic and pine nuts for the sauce that she was sautéing with her right. It was a tradition for Daisy to make a homemade dinner, no matter how busy the day had been.

The jewelry was the sole legacy bequeathed by Rachel, who had died when Daisy was eleven. She wore it daily, much the way that someone else might wear a wristwatch, as a habit and as a requirement. It served more as a tribute to the love that she felt for her mother than it did to symbolize any depth of religious devotion.

In fact, Daisy considered herself to be a non-practicing Jew. This tended to define more of who she wasn't than who she was. From a purely practical standpoint, this meant that, while bacon might find its way onto her burger, no amount of talking would ever convince her that any savior had already come and gone.

It was another tradition with Daisy, perhaps brought about by Rachel's premature death, to try to make every moment count as much as possible. And so, as she seated herself at a plastic table built for two—a heaping plate of pasta in one hand, diet cola in the other—she reached for the top of one of the bottomless stacks of reading material that had always trailed her through life.

The uppermost item brought a smile to her face. It was a copy of *Majesty* magazine, forced onto her by Bonita just prior to Daisy's exit of the shop earlier that evening. The tiny Lotto Lady had advised that Daisy start doing her homework now if she were really serious about taking her winnings to London.

She studied the high-gloss cover just briefly—taking in the dotty but oddly welcoming and ageless blue-eyed smile of the Queen Mother, who was being escorted on the steadying arm of Charles—before rejecting it in favor of the second item in the stack. Oh, sure, it was okay to escape with the Royals during her day job, but there was such a thing as carrying an obsession too far. And this was Daisy's real world. She couldn't be bothered with the likes of *People* magazine. She needed a more edifying fictional escape route. So she reached for Dostoyevsky instead.

Social prejudgments that the cleaning lady does not read *Crime and Punishment*, coupled with the presumed tedium inherent in her job's description, could lead a person to believe, in spite of Daisy's professed doctrine concerning the value of time, that she was wasting hers. Such an assumption would be grossly unfair.

Daisy was already a full year older than Rachel had been when she had died; an odd feeling, that. Thus, she recognized that it was wrong of people to live their lives as if they were part of one big holding pattern, toiling away in jobs that they hated, marking the years off until retirement. The notion that your real life might be starting at some nebulously future time was bogus. Daisy knew that most people never even lived long enough to begin.

You must remember, though, Daisy was a Silverman by blood. She wasn't just marking time. She *liked* cleaning toilets. When she was doing it, her mind was free to go wherever she wanted. Had she been saddled with more creative or intellectual career aspirations, her mind, along with her time, would have belonged to someone else. This way, she got to keep the good part. And the only thing that really belonged to the Bottom-Feeder was the one dish-panned hand.

In fact, the Hand Thing was the only problem she had ever

had with her job. And by "the Hand Thing," she wasn't referring to the fact that her right hand was callused or that the job enforced a radical manicure upon her or that her cuticles were hardened in such a way that she would never be mistaken for any class but her own. No, the Hand Thing was a verbal catchall, encompassing any and every activity requiring the use of both hands at the same time. As long as just one hand was needed for the performance of any given task, she could always continue plugging away at her stack of books. But both?

Were she a circus juggler or a gastroenterologist, her job complaint would be exactly the same.

In spite of the whole Hand Thing, Daisy was grateful for her job. In fact, it was yet another tradition with her to count her blessings every night as she performed the cleanup job on the meager quantity of dishes that she had used. Another reason why Daisy was a non-practicing Jew was that she never could sit still for spirituality. It only came to her when her hands were busy doing something, like working in soapy water.

Daisy turned on the kitchen radio to catch the news as she was washing her pot, her plate, her fork, and her glass. The local segment brought a tear to her eye; the national tipped the tear over the edge of her lower lash; and the international report instigated a steady coursing down the front of her face.

As she turned off the faucet and applied moisturizer to her hands she was more grateful than ever. She gave thanks for her job. She gave thanks for the legacies that she had received from both of her parents. She gave thanks for the Lotto Lady's generosity...

Lotto!

Daisy looked at the clock over the stove and saw that it was 7:59. Pulling the crumpled ticket from the pocket of her jeans, she hurriedly crossed to the small TV set in the combination bedroom-living room, turning it on. She performed this hopeful and energetic little dance more out of habit than out of any concrete expectations. After all, no Silverman had ever won anything. For if they had, even *they* would no longer be cleaning toilets.

On the screen, a lady dressed all in canary yellow let the numbered balls loose in their cage.

The digital timer on the VCR ticked over to 8:00.

And the news that Daisy Silverman heard scattered her previous thoughts, like just so many autumn leaves, out to three of the corners of the globe; while the very same news informed her that her destiny was now firmly pointed towards the fourth.

Daisy's star was rising in the east.

6

"*IT'S THREE O'CLOCK IN THE MORNING! WE'VE DANCED THE WHOLE NIGHT THROUGH!*" The chiming of the ormolu clock on the mahogany dresser signified that the Prince's desperate rendition of the tune was at least temporally accurate, if a touch over the top in the stridently morose department.

"Aye, Sir," said Sturgess. "But some of us are growin' a bit old fer this. And besides, my feet are sore."

Sturgess was wearing his most favored and favorite hat, that of confidant and friend. Just as Elizabeth had found solace in the counsel of the legendary "Bobo"—the senior dresser who had been her principal advisor and companion since nursery days—so Charles felt about his own valet-slash-bodyguard-slash-confidant. Pity, then, that he kept calling him Sturgeon.

Unlike the aforementioned Bobo, Sturgess had no delusions that he would be sitting beside his employer on the throne one day. But, sharing the same country of origin, there was a natural burr and a relaxing lilt to his manner of speech that he only allowed to creep back in when it was very late at night and he was absolutely certain that they would not be disturbed. As was currently the case.

The Prince abruptly released his partner, flopping down upon the velvet spread.

"Man delights me not."

"Well, tha's all right, Sir. Ye know, ye always have been known fer bein' more of a ladies' man."

"Nor women neither."

"Och, well. The whole human race then, is it? Now that could present a wee bit of a problem," Sturgess thoughtfully replied as he removed the Prince's oxblood leather shoes.

"Do you think that I made that up, Sturgeon? That 'man delights me not' nonsense?"

"Sure. Why not? I like ta believe that ye can be that creative with a turn o' the phrase when ye want ta be, Sir."

"Well, I didn't. That phrase was coined by some far more intelligent blithering idiot."

"Ah," came the noncommittal reply.

"Do you know what it's like to be ineffectual, Sturgeon?" the Future Defender of the Faith queried, betraying an acute level of self-awareness far greater than that which he was usually credited with possessing.

Sturgeon deemed it most prudent to stay mum on that one. Instead, he pretended to be thoroughly engrossed in the task of plumping up the pillows. He needn't have bothered with the ruse, however.

"No, of course not," the Prince answered his own question. "How could you? You're the most effective person I've ever known. They should let you run Parliament."

While they had been talking, the Prince had been traveling back and forth between bedroom and dressing room, and he now emerged from the latter, buttoning the top of his pajamas.

"Do you think it possible for a quite sane person to be driven mad by attending one too many embassy parties?"

"I suspect so, Sir," the valet replied, turning down the covers.

"Do you think that will be my ultimate fate, then? To get carted away before God and everybody—starkers—just because one too many horsy debs felt impelled to query me about the world's finest fertilizers?" The Prince climbed between the sheets.

"I suspect not, Sir. Ye're far too practical to let tha' happen ta ye." And, knowing that at certain points in every man's life, that there were desperate times that shrieked for desperate measures,

Sturgess produced the universal panacea. Placing the rather ratty-looking Teddy on the bed beside the recumbent Prince, he tucked the sheets more snuggly up around both of their necks.

The Prince yawned, languorously, his emotions temporarily mollified. "Do you realize, Sturgeon," he wondered aloud, with an almost intellectual detachment to his tone, "that during the entire hellish evening, not once did a single soul even mention world affairs? The whole bloody planet could go to hell, and do you think that any of those people would care? Do you think it possible that nobody cares?"

"At times, Sir, I suspect ye are the only one." Sturgess crossed the room and, as if by magic, the lights went out. "Try to get some sleep now, Sir. It's been a rather long day fer ye and, chances are, there'll be another embassy party tomorrow."

And the Prince who, having found that life raft of a note on his breakfast tray, had begun the day with such an elevated mood, drifted off to sleep the slumber of the damned.

7

MindyLou McKenna's voice screeched down the telephone line. *"What did you just say to me?"*

"I'm sorry. Excuse me?" Daisy asked vaguely. "I got distracted there for a minute. I thought maybe I'd left something still cooking in the kitchen; but no, I realized—my mistake!—that heavenly smell is just another one of my bridges burning behind me."

"I don't know what the heck you're talking about, Daisy. Could you please just tell me what the heck you're talking about? No, on second thought, don't. It'd probably give me a migraine. Just get over to Mrs. Reichert's before—"

"In my heart of hearts, I always refer to you as the Bottom-Feeder, MindyLou," Daisy interrupted. "And I don't believe that I'll be coming in to work anymore," she added, just barely managing to keep the whoop bottled up inside until she had delicately replaced the receiver. She had never realized it before, but that whoop had been waiting all of her life to come out.

8

"Another day, another embassy party," the valet said brightly, drawing the drapes and exposing a stunningly damp view of the Thames Valley.

"Please tell me that your real name is Benny Hill, Sturgeon," the Prince requested, unable to suppress the very unregal modulations of the beggar from creeping into his voice.

9

"Pack your bags," Daisy announced, virtually flying into the shop.

"How long are we staying for?" Bonita asked, as if she had this sort of conversation every day of her life.

"For as long as the first year's check lasts us. If we run out before next year's check kicks in, well... we'll worry about that when we have to worry about it. And not a minute before."

10

"Same time, same place," the bodyguard said as they entered the room.

"Fine," his employer muttered with some degree of asperity. "If you're not willing to be John Cleese, then how about if we just all agree to call *me* Bootsie and have done with it?"

11

Bonita squinted through her glasses, closely examining the extensive selection of keys that were attached to an elasticized cord around her wrist. Choosing one, she inserted it, locking the door behind them. As they strolled down the street, bags in hand, she tossed the cord and the keys into the nearest trash basket.

"Don't you have any family that you need to tell about where you're going?" Daisy couldn't help but wonder out loud.

"Nope."

"No family at all?"

"Never saw the point in it. Figured on just putting one together." she shrugged. "Making it up as it goes along."

12

The confidant closed the drapes.

"Are we in Bedlam yet?"

"Nae. But I'm afraid that we're all on our way."

13

"Just a little advice," Bonita offered. There was a warning note in her voice that Daisy happened to miss, as she hurried through the airport, the topknot bobbing along at her side.

"Shoot."

"Never lose sight of who you are."

"Of course not," came the vehement reply.

They were craning their necks, scanning the departure times on the display screen.

"And never forget where you come from."

"Not possible."

The childlike smile belied the underlying seriousness of the final warning that came just prior to boarding the jet. "And, whatever else you do, never stay too long at the ball."

And Daisy, who, having never traveled very much before, had become temporarily sidetracked by the whole ticket, boarding pass, your copy, my copy process, uttered a distant, "Yeah, yeah; sure, sure," in response.

14

"Is it the Fool's Day again?"
"It can be if you so order it, Sir."

15

In Heathrow Airport, on an early morning late in the month of April, an auburn-haired woman with a baseball cap jammed on her head stood waiting to pass through customs. At her side was an equally short companion, wearing a tweedy green dress and her version of a Victorian 'do made even wilder by a night's sleep on the plane.

"And where might you be going, Miss?"

Daisy Silverman smiled, shouldering her bag as the official waved her through.

"Why, to see the Queen, of course."

Part Two

She Flies Through the Air with the Greatest of Ease

For he that talketh what he knoweth
will also talk what he knoweth not.

from "Of Simulation and Dissimulation"
~ The Essays of Francis Bacon

May

1

The gentleman holding the post of Her Majesty's Master of the Household had, as just one of his myriad responsibilities, the task of writing up the "Court Circular" column which was, in turn, reprinted in the *Times* and the *Daily Telegraph* under the royal coat-of-arms. It catalogued the daily whereabouts of specific Royals in descending order of importance. As such, it functioned as an open beckoning gesture to any moron with the proper networking connections who could thusly obtain the appropriate invitation card. It also set the Royal Family up as sitting ducks, at least for the duration of the event, for any and all gawkers who were in possession of the metaphorical price of admission.

On an otherwise brilliantly fine Friday, smack in the middle of the often dicey month of May, the following item appeared in the column:

"… and, also to be noted, this evening there is rumored to be a positively *stupendous* soiree that is to take place at the Pakistani Embassy. HRH, The Prince of Wales, will undoubtedly be in attendance."

• • •

Daisy Silverman had taken up residence in the British Library during most of her waking hours, when she wasn't out jogging or eating. And the single thing that drew her to the interior of the structure, like a giant magnet operating on a paper clip, was—of course—the Reading Room. The rules stated that you could not gain admittance to the august enclosure unless you were at least twenty-one years of age *and* your research there had been recommended by a sponsor— preferably a renowned scholar. Otherwise, the best you could hope for was a micro-brief look-see with one of the warders as escort. Frustrating.

But rules, thank God, had often been made just for Daisy to break them. And when Bonita, who was fast becoming a source of constant surprise, had learned of the dilemma, she had merely shrugged the problem off. Grateful, and positively reeling from the giddiness brought about by such a voluminous windfall, the naturally inquisitive Daisy had neglected to press for details concerning the origin of Bonita's scholarly underground connections, when the former convenience store clerk had claimed to "know somebody."

Now situated on a regular basis where she had so badly wanted to be, Daisy didn't care if other people found her behavior a tad bit touristy. She loved standing in the circular room, the 106-foot high, pale blue dome soaring comfortingly like a second heaven over her head; loved looking at the spines of the books, the autumnal hues of their bound leather causing her to think curiously of Halloween; loved imagining all of the great minds that had ever done their thinking here: Dickens, Gandhi, Shaw, Thackeray, Yeats. So what if back when they were around it had all been part of the British Museum over on Russell Square, and had since been moved to Euston Street, lock, stock, and carrel? It was still the Reading Room in the British Library.

Most of all, though, Daisy loved—no matter how trite—to fantasize about Karl Marx, sitting in his favorite seat, toiling away on *Das Kapital*.

As she took in the arched windows rising up the sides of the dome, took in the real scholars poring over their tomes at the leather-topped tables, the sight of just a mere fraction of the Library's reputed eighteen million holdings—shelved on three floors and all in one place—was enough to knock Daisy on her literary ass.

Why, then, this special place—the Library, itself—that was always so good at elevating her spirits whenever she got feeling blue (for, in spite of her instantaneous love of the city and that enjoyment that she derived from the quirky companionship of Bonita, she still got a little homesick upon occasion) should let her down, she had no idea. But let her down it did, and badly at that. And quite suddenly, on that same day that the item—which she had not read—had appeared in the daily newspapers, she found herself running from her haven, face streaming with tears.

Her sneakers carried her out of the library, and she collapsed in a heap on the stone steps, the column that supported her back dwarfing her despondent form. So atypical was her total self-absorption on that day that she hadn't noticed that there had been another person contemplating Marx's chair in the Reading Room. Or that the individual had pursued her in flight, scurrying along in his own cross-trainers and straining to keep pace with her surprisingly brisk stride.

"Please. May I please be of some assistance to you, Miss?"

Startled, Daisy glanced up, seeking the source of the Indo-Iranian-based accent. As she raised her head from its dispirited resting place in her hands, her nose wrinkled unconsciously. Whole cashews? And was that, possibly, garlic-steamed artichokes? How could she possibly remain depressed now?

Her uplifted gaze took in the sight of a man about her own age, skin the color of filberts. He had close-cropped, wavy black hair, and a matching pencil-thin mustache that twitched under an inoffensive nose whenever he spoke or smiled. His body had the pear-shaped quality of a drop of water being slowly squeezed from the faucet and, amazingly enough, it did not look as though he would turn out to be any taller than she.

What a wonderful world it's been lately, she thought, obscurely. *All of a sudden, it's as though everything were just my size.* She could have sworn that she smelled just a tiny whiff of a decorated gingerbread-man cookie, too. Yummy.

She wiped at her eyes with the cuffs of her sweatshirt.

"Excuse me?"

"You began to cry back there," he said, indicating the Library with his hand. "When you were looking at Marx's chair. I thought that maybe I could be of some help to you. Perhaps you were lamenting the lot of the masses?"

"Oh, that," Daisy replied, feeling just a trifle embarrassed at the prospect of having to speak about the idiosyncratic nature of her personality out loud. "No. I mean, that could have done it, maybe on another day. And today, it did actually start with Marx's chair. And then, of course, I got thinking about *Das Kapital*—I mean, who doesn't when they go in there? And then," and here she sighed, "I got to thinking about how I had never even read *Das Kapital*—never mind having actually written anything like it. And then," she wound up, "I got to thinking about *all* of the books in there and *all* of the books in the world—history, anatomy, tai chi, even things that I'm not remotely interested in—and I thought how it's just not possible: I'll never live long enough to read everything that I want to read. Don't get me wrong, I don't mind facing the thought of my own death at all. It's just that I absolutely *hate* the idea that I won't get the chance to read everything first. In fact," she shrugged, "it's the only thought that ever makes me feel like just throwing in the towel."

During the entirety of Daisy's speech, the little man had been struggling to maintain an appropriately solemn air of sympathy. But the constant twitching of the mustache betrayed him, and his true feelings finally won out, as a burst of magnificent pearly sunshine forced its way between the curtains of his previously pursed lips. Daisy was unnerved by the impression that the man was laughing out loud at her.

"But," he cried with delight, "that is the most wonderfully delightful and magically delicious thing that I have ever heard! Please to tell me your name, so that in the future I will know how to properly address such a delectable creature."

"It's Daisy," she hesitated, still not completely certain that she wasn't being mocked.

"Well, Daisy," he said, wiping at his own mirthful tears, "you must permit me to introduce myself. My name is Pacqui—never to be confused with Packey or Paki."

Daisy's vacant expression revealed her confusion. It all sounded like *paeki* to her.

His hands moved constantly as he spoke, the conductor of some silent symphony that perhaps only he could hear. "It's spelled with a c-q sequence, rather than a c-k or a lonely k. The Londoners nicknamed me that in order to distinguish me from the other two that they have nicknamed at the Embassy."

Daisy gave a tentative smile of understanding. She thought that, just maybe, she had caught the glimpse of a linguistic point in there somewhere.

"Please, Daisy. You must let me show my gratitude to you for providing me with such a moment of incomparable joy. You must permit me to escort you to the embassy party this evening," he pronounced, his hands describing a final flourishing crescendo.

"But I wasn't invited to any party this evening!" she protested.

"That is of no matter. I was." He paused for just a second, beaming. "Wait 'til they get a load of you."

2

"Tasteful brown skirt and businesslike blouse? What do you think you're going to here—a job interview?" had been Bonita's skeptical reaction upon being shown Daisy's choice of eveningwear. She wrinkled her nose. "Don't think so, dear."

They were seated on the delft-and-white covering on the bed in Bonita's cozy single in the Hotel Russell.

Daisy, not normally given to caring two shakes about what she wore, experienced a peculiar moment of fashion distress at Bonita's critical tone, as she rose and crossed through the connecting door to her own double beyond. "But what am I going to do?" she shouted back, desperately rifling the few items that actually required hangers. A note of agitation crept into her usually more placid voice. "I don't have the kind of wardrobe that gets asked to Embassy soirees."

"Hmm." Bonita consulted the timepiece ticking away on a chain around her neck. It was three twenty-four and the party wasn't due to start until eight. "Might be just enough time." A thoughtful finger stroked the walnut face. "Might know just the right place."

3

If there was any truth to the Harrods motto of Omnia, Omnibus, Ubique—"all things, for all people, everywhere"—then what was now being required of that venerable shopping institution was that it cough up the perfect dress to transform a Danbury toilet bowl cleaner into a princess for the evening. And if the jaded shop clerk, whose attentions they had commandeered for their purposes, thought—wrongly—that she had seen other women like Daisy before, it soon became obvious that she had never encountered anybody quite like Bonita.

The shop clerk, whose own impeccable attire rivaled that of any model strutting her stuff on a Parisian runway, evoked an uncharacteristic frisson of fashion inferiority in Daisy, as she waited obediently in her underthings in the vast changing room. She was dead certain that she would never possess even half as much style as the sales clerk.

Bonita, casting an Ungaro eye on the proceedings, fast rejected everything black that the heretofore unruffled, but soon to be harried, clerk brought in as being "common as fish and chips— everyone who hasn't the imagination to come up with a real color always wears black"; white was for "babies, virgins, brides, and nuns in their coffins," in that exact order; and the one red number that the clerk had brought in, while it definitely passed muster on the "real color" test, was deemed deficient in that it "certainly does make a statement," but "... 'come up and see me sometime?'

Mm… Think not."

And Daisy, changing garments with the speed of a photographer snapping away, rejected anything without at least a crew-necked collar. A slightly darker-hued miniature strawberry of skin had marked her collarbone since the time of her birth. And, in spite of a nature that was otherwise devoid of physical vanity, she had always been reticent about exposing this stain to the probing eyes of the world at large. In her own mind, she explained away this insecure behavior by telling herself that she wasn't exactly embarrassed by her birthmark, but rather that it just clashed with a lot of things.

"Refresh my memory," Daisy was heard to despair at one spiritual low point during her tenure in the changing room. "Just what am I doing here? And why is this so important?"

As the clerk, her French twist now completely uncoiled (it really was amazing how much damage two women from Danbury could cause in the space of one harmless hour) exited underneath the weight of yet another pile of rejected clothing, Bonita—using that rare and wonderful personal referent—declared it time to "do the job myself."

Back in a flash so quick that it seemed scarily inhuman, Bonita hung the lone garment from the hook on the wall, flashing her baby-teeth grin at Daisy. Accompanying the clerk out of the room, Bonita declared, "If this doesn't do the trick, then by all means, go with the dead-nun look."

Daisy found herself suddenly alone with The Dress.

She slipped the gossamer fabric over her head, and by performing just the minimum of contortionist acts, she was able to manage to zip the back all the way up her neck. Almost fearfully, she turned to confront her image in the looking glass.

The material wasn't a single color, and yet there was no discernible pattern to it. Rather, it was opalescent, as if the designer had managed to capture the interior of an abalone shell and had talked Rumpelstiltskin into magically spinning the hard substance into the sheerest of threads. At the neckline, the collar climbed further upwards, protectively embracing Daisy's neck. The entire top half of the dress hugged her form to the waist, but there were no sleeves to it, thus showcasing her athletic and shapely arms to full advantage. From the waist the skirt flared out, ending finally in a hemline that was designed like the layers of a handkerchief, with some of the points extending just below the knee, while others afforded a provocative glimpse of thigh now and again.

As Daisy took in the head-to-toe reflection, absentmindedly tucking the Star of David beneath the collar, it occurred to her that she wasn't in Kansas anymore.

Daisy no longer looked like a Silverman.

• • •

The duo from Danbury flew through the rest of Harrods, the sales clerk a permanent fixture in tow. "Might not think they're all your department, honey, but they will be now," Bonita advised.

Lingerie coughed up silken undergarments, a far cry from Daisy's usual torn and tattered invitations to ambulance embarrassment. Hosiery nobly lived up to its name. And in the shoe department, they managed to track down a lone pair of size fives, whose curved stiletto heels were architectural marvels, and whose color and form would enact a perfect union when paired with The Dress.

Sparing a fleeting thought for the very disheveled shop clerk, who was at that very moment gratefully consuming the dust churned up by the passing of their wake, as they hurried through Knightsbridge, wending their way back towards the hotel in Bloomsbury, Daisy basked in the warm afterglow of shopper's success. It now seemed to her that the initial frustrations of the search had all been part of someone else's bad dream; and the excavation of that most sought after item, that confection of perfection—The Dress—as easy as plucking an apple from a low-hanging branch.

4

It hadn't taken long for Daisy to recover her inherent sense of the proper hierarchical structuring of priorities.

"Substance before style," she informed the protesting Bonita as she did up the neon pink laces on her sneakers. Neon pink meant that nobody could possibly miss you at night.

"But," Bonita objected, trying to interject her own brand of rationalism, "you only have two-and-a-half hours left, and you still need to shower and change and do your hair and—oh, who knows?—mentally prepare yourself or something of the sort."

"Not to worry," Daisy laughed, dismissing her concerns with a mildly insulting, patronizing pat on the topknot. "I'll be back from my run in plenty of time to attend to all of that fashion stuff."

5

Daisy jogged south down Montague Street, heading in the general direction of the Thames. Making a few quick turns, she crossed New Oxford and veered onto Shraftesbury to the right. So far, so good.

She was thinking about how much nicer it was to run in London than it was back in the States. In spite of the city's much-maligned climate, hardly a day passed when it wasn't decent enough out to get in at least some form of workout. Here, men didn't react to her sprinting form with verbal assaults, assuming an exercising female must certainly be in want of sexual solicitation. And, best of all, she found that the idea of falling prey to a drive-by shooting never even crossed her mind.

Sometimes the sidewalks did get a little congested, but she did try to avert knocking other people over whenever possible, and they did seem to appreciate that. As she made her way through Piccadilly Circus, usually one of the most crowded pedestrian areas, a sprinkle began to fall from a suddenly notorious gray sky. In an attempt to avoid being blinded by brollies, she maneuvered her way through the mass of milling bodies and, exiting the other end, turned right onto Old Bond Street.

At this juncture, having passed the halfway point of what she considered to be her short route and thinking herself home free, Daisy let her guard down. Her mind began to wander, her thoughts the victim of random input, which—if you really gave it some serious consideration—some would argue could be far more dangerous than any drive-by shooter.

As Daisy propelled her body north by northwest (*Hamlet*, anyone?) along Old Bond Street, her consciousness began to clear itself of all unnecessary clutter. In fact, such was the vacancy of her meditations that any Zen master might have been proud of the mental vacuum that she had created.

She was ripe, then, as she crossed the line from Old Bond Street into New, for a single item of sensory input to invade her being, temporarily laying siege to the entirety of her existence.

Chocolate? She sniffed the aroma on the damp air. *Violets?* She experienced the bit tightening in her mouth. *Chocolate* and *violets, both, at the very same time?* was her final waking thought, as the reins yanked her back for a 180-degree turnaround, where she would have encountered possibly the finest chocolate shop of her life, had she not, in her haste to discover the source of the unprecedented aroma combo, bumped a brollie, tripped over a Chow, and been sent sprawling rump over teakettle, all before ending up smack on top of a damp sewage drain.

Which, when you really thought about it, wasn't all that far from where Miss Silverman had started.

6

On the floor of the guest room in the Hotel Russell stood a silver champagne bucket, sans bottle and with an overabundance of chipped ice. Encased within the ice and, thankfully, protected from view by the surrounding linen towel, was one formerly delicate, but—for the time being—now hideously swollen left ankle. The form extending upward from the ankle in question belonged, of course, to Daisy, who was holding in her right hand the missing champagne bottle. This original administration of first aid, brought about with the enlisted help of one very startled room service waiter, had all been, of course, Bonita's doing.

As Bonita peeled back the linen to see how the patient was doing, it was revealed that the ice had not caused the swelling to go down one jot. But that didn't really matter much anymore, since the champagne bottle was more than holding up its share of the bargain, and Daisy was no longer feeling any pain.

"What am I going to do?" she asked hazily, bending over to study the ankle with a scientifically inquisitive smile. Daisy, the proud recipient of Rachel's DNA right down to the very last strand, had crossed over the border of tipsy and was fast approaching sloshed on the strength of little more than a single glass of the bubbly. "What will I do about those shoes?" she pressed, as if nothing else had ever mattered quite so much or quite so little to her before.

Bonita pried the champagne bottle away from Daisy, moving it safely out of reach, before crossing to the closet. Turning back again, she offered her idea of a sensible solution. In her left hand, she held The Dress. And from the curved joints of one extended forefinger, she dangled a single neon-pink-laced sneaker. "Just put a sock on the other and no one'll even notice the Elephant Man likeness," was the sage advice.

To which Daisy emitted a groan. It was impossible, really, to tell if it was a groan of dismay at her predicament and the idea of making a stylistic fool out of herself, or if it was a groan brought about by the giddy intoxication of relief; she would not be required to stumble around in public in the unaccustomed architectural marvels, thereby making a tottering fool out of herself.

In fact, all that you could really be certain of was the exact words expressed within the confines of the emitted moan:

"Oh no."

7

The Prince of Wales stood, studying his own image, in front of a mirror that was fit for a king. He was adjusting his own tie.

"Do you believe, Sturgeon, that every now and again, when I disappear from the center of things—as if I've fallen off the face of the earth, as it were..." He paused here, brooding over the exactly correct wording that would complete his thought. "Do you think that people forget all about me, as if I never really existed in the first place?"

Sturgess held open a stupendously well-tailored evening jacket, the sleeves gaping an invitation to the Royal arms. "Well, I certainly never do, Sir."

8

As Pacqui held open the door of the black cab for Daisy, she noted that her escort was attired in a black suit, white shirt, and skinny black tie. The effect created might have been that of an Archie Bunker-inspired hit man, were it not for the pair of unnecessary dark sunglasses that pushed the whole outfit into the realm of Pakistani Blues Brother.

"Your coach awaits you!" he announced, sketching a bow in the air as he ushered her into the back.

Showtime, Daisy thought, grabbing onto his arm for assistance as she dragged the sock-clad swollen ankle into the cab behind her.

9

Daisy always knew that she'd had too much to drink whenever she found herself engaging in philosophical debate with her own contemplated mirror image in a public bathroom.

"We could just hide out in here all night," Real Daisy suggested.

"We could go out there and mingle," Reflected Daisy replied. "How often do we get the chance to meet so many different people?"

"It's kind of cozy in here," the first suggested, wistfully, indicating the commodious expanse of the pink powder room and the generous offering of stalls in the Pakistani Embassy's Ladies' Room.

"Well, it is if we want to spend our entire life in the toilet." This time, Reflected Daisy didn't wait for a response. "I, for one, am heading on out."

"But what about Pacqui?" Real Daisy asked in distress, hand flying unconsciously to the Star of David at her throat. Her hand groped around for a moment, alarm beginning to seep in, until she felt the outline of the reassuring jewelry beneath her dress. She had forgotten that earlier in the evening, while putting on her new things, her tipsy focus had deemed the chain to look "somehow not-quite-right" with the perfection of The Dress and, rather than removing it entirely, had tucked it away safely inside.

"How in the world are we ever going to find Pacqui again among the crush out there?" she persisted. But even as she uttered the words, her focus expanded and she realized that, not only had

Reflected Daisy deserted her, but that some of the other female partygoers, many of whom were now queuing to use the stalls in the loo, were all staring at her.

Oh, dear, she thought, flinging open the door and sallying forth under a pretense of self-confident hauteur. *Did I really say all of those things out loud?*

Unlike earlier in the day, when it had seemed as if everything was for once just her size, as she emerged now on the other side of the bathroom door, it was to be found that the world had grown large once again. The Embassy hall was jam-packed with everybody who aspired to be anybody. Why, a person couldn't swing a stick in there without hitting a marquis, an earl, or a sheik. And every single last one of them was taller than Daisy.

Like a squirrel lost in a redwood forest, she searched in vain for Pacqui, but he was nowhere to be seen. Having sought out liquid sustenance from champagne acquired at the open bar in the corner of the room, she was further diverted from the hunt for her companion by the whiff of sweets she caught off of a passing dessert cart. Bending over it, she studied the selection intently.

Cheesecake? Mousse? Profiteroles? Not exactly the kind of thing that she currently had a hankering for, but it would have to do for now, she thought, as she began loading up her plate.

Straightening up and backing away from the cart—figuring that, probably, it would be fair to give someone else a crack at it— her senses were confronted with the ephemeral, fleeting aroma of exactly what she had been looking for. It seemed to be passing right by her, and she wheeled suddenly, trying to catch onto it before it disappeared completely.

And so it transpired that, as she wheeled, she collided with the Prince who, on this occasion, had opted for making a beeline straight up the middle.

And, for the second time that day, Daisy Silverman went down for the count.

• • •

She came to gradually, revived by the scent that had captured her attention just prior to the collision. Dimly, she took in the sound of a vaguely familiar voice uttering an imperious command.

"Quick, Sturgeon! Fetch a glass of water!"

Eyes still closed, she inhaled a full measure of her all-time favorite combo: chocolate and peppermint. In this particular chocolate, she discerned the musky odor of a high-priced but fun-loving trollop, while the peppermint on offer extended the cleanly virginal promise that one's innocence might be regained. She felt her nostrils quivering involuntarily as the firmly supportive hand under her elbow assisted her to her feet.

Rising slowly, still feeling unsure of her footing, Daisy found herself brown-eye-to-flesh with the largest biological instrument for listening that she had ever encountered in her life. The whorls of the canal seemed to go on forever. It might have been the result of an optical illusion, brought about by such unusually close proximity, but she could have sworn that Dumbo had nothing on this specimen.

The Ear was the single most erotic organ that Daisy had ever seen.

Straightening to her fully extended, vertically challenged stature, Daisy found herself raptly gazing up at the face that was attached to The Ear. It was the face of...

"Oh, my God! Charley!"

"Sturgeon!" he called, unable to tear his own focus away from the sheer openness of the face that was looking up into his. "Haven't you managed to locate a single glass of water in this entire place yet?"

Sturgess, slightly miffed at being drafted into service as a common waiter, deemed it prudent to break the electrical current by drawing the still stunned Daisy off to one side.

"Miss," he began, trying to come across as gently forceful and magisterially suggestive at the same time. He endeavored to keep his voice down so as not to draw undue attention to what was fast becoming A Situation. "One cannot address the Prince of Wales as 'Charley.'"

"Why ever not?" Daisy asked dreamily, staring back at the place where her new acquaintance still stood. She smiled shyly and, lifting her hand, sketched a little wave by wiggling her fingers.

No one, to Sturgess's knowledge, had ever asked that question before. He drew himself up to his full height. "Because it simply is not something that one does." He could see already that lessons in protocol were not going to be easy with this one. "Upon first being presented to the Prince of Wales, one is to initially address him as 'Your Highness.'"

"But I wasn't presented to him," Daisy cheerfully protested. "I fell at his feet."

"Be that as it may," Sturgess pressed onward, clearing his throat. He refused to allow himself to become caught up in the details. "If, following the initial encounter, one is permitted to remain in the Royal presence long enough so that a second address becomes required, one may use the more simplified title of 'Sir.'"

"You must be out of your mind," Daisy laughed, returning to her democratic senses. "I mean, he may be special," she added, thinking of The Ear, "but let's not go overboard here."

The spell broken for the moment, she turned and faced Sturgess, really seeing him for the first time. "And how does one address you? Is your name really Sturgeon?"

"God, no," came the unguarded, and therefore unprecedented, reply.

Daisy looked first at the Prince, then back at Sturgess, and finally back to the Prince again. She was clearly confused. "But I could have sworn he said—"

"Sturgeon is merely the, er, *nickname* that His Highness chooses to address me by," he hurriedly supplied, backpedaling like mad.

"And if one wished to address you by the name that you were meant, and possibly prefer, to be called?"

Sincerely praying that his answer would in no way imply a dissatisfaction or a criticism of his betters, that worthy servant replied, "That would be Sturgess, Miss."

Sturgeon, Sturgeon, Sturgess? Daisy glimpsed an unfortunate

pattern developing here and, deciding that it was high time that someone took it upon themselves to do something about it, called for an emergency nomination. She unanimously—if unilaterally—elected herself, and would have marched straight back to the patiently waiting Prince of Wales were it not for the fact that her twisted ankle rendered the straight march more of a listed hobble, her beeline a pathetic s-curve.

"I can't believe that you do that all the time," she accused, helping herself to a champagne glass that had ventured too close within her orbit.

"What?" the Prince enquired absently. Earlier his stomach had been growling. (Embassy parties were notorious for their meager pickings, and besides, who wanted to eat with all of those strangers staring at you, hoping to catch sight of a Royal with spinach stuck between his teeth or a milk mustache? "Got milk?" He thought *not*. Much better to wait until after.) But now he found his appetite had completely deserted him. He couldn't quite put his finger on what was so bewitching: The Girl or the ethereal-like quality of The Dress?

"I can't believe that you call him Sturgeon all of the time, when his real name is Sturgess."

"It is?"

"Don't you know how important a person's name can be to them, Charley?"

The moonish perplexity on the Prince's face made manifest that, clearly, he did not.

"Even if a person absolutely hates their name, it's still their own." And here, she could feel herself about to fly off on some tenuously related—at least, one could hope—tangent, but was powerless to stop herself.

"When my father named me Daisy, he doomed me to a life that would always be at least partially juvenile. Can you just hear what Daisy Thatcher would have sounded like? Kind of loses something, if you ask me. I doubt that anyone would have ever nicknamed me Old Iron Girdle, or whatever it was they used to call her."

Daisy noticed that a veritable paddock of horsy-looking women on the sidelines were all shooting daggers at her, but she chose to ignore them and barreled blithely on, pursuing instead what she was sure would be her winning point. "I mean, one can only presume that there's a good reason why you didn't name your own two sons Gaston and Alonzo. So, you see then, it would be okay if, for instance, I were to call him Sturgeon. Because then it would be to show that I liked him, not because I couldn't or wouldn't be bothered with remembering his proper name."

The Prince suddenly found himself in need of a glass of champagne after all. Badly.

He thought that he could glean just the dimmest outline of a point that he could respond to in there, somewhere. But then, he thought, looking at her, did it really matter?

Leaving Daisy and Sturgess to fight it out for supremacy of the satay tray, he flagged down a passing waiter and, helping himself to a glass, decided that it was time to respond to something. Anything would do, really. The important thing, at this juncture, was merely to get the point across that he was not a mute.

"I could try to change." He was surprised to hear the spoken words offered in his own voice, tentatively.

"Hah!" she returned with a mildly mocking laugh. "Almost no one ever can, even if they want to. It's only when you're not trying at all that those things seem to just happen to you." She gave the matter some further thought. "And often, it's a change for the worse."

"You know this whole name thing, which you have so kindly brought up, has called to mind a memory from my youth," the Prince confided, choosing to drive down a different street. "As a child, I always imagined that my real name was something more sturdy, like Richard Blake, and that I'd been switched with Charles Windsor at birth."

Daisy grabbed onto his sleeve, laughing. "And I always pretended mine was something more sophisticated, like Catherine Harkness!"

The Prince laughed along with her. "And is that your family name, Daisy? Harkness?"

The lights in the hall had dimmed and a quartet, set up in one corner, launched itself on a showcase of Billy Joel tunes. Daisy—uncertain if the nausea aroused in her stomach was the result of too much champagne or if it had been brought on by the cellist's overly zealous rendition of "Uptown Girl"—snagged a healthy slice of mille feuille off of the pastry trolley before answering. Unfortunately for her, she committed the tactical social error of trying to speak with food in her mouth.

"No, it's Daisy Sil—" And this was where she began to choke, one of the thousand layers of feuille having become as firmly lodged in her esophagus as it is possible for pastry to become lodged.

As her face turned blue, the Prince's blanched white with worry. "Sturgess!" he demanded. "Do you think that we could have a little Heimlich over here, please?"

As Sturgess administered the required first aid, Daisy tried valiantly to complete her sentence, but the only thing that she was able to come up with—immediately subsequent to the ejection of the offending pastry—was a single sibilant "S—"

"Ah, I see," said the Prince, putting one and two together, as he rubbed her back solicitously, the concern still evident on his face. "Daisy Sills is it, then? What a perfectly charming name." He was relieved to see that his patient was looking much better, and he gratefully accepted that single glass of water that Sturgess had finally managed to procure. Using the sky blue silk handkerchief from his breast pocket to daub at the stain on his lapel, he wondered idly if the palace dry cleaner would be able to remove saliva and pastry stains from wool. Well, no matter, really; there were, after all, a lot of other suits in the world, he concluded, passing the silk handkerchief along to Sturgess who, having momentarily disappeared again, had re-materialized with an amazing second glass of water for Daisy. "I believe that I used to know a Major Sills in Dorchester. But probably no relation, what?"

Daisy, who would have liked to have cleared up the mix-up concerning her family name, had just taken a big gulp from her own glass of water and, now reluctant to speak with any consumable at all in her mouth, felt the moment pass her by.

Meanwhile, the Prince was experiencing his own technical difficulties concerning the mechanics of polite conversation. Completely taken by the charms of Daisy—which were beginning to outweigh the opalescent splendor of The Dress—for once in his life, the King of Small Talk was at a dead loss as to what to say to a relatively strange woman at an embassy party. The old fertilizer standby probably wouldn't do here. And, the quartet having now embarked on the "Delilah" portion of their Tom Jones retrospective, well, there was clearly nothing neutrally inoffensive that one could say about *that*.

Casting about for a source of inspiration, the Royal glance chanced to fall upon Daisy's most original choice of formal footwear. Noticing the sock and neon-pink-laced sneaker for the first time, he commented brightly, "Oh! Aren't you clever to have worn your trainers? I wish I'd thought to do that. My feet do get so sore at these things. Sturgess, make a note."

What? shrieked the blatantly bewildered expression on Daisy's face.

Perceiving that, perhaps, his conversational gambit had not been received in quite the manner in which it was intended, he plunged ahead. "So, Daisy Sills, where do you hail from?"

A part of her still wanted to correct the whole name thing, but she found herself, curiously, just answering the question that had been asked. "I'm from Danbury; it's in Connecticut." She was about to explain where Connecticut was, when the Prince interjected robustly.

"Ah, yes!" he cried, glad to find himself in the comfortable midst of a topic of which he knew something. "Hat City! How your people must have despised President Kennedy."

Realizing that he must assume that "her people" *owned* Danbury, Daisy replied, "Well, it did devastate the industry, but somehow Daddy managed to survive with his fortunes intact." Daddy? Now where had that come from? Could Mumsy be so very far behind?

Which was kind of the truth, since Kennedy's refusal to wear a top hat to his inauguration really had had no discernible effect on Herbert Silverman's economic status as a septic man. Silverman's Septic had muddled through far worse.

"And the rest of the city?" persisted the Prince. "How have the rest of the citizenry managed to hold up?"

"Well," Daisy replied, tentatively, cognizant of the fact that the incident to which he referred had taken place nearly forty years ago. "I do believe, Charley, that most of them have managed to get on with their lives by now." Not wishing to pursue the idea of "her people" any longer—although, technically, she did have people, only not quite in the sense that he meant and, anyway, they were all dead—she decided that it was best to turn the conversational tables on him.

"And how about you? What was it like growing up in the palace, knowing that some day this would all be yours?" she asked, her gesture only wide enough to encompass the immediate vicinity, but intended to convey the vastness of Great Britain and the Commonwealth.

Regardless of the fact that the earnest query was a tad bit Oprah, the Prince found himself smiling inwardly at the refreshing display of candor. He knew that this was the question that piqued the curiosity of everyone who had ever met him, but that they were invariably too intimidated, or too intent on appearing blasé, to ask. This reticence on the part of others had proven just as well—at least, in the past. For it had prevented him from having to disabuse people of their dearly cherished illusions.

The truth of the matter was that his existence, to date, had been neither as hedonistic nor as dreadful as most people suspected. Rather, it had mostly just been boring. Until now, at any rate.

Still, in spite of his previous reluctance to publicly delve into his own past, there was something about this upturned and open face that made him want to answer Daisy as honestly as possible.

"Well," he began slowly, with a self-effacing grimace, "it's actually a terribly long story. Are you certain that you would be up for it?"

"I've got all night," Daisy replied, not even thinking about what she might be letting herself in for. "And I'm all ears," she added hastily.

"Oh," the Prince responded, his lips parting to evince a smile, the unguarded radiance of which the world had hardly ever seen. The effect was dazzling. "You too?"

* * *

"Mother always said that she wanted a normal, ordinary life for her children."

What was she, nuts? was the very first thought that popped into Daisy's mind. But for the time being, Miss Sills—nee Silverman—was wisely keeping her own counsel.

* * *

"Then it was off to school when I was eight. That was all Father's doing. You know the old story: If it was good enough for him… God, how I hated it there." The Prince sighed heavily, attempting to shrug off the memory as if he were having a bad LSD flashback. "Still, I don't suppose it was his fault, really. After all, he did have his own difficult childhood to contend with."

He was trying to put on a good face, but Daisy wasn't having any of that. Besides, she could clearly see Sturgess, who was standing the requisite three paces to the rear, begin to roll his eyes.

"Your father sounds like the ultimate doctor's wife to me," she put in, helping herself to just a little bit more of that lovely champagne. She wasn't usually much of a drinker, but while she was imbibing this stuff, she didn't seem to notice the throbbing in her ankle. So, you could say, that it was actually keeping her on her feet. That is, of course, providing that it didn't knock her on her butt again.

* * *

"The investiture—not to put too fine a point on it—was a bitch. One might imagine it to be a moving experience, but one would be quite wrong. Why, you should have heard the razzing I took about it at school. 'Saw you on the telly the other day with your mum, Charles. Lovely hat you had on. Looked quite a bit like my aunt, Hermione. Was that real ermine on the collar of your dress, then? Must have killed an awful lot of poor defenseless animals for that one.' Mind you, this was back at the end of the sixties, everyone's consciousness was being raised—love and equality for your fellow animal and all of that. Of course, they didn't actually say all of those things directly to my face, but I could hear them. At any rate, my therapist says— considering what my life has been like so far—that it is truly amazing, but that I don't seem to be suffering from paranoia in the least."

. . .

"You know, when I was really small, I suffered from knocked knees; had to go around wearing these dreadful orthopedic shoes. It was something of a relief, really, when my sister Anne came along and proved to be quite a good rider and sailor. Took a bit of the pressure off. But then, of course, it did become a smidgen old quite fast, Father always going on in that obnoxiously hearty way that he has—perhaps while he was plugging a pigeon over the palace or something—'Why can't you be more like your sister, Charles?' One tries to exercise patience, but it can be tiresome."

. . .

"Bringing girls home was never easy."

Daisy's ears pricked up at that.

. . .

"It is difficult, always having to keep a detective with one. Although," he hastily added, "I must say, that Sturgess is, by far, the very best that I have ever had. Still, there is a loneliness that is peculiar to an existence that must always be lived out in the presence of other people. I find that I am never so alone as when I am in a crowd. The handful of times that I have ever been permitted to be completely and physically alone have proven to be the few times that I have ever felt remotely at home in this body. Or as if it even belonged to me."

*   *   *

"Bad at maths; loved history—well, hardly surprising, that." The Royal face lit up here at the memory. "And astonishingly good at charades and playing dress-up."

*   *   *

"I sometimes think that, were it not for the fact that I was groomed to become a human Switzerland, I might have become something of an adventurer. I jumped out of a plane once; and I loved to fly. But I had to give all of that up. You see, it took all of the fun out of it, always feeling as though I should be worrying more about what I was doing, because whenever I was doing anything, there were always at least a couple of million people worrying about what I might be doing." The Prince gave a puzzled frown of his own. "If you take my proper meaning."

*   *   *

He stole a peek at his watch and then crisply shot his cuff, discreetly re-covering it. *My, I have been nattering on*, he thought to himself. Out loud, he said, "Oh sure, there are other family members that I could go on about. My grandmother, for instance, is an absolute honey." His face clouded. "Although, one does find oneself wishing that she wouldn't drink quite so often or puff on those cigars." But then the resilient smile made a comeback. "Still, she is nearly one hundred, so perhaps she knows something that the rest of us don't."

"So, when one gets right down to it, those are the nuts and bolts of the whole affair: Father could be a trifle chilly, while Mother was just a wee bit preoccupied."

• • •

Daisy, who had remained inordinately silent during this Monarch Notes version of the princely bio, had been ingesting all of this with just a modicum of salt. It didn't do to pass judgment without first hearing both sides of a story or, at the very least, observing all of the principals firsthand. Besides, she held her own preconceived notions concerning the functioning of dysfunctional families.

Biology was not destiny and, as far as she was concerned, people could not be preprogrammed in, say, the same way that a computer could be. Despite the almost overwhelming evidence to the contrary—what with the apparently Rachel-like effects of alcohol on her own system and her aberrant attraction to all things septic—she believed that a particular set of DNA or, for that matter, the circumstances of a person's individual upbringing (both familial and societal), merely predisposed one to be a certain way. But a propensity in one direction was not the same as an actuality, hence the scientific distinction between potential energy and kinetic energy.

Daisy herself could be said to be a classic case of unexpressed potential energy.

So, as anybody with half a brain could clearly see—was how the mental debate that was going on in Daisy's slightly pickled brain wound down—the combined double whammy of nature and nurture necessitated nothing.

And, in the best of all possible worlds—one without twisted ankles or expensive champagne—she might have voiced all of this far more cogently and graciously to the Future King of England, had it not been for her damned furry tongue. What she came out with instead, in a sentence eerily reminiscent of Bonita, sounded more like: "Even Jack the Ripper's mother was not completely to blame."

Then she raised her hand delicately to her mouth and, quite demurely, hiccupped up some Perrier Jouet. As she did so, she caught sight of the time. "Gotta run."

Her choice of words was uncharacteristically inaccurate, but they served their purpose in extricating her from the Royal presence, returning her to Pacqui's side, and freeing her to face the night.

The British Monarchy—for the time being, at least—was none the worse for wear.

10

In the cab, Pacqui commented on the oddness—and odds—of the fact that he hadn't run into Daisy all evening. "It was truly as though we were living in parallel universes. But," he added, laughing at his own joke, "the honor was all surely in the opportunity of being permitted to be driving Miss Daisy."

A most preoccupied Miss Daisy failed to respond.

"I wish that the evening did not have to end," Pacqui lamented a short while later, scampering ahead to open the door of the Hotel Russell for his lurching companion. "Perhaps," he asked, hopefully, eyeing the sneaker, "you might be so kind as to consider going for a jog with me tomorrow morning?"

Briefly recalled to reality, Daisy ruefully glared down at the other foot, the ankle still visibly swollen beneath the sock. "How about a brief stroll through Hyde Park instead?"

11

"Find me the woman who was wearing the trainer with the pink laces!"

"An' when I find her fer ya, Sir?"

"There is a message that I should like for you to give her for me. Bring me some writing paper and a pen."

The necessary materials having been produced, the Prince set about composing his missive. Periodically, he could be seen to be chewing on the top of the pen. And, providing background entertainment, he could be distinctly heard to be muttering throughout.

"Ask her... ask her... Oh, dear God! Do you think she could possibly be married? Did not see a ring, but then, whoever knows? How to circumnavigate that sticky wicket. Hmm... A guest! Invite her to bring the trusty old guest! If she brings a husband, then my goose will definitely be cooked, as Father is so fond of saying. But then, I suppose we could always... No, no, must not purchase trouble. We shall cross that drawbridge if and when our carriage delivers us there... Done! What do you think?"

Sturgess read in silence for a moment, finally answering with a certain degree of pride. "I do believe that ya have a wee touch o' the Robert Burns in yer soul, Sir." Then he thought again of the highly irregular young woman that they had encountered that evening, and for whom the letter was intended. "But are ya quite certain in yer mind, Sir, that ya do not want ta sleep on it fer a coupla nights?

Perhaps, it would be wiser ta... shall I send fer Teddy, then?"

"Blast Teddy!" There was a wild gleam in the Prince's eye. "Full steam ahead!"

12

As Sturgess exited the Royal bedchamber, gently shutting the door behind him, he determined to put the Master of the Household onto the task of running Daisy Sills to earth.

Sturgess's own official responsibilities were quite sufficient to occupy all of his time, what with always having to attend to the Prince's needs, not to mention the personal responsibility he felt about keeping His Highness out of trouble.

Besides, it was high time that the Master did something to earn his keep.

13

The Master of the Household, not used to being roused out of a sound sleep at four o'clock in the morning with a Royal request, was grumpy nonetheless. Replacing the receiver with a clatter that was loud enough to wake his equally grouchy wife, he grumbled aloud something to the effect that Sturgess had, yet again, overstepped his bounds. Not only that, but the man was clearly barmy. For, as anyone with half a grasp of palace protocol could tell you, it was the proper duty of the Chief of Palace Security to run human beings to earth, *not* the Master of the Household. When the Master arose, in an ungodly short period of time, he would be passing the champagne bucket in that general direction.

"Damned Scots," the Master muttered, punching his pillow—as opposed to, say, his wife, who had an unfortunate talent for always managing to punch back even harder. "Share a stinking Parliament with them, and they bloody well behave as though they thought that it was *them* what owned *you*."

14

Daisy was dreaming about Determinism.

The inevitability of events? the Dream Daisy pondered. Day following night? Who needed it?

There was a man singing something. And the sounds seemed to be coming from outside.

Entering through the connecting door, Bonita crossed to the window by the bed, where she benevolently proceeded to raise the window itself without drawing the blinds—the better to hear what the man was singing without actually allowing in any invasions of sunlight.

"'Daisy, Daisy, give me your answer, do...'" This lyrical, if somewhat strident, Pakistani rendition came wafting in through the crack.

Bonita, peeking through a gap in the drapery, beheld the form of Pacqui, who was joyously serenading from the pavement below.

"My, we were a busy little beaver last night, weren't we?" she enquired of the nearly comatose form beneath the sheets. Her hand hovered threateningly close to the cord that hung beside the sash. "Shall we just draw these nasty old drapes, then?"

Daisy, ungluing her lids, fixed her friend and companion with one very bloodshot eye. "Don't even think about it," she glowered.

"And how are we feeling today?" Bonita seated herself on the edge of the bed. "Fresh as a dai—"

"Oh, put a sock on it," came the uncharitable reply, as Daisy clutched onto her head with both hands as if, somehow, were she to hold on tightly enough, she might be able to prevent the whole thing from splitting apart.

A knock came at the door, adding mental insult to mental injury, and Bonita accepted the proffered item from a green-liveried porter. She examined the stunningly red crest of the Royal Family, as it appeared on the most impressive and official Buckingham Palace stationery, before relinquishing it to a suddenly much more conscious Daisy. "What *did* you get up to?"

Daisy tore at the seal on the creamy envelope and read the following in silence:

> *Dear Miss Sills,*
>
> *How lovely it was for me to make your acquaintance last evening. I am hoping that the encounter was not entirely unpleasant for you, and that I will be successful in persuading you to repeat the event. That is to say, not the exact same embassy party—for, they do tire one so; and besides which, even those who are blessed with the staunchest of constitutions at times can grow weary of satay. But, perhaps that is neither here nor there. Rather, I had in mind the notion of pursuing our acquaintance at some other, as yet to be specified, event.*
>
> *In the not too distant future, I shall be playing in a polo match at Smith's Lawn. Perhaps, if the idea does not seem too tedious to you, you might consider coming to watch me compete? Or, conversely, if that does not suit, perhaps you might do me the honour of accompanying me to the races at Ascot in a few weeks' time?*
>
> *I look forward with eagerness to hearing from you. You can reach me at any time at the above address. Just send your messenger around.*
>
> > *Sincerely,*
> > *Richard Blake*
> > *or, if you prefer it,*
> > *Charley*
>
> *P.S. Oh, by the way: Should you feel the need to bring a guest along with you, I would understand completely. All appropriate accommodations would, of course, be provided.*

"I think that I've just been invited out on a date with the Prince of Wales," a stunned Daisy commented, passing the pages back for Bonita's perusal. "And I'm taking you with me."

Bonita was puzzled. "But why does he call you 'Sills'?"

Daisy gave a noncommittal shrug, as if to say, "Who can tell with those madcap Royals?"

Bonita busied herself rummaging through Daisy's meager wardrobe. "Tsk, tsk. Won't do. New life; new clothes." She poked her head out of the closet. "Have to do something about that ankle, too." Diving back in again, she began tossing out garments right and left. Daisy thought that she heard her friend merrily singing something along the lines of, "Hi-ho, hi-ho, it's back to Harrods we go…"

And her foggy brain perceived it as being distinctly peculiar that Bonita's song was in no way inharmonious with the tune that was still making its way into the room through the scarcely opened window.

"'I'm half crazy…'"

June

1

A cloud-challenged, cerulean sky hung over the emerald expanse of the Guards' Polo Club at Smith's Lawn, not far from Windsor. Trite, perhaps, but what the hey?

If anyone had been paying attention, they might have noticed that a man in a navy-and-white player's uniform could be seen trotting up to where two women stood waiting on the sidelines.

"Charley!" Daisy called, waving.

The unrefinedly sweating Prince broke into a wide grin as he pulled up short alongside of the duo. "Miss Sills! How splendid of you to come!"

Daisy could feel Bonita's eyes boring a hole into the side of her face at the mention of "Miss Sills." Turning her attention briefly to her friend, she shrugged her shoulders as if to indicate that people were always making such mistakes in life and, anyway, certainly one name was as good as any. Then she decided it was high time to nip this problem in the bud. "Make it Daisy," she said, turning back to the Prince. "I think Miss Sills was an opera singer."

"And a wonderful one, too." The Prince gave Daisy as covert as possible—but still, a rather unregal—once-over. "What a lovely dress," he commented.

The teal-and-white polka-dotted dress that Daisy wore created a startling counterpoint with her auburn hair. It was a good thing for her that Harrods had such a large stock of sleeveless summer dresses with crew-necked collars, she thought, feeling for the talismanic Star of David that was hidden beneath the material. That almost nonexistent birthmark was still troubling her, and it was a great source of comfort to know that she would be able to, so stylishly and so easily, cover it up—for an entire summer, in fact, should it prove necessary.

On Daisy's feet, the ankle having since healed, were a pair of matching spectator pumps. "So this is why they call them that!" she had interjected that morning, putting them on prior to leaving for the match. "They're so that you'll look good, just in case anyone else is watching you, when all you're really doing is watching someone else doing something!" To one who did not know her, she could at times appear to be something of a fashion Neanderthal, but it was, quite simply, that her life had never had a call for any such items before. And yes, a rather lengthy expedition to Harrods had taken place just as Bonita had promised. Only this time they had left no survivors.

Bonita, in her new orange tweed, was dressed in a manner completely out of sync with the time of year and the temperature but that somehow, as ever, perfectly suited her character. She cleared her throat loudly, in a studiedly obvious manner, in the hopes of drawing some of the disgustingly besotted couple's attention onto herself.

"Oh, how rude of me!" Daisy cried, acting quickly to correct the error. "Bonita, I'd like you to meet Charley; he's the Prince of Wales. Now, then: Sturgess says that we have to call him Your Highness or Sir, but I don't think that's going to be necessary."

The confused look on Bonita's face informed Daisy that, in the fuss of the last few weeks, she had somehow neglected to mention who Sturgess was. *Oh, well,* she thought. There would be time to get into all of that later.

"And, Charley, this is Miss…" And here Daisy pulled up short, for once totally at a loss. She realized with a certain degree of astonishment that, in all of their travels together, the opportunity had oddly never arisen for her to learn of her friend's last name.

"Chance," Bonita filled in the blank, shooting Daisy a quick glance and giving a disturbingly familiar shrug to her own shoulders, as if to indicate that Daisy was right and that one name might serve as well as another. She extended her hand, flashing the tiny-teeth grin. "*Miss* Chance."

"Charmed," came the accurate response, as he graciously accepted the hand. "And you are...?"

"Daisy's governess."

"You could say that she taught me everything that I don't know," Daisy put in.

Charles was feeling relieved. For, although Miss Chance appeared as though she might be politely termed "formidable" at best, at least her name wasn't "Mr. Sills." Surely, that had to count for something.

"You ladies must be tired from standing for so long. Would you care to sit down?" He indicated the lawn, but then, eyeing Daisy's dress, he shook his head as if at his own stupidity. "No, that will not do at all. You might get that lovely frock soiled."

He cast about, seeking a suitable solution, and he surprised himself with his own alertness by coming up with something right away.

"Upsy Daisy," he said. "On to the bonnet." And he placed his hands around Daisy's waist, lifting her up onto the hood of a sleek silver car parked nearby on the grass. A quick shake of the topknot indicated that Miss Chance had no desire to be similarly hoisted.

When Sturgess came upon the odd little grouping a short time later, carrying the requisite post-match fresh towels and limeade, he was shocked to find that American woman seated on top of the Prince's brand new Aston Martin, with His Highness hopped up there alongside of her. And on the ground beside them stood another woman who, from what Sturgess could see of her, only presaged even worse things to come.

As the appropriate introductions were made, Sturgess cast a withering glance on Daisy and her equally diminutive companion. Weren't all Americans supposed to be tall, like Texans? Perhaps the Yanks' overzealous passion for compact technology—computers, discs—had finally crept into the gene pool. For it appeared as though they might, at present, be breeding dwarfs over there.

"Love your country," Bonita said, extending her hand.

Sturgess studiously ignored the offering. Didn't these people know that bodyguards were not meant to be treated as social entities? But, then, Americans were such a funny sort. Whenever they encountered anyone with an accent—which included anyone who spoke at all differently from them, no matter whose native soil they happened to be standing on, home or abroad, it made no never mind—they immediately held the so-called foreigner one hundred percent accountable for any and all actions of that person's homeland government and culture. "I do so love your country," Anglophiles would say, as if the person whom they were addressing were William of Hastings or something. And, heaven forbid if they had found something that was not entirely to their liking, *well...*

Sturgess sniffed at the air above her head. "Thank you for your kind words. I shall endeavor, should the opportunity ever arise, to pass those sentiments along to the appropriate authorities." He sniffed again, only this time it was from incredulity rather than, say, the affected snobbery that only the lower-rung members of a clear-cut class structure were ever any good at projecting. Could any woman really give off such a strong scent of barbecued chicken? The aroma of it was invading his senses and positively destroying the aftertaste that he had been savoring all day from the leftover satay that he had enjoyed for breakfast that morning. He couldn't wait to get away from her.

For her part, Bonita squinted up at the bodyguard through her frameless spectacles, rather rudely eyeing with suspicion the man who had just snubbed her. Not much to look at, was he? Much more height to him than any practical person ever needed to get the job done. Could do something a little more imaginative with that lack of hair. What was wrong with the Royal Family anyway? Didn't they care what they had to look at all day long? Go figure. Probably hang Warhols in the palace next. Thank God, not her problem. Conclusion: rumor proved as truth—good help *was* hard to find.

Charles had meanwhile taken a towel and was using it to mop at the perspiration that was still beading up on his neck. He took a healthy swig off of the bottle of limeade, before holding the bottle out to Daisy. "Care for some?" he offered, not entirely successful at stifling a most indelicate belch with his other fist.

Daisy, who had concluded in advance that, based on recent experience, it would not be wise to consume anything in front of the Prince for the time being, shook her head in polite demurral. Besides, it was all she could do to tear her eyes away from the draw of The Ear. She kept waiting for him to ask her a real question, so she could see how it worked.

But he was apparently too preoccupied. He was examining the remaining spectators and players who were still milling about, searching. His face brightened.

"Ah, yes… Over here, boys!" he beckoned loudly, waving his arms in the air. In a more subdued tone of voice, he spoke to Daisy. "There are a couple of people that I should like for you to meet as well."

Two extraordinarily tidy young men made their way over to where Charles and Daisy were seated. The taller of the two was such a crisp thing, that he positively squeaked as he walked.

The Prince hopped down off of the Aston Martin. "Daisy Sills," he announced, "I should like to present my eldest boy, William. The sloucher," he added with obvious affection, "is Harry."

And so it came to pass, that Daisy Silverman found herself face-to-face with The Heir and The Spare.

Were these things all really happening to her?

Amazingly enough, this incredible scene—much in the same way of many things that had transpired in the Prince's life during the last twenty years—went wholly unremarked by the members of The Press.

Talk about a fairy tale.

2

A phone was ringing at the Hotel Russell.

"Hello?"

"You think that nobody ever sees you. But I was there today. And the rest of the world will not remain in the land of dreams forever, my dear."

Ominous.

"Pacqui?"

But the line had already gone dead.

3

Defender of the Faith. Head of the Commonwealth. Supreme Governor of the Church of England. CEO of the largest tax-exempt non-charitable organization in the world. Queen. Call her what you will, but there were times when all of her titles weighed down on her as heavily as a crown.

Yes, it was sad but true; even queens sometimes got the blues.

Well into her morning routine—having already bathed, dressed, and quickly gone over her personal correspondence—she was now studying the card that contained the day's agenda. She glanced at it only briefly, before discarding it in disgust. What she had beheld there prompted the Reigning Monarch (simply another, albeit more transient, way of putting it) to hope that she was correct in her religious beliefs and that there indeed would be a sweet hereafter, a day of reckoning, a justification—a final reward for a life well and dutifully lived.

There had better be, because she certainly wasn't getting any here.

In fact, it was a good thing for the card that it wasn't a real messenger, because, otherwise, it might have been shot. For the offending item carried the rather disturbing information that the Queen must soon begin preparing for her next birthday celebration.

But, was it her Real one or her Official one? Time, and the ceremonial duties that went hand-in-hand with the mantle of sovereignty, had managed to finally blur her mental answer to that internally asked question. She must take care to never give voice to such a notion. Why, if she ever did, people might begin to think that she was losing her hold on things. And there would ensue— again!—all of those unpleasant speculations about it being time to step down a little early. Perhaps give the next generation—or, better still, the one after that—an opportunity to carry on with the scepter of tradition.

Over her dead body.

If she just remained calm, and carried on with her morning routine as if there were nothing amiss, surely, in time, the entire birthday matter would sort itself out.

It was 8:45, and she proceeded to her breakfast of sausage and kippers. She was halfway into it, when she decided to go the whole nine meters, opting for toast with Harrods' marmalade as well. Might as well enjoy it while she still was able to. Before one knew it, it would be March again—whenever that might be—and time for Parliament to publish the Civil List, in effect informing the Royal Family of what their allowance would be for the coming year. They had become increasingly tightfisted of late (things certainly had changed considerably from when *she* had first started out) and it was anyone's guess how long the favorite marmalade would survive as a necessity rather than a luxury. Why, it could fall prey to the assessor's axe any year now. Really, how anybody expected a woman to be able to afford pins on only $13,000,000—per annum—was quite beyond her.

She spread an abstemious quantity on her toast (so much fuss about nothing, really) and put on her reading glasses, so that she might peruse the latest racing news in *The Sporting Life*. As she turned the pages, a reference to the upcoming events during Royal Ascot Week caught her attention. Ascot was always held in June.

This was good news indeed, for it gave answer to the thorny birthday question. If the month were June, then that meant that April 21st—and her Real Birthday—had already passed (which made abundant sense, since it hadn't seemed as though it were that long ago since the last brouhaha had taken place). The bad news, then, was that she was, in fact, already older and had been for almost two months' time.

She put aside the racing news and reached instead for the card with the day's agenda again. Ah, yes, there it was. If she had looked at it more carefully the first time… but that was neither here nor there. Besides, surely it was somebody else's responsibility to more prominently display the fact that she would be required to don her uniform for the occasion. Had she seen that tidbit of information earlier, she would have known instantly that it was the Trooping of the Color Ceremony, performed annually in honor of her Official Birthday and mounted by the Brigade of Guards, that she was to be preparing for.

Yawn.

She sat back and listened to the bagpipes being played by the man who paraded up and down the walk outside of her window every morning for fifteen minutes. While the rest of the palace groaned with its displeasure at the sounds, the Queen gave a satisfied sigh, her equilibrium restored.

First, she would take her nine corgis for their daily walk through the gardens and on to see the lake and the flamingos. Then, only after that pleasant task had been completed, would she return and commence worrying about what to wear.

For the Trooping of the Color Ceremony, it was essential that she appear in appropriate regimental dress, depending on which regiment of the Guards Brigade was being so honored that year. It was always so important that she get everything just right. As the Queen mentally reviewed her vast uniform wardrobe—really, that Michael Jackson character had nothing on her—she sent a mild thanks to her own sovereign power that the card had also informed her that this year it was to be a regiment of Scots coming under review. She had always found the Scots, in spite of an inordinate amount of bad press, to be a most forgiving folk. Not at all like the Welsh, for example.

A few years ago, when it had been the Welsh, there had been one button on her uniform that had been stitched on to the wrong spot. Why, the resulting furor had almost equaled that of the Boston Tea Party, she remembered with a certain degree of asperity, holding on to the leash firmly in one hand as the corgis yanked her across the lawn behind Buckingham Palace. With her free hand, she adjusted the scarf that she was hoping would protect her coif from a most inconsiderately persistent drizzle.

The Welsh… hah! One would have thought that she had tried to unlawfully seize their lands or something!

4

Back at the palace, the Duke of Edinburgh had been roused from slumber by his wife's bagpipe player.

Damned palace walls were so thin that there was simply no avoiding that wretched noise, he thought. No wonder the Empire was crumbling.

He tried to return to bed, but, in the event, the ensuing barking made any thoughts of further sleep impossible.

The Duke threw the covers back and, rising, strode to one of the long windows in his own chambers. He pressed his fists firmly onto the sill, doing his best Yul-Brynner-in-the-*King-and-I* imitation—except he wasn't—and glared out into the cold, gray drizzle. In the mist, he could dimly make out the tenacious little figure trotting along.

Yes, there went his ever-loving wife and her armada of yapping Corgis again.

5

Much later in the day, following the ceremony, all of the Royals who happened to be in residence at the time stood on the balcony of the eastern facade, with its forecourt view of the Victoria Memorial. They were waving to the vast crowds of the birthday well-wishers.

Hearty wave.

Andrew wondered why, if they were going to move his mother's birthday around in the hopes of getting better weather for it—much in the same way that the Americans now believed that every holiday should occur on a Monday; really no telling how long it would be before they decided to replant Christmas there—the very least they could do was spring for July or August, when there really was a better chance of seeing the sun shine. It always seemed to be so damp on the second Saturday in June.

Good-natured wave.

Edward was hoping that there would be Yorkshire pudding with the birthday supper afterwards. A tiny frown crept over his features, when he thought that the overwhelming worldwide preoccupation with heart-healthy eating might prevent such a glorious eventuality. But he shrugged all such nasty notions aside.

Wistful wave.

Anne thought ruefully how her time could definitely be better utilized with riding or working on one of her many charitable missions instead. Definitely the last year.

Slightly tozzled wave.

Princess Margaret was wondering what the hell she was doing there, when she'd much rather be back at Kensington Palace. Why did Mother always have to insist that she be there for Lizzie's parties? It might be nice to stay at home every now and again. And it wasn't as though anyone ever made such a great do about it when it was *her* turn.

Much more tozzled wave.

The Queen Mother was thinking how simply lovely it was to have children.

Grim wave.

The Duke of Edinburgh was mentally figuring out just exactly how much poison it would require to kill that bagpiper. Would a similar quantity prove sufficient to take care of the corgis as well? And, most important of all, could the crimes ever be traced, beyond the shadow of a doubt, to him?

Tired—but pretending not to be and with determined cheerfulness—wave.

Couldn't they ever just get on with it, the Queen thought.

Absentee wave.

Where the devil was Charles?

Come to that, nobody could recall having seen him for days.

Just what the devil *was* he getting himself up to?

6

In the stands, women carrying racing cards were seen to come and go; not one of them gave a flying fig about Michelangelo.

• • •

It was the second of the four days in late June set aside for the Royal Ascot Week Race Meeting in Berkshire, signifying the beginning of the English summer social season, and the Prince of Wales could be seen to be traveling incognito. In addition to the expected top hat, lengthy morning coat, and cane, he was also sporting a full set of phony whiskers. Combined with the fact that the round sunglasses that he wore managed to camouflage the true color of his eyes, the entire effect of the costume went over as being just a teensy bit Lincoln-esque.

At his side, and doing her part to uphold the traditional dress of the lady spectator at Ascot, Miss Silverman was wearing the requisite pumps—amazing how much spectating was going on in her life all of a sudden. The pumps matched the salmon-and-white summer frock that, in turn, matched nicely with the wide-brimmed hat that—Daisy had learned much to her horror the day before— was *de rigueur* for the fashionable at the Race Meeting.

An emergency call to Bonita back in London on the previous evening had elicited the domino effect of a call from Miss Chance to the lovely people at Harrods, thus proving to the staff there that the

Americans could serve just as effectively as tormentors over the wire as they could in person. (Equally amazing to Daisy was the speed with which accessories were becoming necessities; if Charley looked like Abe, then she was beginning to feel like a dwarfish Barbie.)

In addition to Bonita, Sturgess had remained in London as well. By using the persuasive argument that provided he kept his disguise on in all public places he would be safe, Charles had managed to prevail upon his protector to stay behind for once. For the first time in years, then, the Prince was out on a date with a woman whom he had not known practically since pram days, and there was not a chaperone in sight.

"God, I hate horse racing. Always was more of Anne's thing, really."

"Why are we here then?" was Daisy's question, but the Prince's mind could only seem to operate on a single track at the moment.

"And the absolute utmost in dreadfulness is the Royal Windsor Horse Show in May. Fortunate you," he added, giving her hand a patronizing pat, as though she were a child who had barely and obliviously escaped a fate worse than boarding school, "you just missed that one. They hold these awful Gymkhana Championships and Father insists on participating in the National Carriage Driving Competition. It always puts him in such a foul mood when he loses."

Prompted by the bemused expression on Daisy's face, he quickly explained just what exactly the sport of National Carriage Driving entailed.

"I hate to play the philistine," she responded, her stupefaction having dissipated not one iota, "but I just don't get it. What's the point?"

The stark expression on the Prince's face indicated that, clearly, Honest Abe had never been quite able to fathom it all either.

As the day wore on, Charles, having apparently forgotten all about his disguise, proceeded to proudly introduce Daisy to any and every passing lord and dignitary who, for their part, cast many a startled backward glance upon the unusual pairing.

Daisy was fast learning that whom you knew was far more

important, in this world, than what you knew. For example, in doing her research, prior to attending Ascot—and armed with the knowledge, gleaned from the *Times*, that a visiting legation from the relatively new country of Butterundi would, in all probability, be in attendance—she had boned up on the politics of that minuscule protectorate and its efforts to gain a toehold in the lucrative field of exportation of palm products. Feeling confident that her recent acquaintance with the shipping methods employed for the palm items would stand her in fine conversational stead with the best of them, imagine then her consternation when upon being presented to the Marquis of Butterundi, he proved to be far more interested in learning if—being from the U.S.—she were a personal friend of Kevin Costner.

As yet undaunted, however, Daisy was never one to feel that any information, acquired when her two hands were firmly wrapped around a book, was ever a total waste. While doing her digging at the British Museum on the topic of Butterundi, she had also taken the time to sift through some material on the Royal Family. True, like all of her fellow countrymen, she had preconceived notions about the Royals, but this was the Real Thing. And the *People* magazine version would, quite simply, no longer do.

And, as Charles introduced her to a seemingly endless stream of the nobility, she was glad of the reading she had done. She was easily able to identify Princess Michael of Kent. And Charley's aunt, while she looked as though she could use a few cups of coffee perhaps, was also a snap. But as the hours ticked by, and with the titles still flying fast and furious, her head began to swim.

"The Earl of Essexshire," the bearded Prince went on. "The Duchess of Duncansville. Oh, and look," and here he pointed in what some might say was a rather rude sort of way, "there's the Laird of Loch Labian. Huh. Rather a nerve, calling himself that. Never does anything for those poor blighters anyway. One would think he should be too busy to venture so far from home."

Daisy felt as though she had accidentally stumbled into Warp World. Out loud, she said, "What does that mean, the Laird of Loch

Labian? I keep getting this strange feeling, like I should be asking somebody 'What's the frequency, Dan?'"

But the Prince had become distracted by the flight of some speckled bird, soaring over their heads. "And there's Charon," he said, his still upward tilted chin indicating a rather dour looking little man in one of the upper boxes. "Funny, I never noticed him there yesterday."

"Who?" There really were so many stupid things to know here.

"His official title is that of Her Majesty's Representative at Ascot. He is the man who arbitrarily controls who can and cannot enter the Royal enclosure."

"Charming." Daisy squinted into the sun. "Is that your mother up there?"

The Prince looked at her, an enormously contented smile playing around the corners of his mouth. "How do you and Miss Chance feel about Scotland?"

It might have given Daisy more than a moment's troubled pause, had she had time to spare a thought for the fact that the Star of David had now apparently taken up permanent residency beneath the front of any garment she happened to be wearing. But she'd had that nasty hat dilemma to contend with of late and, besides, it was tough thinking ethnic when the horses were running. She might not be conscious of it, but she had evidently made the decision to let sleeping religions lie.

She turned her head to meet another Earl, smile at yet more Duchesses, become totally confused by her very first Laird.

She was too busy talking with crowds to be bothered much about her virtue.

Daisy Silverman was now walking with kings.

And one could only pray that she wasn't losing the common touch.

• • •

The Queen was viewing the proceedings through her binoculars. Having failed to attend the first day at Ascot due to a beastly head cold, probably acquired during the celebration of her Official Birthday, she had pooh-poohed her personal physician's advice that she spend another day cooped up in bed. She could give a fine fig for the fashionable aspect of the Race Meeting, but she would be damned if she would miss viewing the horses.

Still, it was hard that the racing couldn't be constant. She felt the need to keep her spyglass glued to her face even between the runs, in order to avoid the boredom of being drawn into unnecessary conversation with the motley crew that her representative had chosen to admit to the box that year. If she could just maintain the pretense of being so wrapped up in anticipation of the next event on the field that she simply could not bear to tear her eyes away, perhaps none of them would try to talk to her.

But try as she might, even that normally indefatigable horse watcher could not keep her eyes peeled on an empty course for very long. Inevitably, the spyglass moved.

"Good God!" she exclaimed, not conscious of the fact that she had uttered the words out loud.

Her Majesty shifted the binoculars downward, peering out over the top as if in an attempt to see something better. She wiped furiously at her cold, damp nose with a linen handkerchief that bore her crest. Unsatisfied with what she had seen, she quickly replaced the glasses for a second look, only to find that her eyes had not deceived her the first time.

A mother would know those ears anywhere.

What in the world was Charles doing with that ridiculous false beard on? Why, along with that nose of his, it made him look downright Semitic, like he could be a rabbi or some other awful thing.

And who was that woman with whom he was so thoroughly engaged in conversation? The Queen had never seen her before.

Peer, wipe. Peer, wipe.

Who was This One?

She was a tiny little thing, so small that one would hardly deign to notice her, were it not for the fact that the heir to the British throne was busily presenting her to anybody who would pay even the slightest attention.

Practical haircut; strong teeth when she smiled, which was often; that nose looked suspiciously Semitic, too... But, no, surely even Charles would not go that far. Didn't look to be much of a breeder, thank God; an acceptable, but completely unostentatious dresser. Well, the Queen conceded grudgingly, one had to respect that. This One, except for the strength of that smile, did not impress as being at all like The Other One.

The Queen suddenly found herself clutching onto the spyglass with a vise-like grip.

7

It took the castle switchboard a good five minutes hunting, but they were finally able to patch the call through to the Prince's special friend in the guest suite at Windsor, where he had granted her lodging unbeknownst to his mother.

"Hello?"

"Other people are beginning to watch now. You must learn to be more careful." *Click.*

Gee, for such a cute little guy, Pacqui sure was going in for this menacing stuff in an awfully big way.

July

1

From "The Court Circular", the *Times*:

> ... and, in spite of the fact that the inclement weather forecast, predicted for that region, shows no appreciable signs of changing in the near future, select members of the Royal Family will be making the annual pilgrimage to Edinburgh, Scotland. The Queen, Prince Philip, and the Queen Mother are all expected to be in that notoriously wet city for the entire first week in July, conducting business as usual from the Queen's official residence, the Palace of Holyroodhouse. In a most unusual turn of events, Prince Charles is rumoured to also have plans of being in residency there...

2

As few as twenty-four hours previously, there had been absolute strangers tramping about in Her Majesty's Scottish digs.

Open daily to the general public, for a modest admission fee, Holyrood was closed during all Royal visits. The house staff, having arrived the evening before in order to commence preparations, had removed all cigarette butts from around the entryways, every guide brochure that they could find (some of which turned up in the most startling of places), and one particularly persistent tiny set of chocolate prints from the braided cord of a fragile pair of tartan draperies dating back to the time when the palace was inhabited by Mary, Queen of Scots. Yes, an optimist might say that the nearly 500-year-old edifice had been exorcised of all evidence of alien intrusion.

Nonetheless, there was one American who, having traveled for ten hours from London by train, was so totally enthralled with the 150-foot-long Picture Gallery, that it would prove difficult to separate her from it; and one very tenacious Scot, with his own agenda, who had every intention of holding a war council there.

"She must always be addressed as Your Majesty, *never* Your Highness," was Sturgess's advice, an item that he had mentioned to Bonita, oh, perhaps a good half-dozen times already, as he hustled to remain in her wake as she traversed the length of the gallery. It truly was amazing to him how brisk the stride was on this relatively Lilliputian being. "You must see to it that your charge is cognizant of that fact, Miss Chance, and that she behaves accordingly and appropriately."

"People are themselves. Right from wrong. Certain point? On your own." She squinted up at the vast melancholy face of a purportedly Scottish monarch. "Huh. These are really all fakes? Or are you pulling the leg just to see what it feels like?"

Sturgess reddened. "I assure you, Madam, that I would never presume to make such a ridiculous thing up. And certainly not for such a purpose." He indicated the long line of portraits and continued in the tour guide tone of one who had already covered this ground many times.

"What you see before you is a prime example of Scots humor. The nearly ninety oil portraits of Scottish monarchs ranged here were all actually painted by the same Dutchman. They were mass-produced by him—pumped out, *you* might say—at the rate of over one per week. A large portion of them is, in fact, fictitious—"

"Don't get it at all. What's so funny about bad art? Foolish him to waste a year doing this in the first place. More fool, you folks, to hang the art and not the artist." She shook her head. "Don't believe it. Never held with capital punishment, even for bad art." She continued her fast-paced patrol of the gallery. "Can't believe you'd let it hang here for so long. Like any joke: okay, maybe mildly amusing the first time, ha-ha. But letting it hang for generations? For *three centuries*?" She shook her head, and a huge hank of hair unfurled from the precarious topknot. "Can't think what you were thinking of, thank God. All must be out of what's left of your minds!"

"Be that as it may, Miss Chance," Sturgess sought to yank the conversational flow back to the pressing matter at hand, "someone must speak with Miss Sills."

Sturgess had originally determined to pull Daisy aside for another informal tutorial, in this instance regarding the proper form of address when speaking with the Ruling Monarch. He had been aimlessly pacing about the rooms of Holyrood, crossing his fingers that, this time, the talking-to would take, when he had fortuitously stumbled upon the gallery-stalking form of Miss Chance. Being greatly worried about the unpredictability of Daisy's behavior upon being presented to the Queen, he hoped to find in Daisy's traveling companion a co-conspirator to join in the mission of bringing Daisy to heel in the delicate matter of court protocol.

Bonita, keenly attentive to the frayed note of desperation that had crept into the normally stalwart valet's voice, tore her gaze from the latest in the long line of phony Scottish monarchs, and fixed it firmly on him instead. Bewildered by what she saw, she moved closer to him for a better view. Huh. He didn't come across today as being as obnoxiously tall as he usually did.

Feeling sympathetic, she shrugged a peace offering. "What help?"

For his part, Sturgess thought that the wee American might be just barely tolerable, were it not for the aromatic halo of salt and vinegar potato crisps that was orbiting around her.

"Perhaps, it would be best if *you* were the one to speak with her. She cannot very well address her as 'Lizzie.' Surely, even you must realize—"

Bonita snorted. "What does this body look like to you—a turnip?"

Failing to grasp the obscurely allusive Yank reference, but deeply embarrassed by the creative visualization of the naked physicality evoked, he elected to plunge on, despite the sense that he was being sucked into a circular verbal morass. "Root vegetables being neither here nor there, Madam…"

3

The Queen was daydreaming of Balmoral.

Unfortunately for her, that favored haven lay one hundred and fifty miles to the north, while she was stuck within the confines of Holyrood, a place that always succeeded in putting her in a foul frame of mind. She positively hated it there, even if it was for just one short week out of every year. It was cold and damp and draughty and, as if that were not all bad enough, the archaic heating system and electricity were always going on the fritz. Were it not for the fact that the call of duty demanded her annual presence there for such important events as the Ceremony of the Keys, she would have given up a goodly portion of her Civil List allowance in order to find herself elsewhere.

"Did you shoot this, too, Philip?" innocently enquired the Duke's mother-in-law, indicating with a nod of her head to the waiting server that she would very much like some more of the sherry.

The grim person being so addressed took another violent jab with his fork at one of the tough birds that the three elder Royals, with some degree of difficulty, were dining on. "No, I did not," the Duke of Edinburgh, who had been having a rather rough go of it lately in the bird-bagging department, groused huffily.

The Queen swirled the wine in her own goblet, studying the play of flickering lights on burgundy liquid, before taking a fortifying swallow. "Do you think, perhaps, that we should show some sort of—oh, I don't know—an interest?" She reached for her glass again, one slug having proved insufficient. "That is to say, do either of you think it necessary that we meet Charles's new friend this evening?"

Earlier that same afternoon, the Queen had observed Daisy's arrival. By peeking out through a crack formed by heavy tartan draperies, she had witnessed the convergence of the Americans as they had passed Queen Mary's Bathhouse, the turreted lodge on the left-hand periphery of the grounds, approaching from Canongate.

Charles cannot be serious, she had thought, upon this second inspection of Daisy. This One was far too short. Why, put her behind a podium with a microphone, and This One would be no more than a talking hat.

Experiencing a rare reversal of opinion, the Queen had groaned inwardly. At least The Other One had been tall enough for making fashion statements; This One looked to be only capable of fashion clauses, at best.

Thankfully, however, the nostalgic reversal proved to be merciful in its brevity. One would simply have to wait and see.

The Queen was called back from her reverie by the grunting sounds that her husband was making as he bared his teeth, rending the last shreds of meat from the carcass.

"If you're asking for my advice," he said, "I say that it's best to leave it for as long as you possibly can."

"He's right, dear," said the Queen's mother. "You know that you always dread coming here enough as it is. No point in spoiling the entire holiday for everybody else by becoming intolerably pettish before you absolutely have to."

The Duke of Edinburgh, basking in the warm glow brought about by his mother-in-law's rare concurrence with his point of view, waxed expansive. "Leave it until the party, day after tomorrow," he generously suggested, referring to one of the four Garden Parties that the Queen hosted each year.

He picked a stubborn piece of pigeon from between his teeth and sat, examining it where it was now wedged beneath his fingernail. "That way, we can enjoy at least one or two nights' good rest, before learning what fresh horror that son of yours has chosen to visit upon us this time."

At last, he succeeded in dislodging the last smidgen of pigeon from under his nail, and dismissively flicked it away. "Surely, even this palace is large enough to avoid her until then. Isn't it?"

Before the Queen had the chance to respond to this query, the questionable light fixtures flickered once (ominously), twice (dangerously), before the entire structure was plunged into darkness, granting dismal gloom free reign for the remainder of the evening.

From out of the encroaching darkness, as servants scurried to locate candles, there came a single plaintive request from the Queen Mother.

"Has anybody seen my wineglass?"

4

"Well, there goes Mother, off to work again, I see," the Prince said, indicating with his chin the water-blurred but nonetheless purposeful stride of the stolid figure as glimpsed through one of the rain-drenched windows.

What did *she carry in that bag?* Daisy silently wondered, referring to the inevitable purse that could be seen dangling from the Royal wrist. *A spare lipstick? A dime for an emergency phone call? The world's finest electronic organizer?*

Daisy had always previously assumed that the Queen carried her tampons in there. But, surely she was past that point at this stage, no? Not to mention, that it was difficult to feature the Monarch as ever having been the victim of bodily functions. What was the protocol, for example, if the Queen were to fart?

Then Daisy remembered something that she had read somewhere. Out loud, she asked, "Charley, what does the Chief Clerk of the Privy Purse do?" Perhaps this would provide the answer that she was looking for. "Is he the man in charge of that little bag that your mother's always clutching?"

"Not at all," a bewildered Charles replied. He failed to see any connection. "Actually, his duties involve…"

But Daisy was off again in handbag speculation land, and would thus never know what the Chief Clerk of the Privy Purse's job description entailed. *An emory board? Mace? House keys?*

"… so, as you can readily see, to some people's way of thinking, he is a very important man."

The Prince leapt down from his perch on the back of a velvet sofa, where he had been sitting, feet dangling over the side.

"At any rate," he said apologetically, "I'm afraid that I shall have to leave you for a few hours, as I must be off to work as well." His brow furrowed. "A distillery opening? Ground-breaking for an orphanage?" He shrugged. "Well, no matter. Sturgess will have it all written down for me somewhere. Speaking of whom, I shall leave him behind with you. Should you require anything, do not hesitate to call upon him. I am sure that he would be only too glad to help you out. I shall try to return as early as possible. But until then, by all means make yourself at home."

Hmm. What to do, what to do, Daisy wondered. Left to her own devices, she was idly swinging her arms back and forth, clapping her hands together.

Then her eye chanced to fall upon a discarded tour brochure, sticking out from underneath the drapes. It had been abandoned there by one of Daisy's fellow countrymen, the same little urchin who had deemed it necessary to also leave behind his chocolate mark.

Daisy thought of the oak-paneled walls of Holyrood, the portraits of Scottish nobles, the oak chests, the candles, crepitating floorboards, and small windows. Not to mention, enough tartan to gag a warhorse.

She thought of the howling wind. Thankfully, the on-again-off-again heating system was presently in 'on' mode, because the downpour was turning it into a particularly frigid day. Even Edinburgh did not normally get this chilly in the month of July.

She listened for a moment to the creaking of the ancient wooden structure. If a palace could be said to quiver, then this one was doing it.

Okay. So, maybe it was all a trifle over-the-top; just a tad bit Orson Welles on a plaid acid trip. But Daisy decided that she liked it.

Stooping, Daisy snatched up the surprisingly thick pamphlet. She flipped through the glossy pages that made it look as though the sun shone over Holyrood at all times. She was thinking that some tiny tourist's mommy or daddy had forked over a pretty pence for this souvenir, only to have it tossed aside, along with the gummy candies that she had found tucked up under the hem of the curtain.

Well, why the heck not? Daisy asked herself, fishing out the red candies first, with the intention of leaving the licorice ones for last, an eventuality of final resort that would be called into service only in the event of absolute sugar privation.

Charley had said that she should make herself at home, *mi casa es su casa* and all of that. And what better way for a Silverman to make herself at home than wrapping her hands around some printed matter and reading her way through it? She would take herself on a self-guided tour, she decided. Surely, she could amuse herself for a few short hours. After all, she had never needed a Sturgess to take care of her before. And, even if you were only planning on stopping at a certain place for a short period of time, it still always made sense—at least, to her way of thinking—to find out something about where you were, so that later on you would always know where you had been.

Hmm. Let's see…

Holyrood was located at the Canongate eastern end of the Royal Mile, which began at Edinburgh Castle. Peppered with interesting old structures—replete with turrets, gables, and chimneys—the quaint little shops that now studded the Mile sounded to Daisy to be no more than an aesthetically pleasing architectural device, employed to wean people from their own presumably hard-earned cash.

Adjacent to Holyrood Abbey and dating back to the early 16th century…

Yawn. Chomp, chomp. Flip the page.

Mary, Queen of Scots had moved there from the French Court, already a widow for the first time at the age of nineteen. Well, now, that was a bit more interesting.

Chew, chew.

Daisy paused in her strolling and reading to study a marker that recorded the spot where David Rizzio had died on 9 March, 1566.

Nothing like having a veritable tombstone smack in the middle of your home, Daisy thought.

Mary's Italian secretary, Rizzio, had been murdered, assassinated some said by Lord Darnley—Mary's second husband—along with his cohorts. The dirty deed had taken place in this, the audience chamber of Holyrood. The rather—as all reports agreed upon—shrimpy form of Rizzio was said to have been stabbed fifty-six times. A nice round number, that.

The syphilitic Lord Darnley (the brochure didn't exactly refer to his medical condition in so many words, but Daisy had remembered reading something once) had been, in his just turn, also murdered. The same some, who always seemed to be saying something, this time said that Mary's hand was the guiding force behind the plot.

So, plenty of murder and mayhem. A little grim, perhaps, but nothing really out of the way there either.

Yuck, how bland: an orange one. Daisy swallowed. *Flick of the page.*

Bonnie Prince Charlie had hosted one whale of a rip-roaring ball there in the mid-eighteenth century.

Now, that sounded a little more uplifting.

But then, not long after that, the circumstances of his own existence had undergone a distinct reversal of fortune.

And, of course, Mary had also wedded her beloved Bothwell there, an obscenely short time after the murder of Darnley. This union was the signal event that many historians agreed had precipitated her downfall, but it was also one that Daisy had always found to be romantic, if only in a remotely 'other time' sort of way.

The way that Daisy had always figured it, Mary's first husband—the childish French King—had probably played with her; Darnley had provided her with great sex—at least, initially; while Bothwell had, in all likelihood, been the only one who had actually listened to her (for about five minutes, at any rate), thereby explaining just about everything.

But, as anyone at all familiar with Scots history knew, practically even before the third honeymoon was over, Mary's own life took a decided turn for the worse.

In fact, Daisy thought as she flipped the pages more rapidly, it would appear that quite a few people who had entered at the portals of Holyrood had found themselves meeting their own untimely demise. Was it not possible to, having once walked in, walk out again?

Daisy shuddered. The implications of history could be frightening.

Feeling somewhat relieved, she found herself at the last number in the brochure. The entry pointed her attention to a curious piece of needlework, executed by Mary during her twenty years spent as the "guest" of Elizabeth I, while waiting for her own execution. The stitched scene was that of a cat-and-mouse game, with Elizabeth I sewn as being the cat.

Daisy immediately thought of the present Queen.

It must be trying after a while, to always be seeing your progenitors depicted as being wantonly cruel or in any of a number of other despicable lights. Surely, it must make you begin to wonder what they would all be saying about you once you were safely in the ground.

Never having given much of a damn before about what others thought of her, Daisy gave a second shudder, this time in sympathy for the woman whose image appeared on all of the coins in her pocket.

Happily, she discovered that her guided steps had soon led her back to the point from which she had begun, just as Charley was making his own return from another doorway in the room.

"It seemed as though I was gone forever," he said. "Did you have any trouble keeping yourself occupied?"

Not waiting for an answer, he crossed to the window that they had been looking out of earlier.

"Oh, look," he said, parting the curtains. "Mother is back from work as well."

Daisy ducked her head under his arm and peeked out, watching the Queen's approach. From the slight droop in the normally military bearing, it looked as though the Ruling Monarch had experienced a particularly trying day at the office.

Doesn't her left wrist ever get tired of holding that handbag up? Daisy wondered. Surely, there must be a permanent mark tattooed onto it.

Daisy realized, with a mental thud, that the Queen must have been about eleven years younger than Daisy was now at the time that she had ascended the throne. Why, she'd been a baby! What must that have felt like?

Still feeling very much a kid herself, she couldn't imagine.

5

It was payback time for the Queen.

Hostesses in Scarsdale knew about payback time; in Frankfurt, the social laws governing it were followed to the embossed letter, and the French had their own phrase for it: *l'argent de la derriere*.

It was therefore inconceivable that the Queen, being the world's most commonly hosted and hosting woman, should not be aware of a tradition that was practiced even by the Inuit who knew enough to reciprocate in terms of whale-blubber barbecues outside of their igloos.

One could hardly expect less from the Queen.

In exchange for the countless teas enjoyed at the domiciles of others during the course of the year, the Queen herself hosted four Garden Parties during any given twelve-month period, and one of these was always held during the week that she was in residence at Holyrood. But, more than just a tit-for-tat affair, stocked solely with nobles and dignitaries, it was also an opportunity for the Queen to acknowledge the good works of ordinary citizens. Also invited were any number of riffraff, all for no apparent reason other than the fact that they had either enough pull or enough push to wrangle their way in.

This year, the Queen was having 4,000 guests over for her July tea.

And they were all going to have to fit under the tents that had been set up all over the back lawn of Holyrood and which would, pray God and Queen, protect their coifs and top hats from the torrential downpour.

The men, for the most part, knew enough to show up wearing the expected morning suits. The ladies, for their part, were attired in hopeful light dresses and flowery hats, behaving as though they had been delivered of the perfect summer day that they had every right in the world to expect.

The aristocracy was therefore, as was required of them on this occasion, rubbing shoulders with the so-called "little people." Or, to put it more bluntly, with people like Daisy.

For a personal introduction to the Queen—for even that capable little Stateswoman could not be expected to greet each of four thousand individuals in a single afternoon—a card was supposed to be filled out weeks in advance and delivered to the Lord Chamberlain. But today Daisy Silverman would be meeting the Queen, having leapfrogged such banal formalities. For the first time in her life, Daisy could be said to be well connected.

And she—standing nervously with her own entourage of Charley, Miss Chance, and Sturgess—along with everyone else squeezed in under the canvas, was impatiently awaiting three o'clock and the expectedly prompt arrival of the Queen.

As she poked her head out from under the tent, Daisy could see that the cats-and-dogs thing that it had been doing out there had devolved to the inevitable dismal drizzle. *Well,* she thought, looking at the gray sky, *at least it isn't plaid.*

Like clockwork, the Queen could be seen to be making her slightly sodden way across the lawn, trailing her own ambulatory flotilla of hangers-on. The Queen had never been one to disappoint the fans.

There were bands playing under the tent, and a small fanfare went up, as Daisy watched the Royal entrance.

The Gentlemen Ushers leapt to attention, stepping to the front to escort the Queen and other important female persons, and deliver them from the moment of their entrance to the individuals selected for special introduction who were waiting amid the throng. Those flanking the Queen, on this occasion, included the Queen Mother and Princess Margaret. The latter had grown bored early with the London season and, at the last moment, had elected to motor up to Edinburgh, springing a surprise visit on her sister and keeping one eye out for a spot of fun.

As she tracked Margaret's (only mildly teetering) progress around the perimeters—not to mention Margaret's covert glances at her sister, the Queen—Daisy decided that she must be witnessing the Guinness World Record case of Longest Maintained, *and* Most Justifiable Reason for, Sibling Rivalry. But, all voyeuristic cheap thrills aside, a part of her longed to reach out and, grabbing the sure-to-be-startled shadow-dweller by the shoulders, urge her to "just get over it!"

Daisy found herself wincing now as the Princess caught her low heel in the muck. Perhaps reinforcements would be required before the day was out.

At any rate, the primary function of the Ushers as a unit was apparently to ensure the Queen's most efficient and accurate advancement through the waiting four thousand. Once she had successfully traversed the line and, having achieved the end of the marquee, the Queen might accept a cup of tea, but she would *never* eat anything, not wishing to be stared at should it prove necessary for the Heimlich Maneuver to be called into play. *So, that was where Charley got it from*, Daisy thought.

As Daisy observed the slow but steady progress, measured out at a rate that was sure to win the ultimate race, Daisy thought that there were times when the Queen looked peculiarly like an ingénue in an off-Broadway play: hopelessly trying to hit her mark and unsure where she was supposed to place the prop; or, to put it in Drury Lane terms, uncertain if her smile were too wide for the pits or not wide enough to play to the gods.

* * *

If the Queen, whose color could be said to be royal red, was having a tea party, then it would appear to be a requirement that there would have to be at least one mad—in the sense of angry—gentleman present who also happened to be in possession of a hat. In this instance, that Mad Hatter would be Prince Philip (Prince of Corfu by birth; Prince of England only by way of a politely accidental reference on the part of those who really could be expected to know no better; Duke of Edinburgh by created title and, especially, here).

Or, to flip the coin in the other direction, the Queen Mother was attempting to sneak a cigarillo in plain sight at her daughter's tea party, and her son-in-law—a rabid anti-smoker—was royally pissed.

In fact, the claim could be made with complete accuracy, that the two—lashed together in this world solely by the marriage of the one to the daughter of the other—were both fuming.

The Q.M. (as she liked to refer to herself in her own mind, feeling that a good acronym could help define one, as P.M. had done for Margaret Thatcher, or J.R. on that American soap import a few years back) thought, not for the first time, that the world would be a happier and healthier place were it not for the presence of nonsmokers, who were always getting so worked up over everything, thereby causing heart attacks in themselves as well as in everybody else. But, with the way that the world happened to be turning, at present—especially in America where, if rumor could be equated with accuracy, people were practically bearing arms over the issue— it would appear more likely that the anti-smokers would succeed in forcibly excising the other side, before the smokers woke up and smelled the tobacco.

The Q.M. had of late been mulling the issue over. She still couldn't quite figure out what the Antis would do once they had finally succeeded in jettisoning all smokers right off the face of the planet and were forced to face the fact that they were still mortal themselves, but now they had millions fewer people to blame for that unfortunate byproduct of life: that they still suffered from heart disease and cancer, having never given much thought to personal responsibility or—say—giving up double mocha lattes (whatever *they* were) or taking up regular walks out of doors; that they were, ultimately, no closer to happiness than they had ever been, only now there was just one less excuse for it.

Oh, what the hell, the Q.M. thought. Once that had all occurred, the sourpusses would, in all probability, then take up the long overdue crusade of forming a witch-hunting party, with a view to running to ground the rascal responsible for the invention of the Twinkie.

If other people hadn't acquired the sense to make the connection yet that it was undue anxiety that killed, then more fool them.

Being a naturally peace-loving individual herself, the Q.M. was more than willing to do her part to avert the inevitable Armageddon. And so, in order to avoid her son-in-law's further wrath, she would make good her escape into Holyrood in search of a fast game of snooker.

Besides, there was a blasted hole in the tent, and her cigarillo was getting soaked. Not to mention, that they never served anything to drink but tame tea and soft drinks at these ridiculous afternoon affairs.

She glanced out at the downpour, vaguely remembering a schoolgirl quote, something along the lines of there being "water, water all round, but not a drop to drink," but she gave up on trying to recall the origins of the reference when her head began to ache from the effort.

A body could certainly use some fortifying libation, to go along with the snooker, if it were intended that the body in question were to be later thrown back in like a sardine with the rest of the Prohibition Four Thousand.

Now, then, she thought with a renewed sense of purpose— the only really effective device known to mankind that kept a body going strong for over a century. Where was Charley's new little friend hiding herself?

• • •

The Queen Mother had slipped into something a trifle more comfortable.

Considering herself to be too old to have to worry about the newfangled concept that was embodied by the acronym of P.C., the Q.M. thus wore her ermine proudly in spite of the Royal—and politically correct—eschewal of fur. There were an awful lot of dead animals from the Queen's own old wardrobe at B.P. that were now inhabiting the cold storage room back in London, and they would probably never see the light of day again.

Having donned a royal purple full-length stole with ermine trim, along with an evening tiara, the Q.M. was now chalking her cue stick, as she waited impatiently for her turn. She might have known that the American girl wouldn't be up to snuff on the rules of snooker. Still, Charley's girl seemed a nice enough sort and, having confessed after the second snort of whiskey to being something of a "pool shark" back in the States, she really did have quite a deadly aim on her.

Observing Daisy as she sank another ball, the Q.M. decided that it was time to create another diversion. She pulled the sterling silver flask from out of her voluminous purple robes.

"Single malt, this," she said, proffering the flask and inviting Daisy to take another swig. "Couldn't get through one of these ghastly affairs without it."

She keenly eyed Daisy's post-third-shot befuddlement. "Well, then, whose turn is it?" she asked innocently, stealing opportunity and moving towards the table herself.

Daisy stepped back and monitored the Queen Mother's progress to the green baize of the billiards table, its mahogany sides gleaming, the leather mesh pockets gaping enticingly. She couldn't quite decide if it was her own vision that was wobbling or if that was just the natural stride of her opponent.

Back home in Danbury, Daisy'd had a friend—well, more like a pool hall acquaintance, actually—of whom the Queen Mother was oddly reminiscent. It was eerie the resemblance between her and Taffy, the forty-seven-year-old grandmother of five, who still liked to wear mini-skirts and thigh-high leather boots and who believed in family, friendship, and Harley Davidson, but just barely in that order. Taffy liked to shoot pool, liked to shoot it with one cigarette dangling out of the corner of her mouth, and was impossible to beat.

The remarkable thing about getting beat regularly by Taffy, at a game that had the two basic requirements of luck and some sort of aim, was that the woman was a souse. Along with the dangling cigarette, there was an ever-present smudged glass of whiskey at her elbow which, as she bent over the table, could have come from anywhere along the continuum of the fifth that she liked to consume daily. And it was often a tough call to make, which was more precarious: the glass perched on the very edge of the table, or Taffy, tottering woozily up to it to take her shots.

But, no matter how uncertain or circuitous the approach—no matter how long she spent, suspiciously taking in the lay of the balls with one eye squeezed shut, as she swayed on those high-heeled boots like a metronome—when she finally bent over to shoot, it was as though the aging cycle queen had been flash-frozen in space and time, the nanosecond of lucidity elongated just enough to ensure that she would hit her mark with deadly precision.

And now, here was the Queen Mother, who could also bang balls like nobody's business.

"What are your intentions with my grandson?" the Q.M. asked, slamming another shot home while, at the same time, yanking Daisy back from Reverie Lane.

"Intentions?" Daisy echoed, her confusion brought about by a combination of factors, those being that a) she was not now, nor had she ever been, the type of person who had ever intended anything in life; and b) the fact that she was herself now drifting off somewhere, floating out to sea on an ocean of whiskey.

"What are your plans for him?" the Q.M. reiterated, accompanying the surprisingly crisp enunciation of each word with a bang of the cue stick on the floor. But the look on her face gave away the fact that the banging resulted more from an eager anticipation to learn the answer than it did from any presumptions of the right to make imperious demands on Daisy. "What do you want from him? What is it that you see in him?"

Having no clue as to how to properly execute a plan, even if she did have one, Daisy ignored the first question. And, never having been the sort who wanted anything *from* anybody, she also bypassed the second, thereby mentally leapfrogging her way to the end, where she landed somewhat uncertainly at the base of the third.

"His ears?" Her response, were there a keener observer in the room, could have easily been described as answering a question with another question.

"How splendid!" exclaimed the Queen Mother, evidently relieved that now she was able to understand everything. "I fell in love with his grandfather in exactly the same way. What extraordinary coincidences the world so often seems to be made up of!"

Daisy had found, since arriving in London, that whatever meager interest she did possess for introspective examination of her own motivations had been placed indefinitely on hold. And she had no desire—at least, not at the moment—to resuscitate them.

"What was the war like?" She virtually hiccupped the question, hoping to draw the Queen Mother away from the brink of the subject of Charley by substituting a relevant topic from her own reading of the Q.M.'s past.

"Which war?" came the bemused reply from one who was clearly stumped by the frequent obscurity that was Daisy. Surely, the American girl didn't believe that she was old enough to fill her in on the details of the altercation between George and the colonists, did she?

"Why, World War II, of course." Daisy, like the vast majority of her countryfolk, believed that there had only ever been one good, true, and *real* war (the one where their involvement had mostly been reinvented by Hollywood and writers of fiction), while all of the others had merely been the product of grim historians with less than vivid imaginations (with the only other notable exception being the Civil War—at least, in the vividness department).

The Q.M. still failed to see how the question was in any way germane to what they had been discussing, but she found, suddenly, that she no longer cared for relevance in the slightest. It was such a novelty these days, when the press only seemed interested in the doings and opinions of younger generations, to be asked a sincerely felt question of any kind. In fact, the only thing that anyone really seemed to ask her about anymore was how she had managed to stick around for so long. People were always regarding her with unconcealed surprise at the prospect of finding her alive, looking at her as if to say, "What? *You're* still here? Well, if you're not going anyplace, the very least you could do is fill the rest of us poor slobs in on how you're not doing it, so that we might have a go at it as well."

"Actually," began the Q.M., hoping to strike the right tone now that she had an audience, "it was quite a pleasant time, really. Oh, one doesn't mean the actual bombing, per se," she hastened to add, seeing the startled expression on Daisy's face. "The Blitz was hardly a day at the polo grounds. But rather, it was so…" and here she paused, leaning on her cue stick as she searched the high ceiling for the right word, "*nice* to feel as though one were needed, do you know? My husband, the King, and I used to go out to see the people after the bombs had fallen. And for some strange reason, our just being on the scene seemed to make people feel better about it all, safer, as though we were the British version of your American Marines or something of the sort." She sighed heavily. "Now all that anybody wants from me is to find out what kind of magic dust I've taken, as if the only object of anything were the ability to stay at the party longer than anybody else." She paused, considering again. "And the only one that the people have seemed truly interested in for the past two decades was of a much more recent generation, and her not even really one of us."

Daisy would have liked to offer something reassuring here, but her tongue had grown too furry from the whiskey. And besides, the only potentially reassuring thing that she got the chance to say was, "Well, it doesn't really matter all that much anyway, does it? I mean, you mustn't miss the bombs so much. After all, just so long as *someone* is making the people feel better, does it really make that big of a difference who is doing it? Or why?"

Because, before she could get her tongue to perform any more tricks, the Queen Mother had done her wobble-walk across the room, and had taken Daisy's hand impulsively in her own.

Daisy noticed for the first time, that the Queen Mother smelled... not precisely like a food item, but rather, more like a person's most favored garment; one that had been stored away in mothballs until almost forgotten and that now, rescued just in the nick of time, had been brought forth in all of its former glory, but this time comfortingly enrobed within a cumulous cloud of whiskey.

"You know, dear, speaking of making people feel better, Charley has been so changed of late—" the Q.M. began.

But before *she* could go any further, the gentleman just named entered the room in a burst of energy.

"Ah! Daisy! There you are. I have been looking for you everywhere." With a loving nod of acknowledgement towards the Q.M., he added, "I sincerely hope that Grandmother has not been filling your head with a lot of silly stories about what a wretched child I was. Come," he added, with a twinkling smile of expectation, taking her other hand, "you must rejoin the party."

And Daisy, who no longer trusted her own desires around this man, especially not when under the intoxicating influence of whiskey, entwined her fingers in his and allowed herself to be silently led away.

• • •

Daisy decided that the Queen Mother had the right idea. It *was* really difficult trying to deal with these affairs without benefit of additional alcoholic support, and the natural byproduct of the New Puritanism—a Garden Party with tea being the most radical beverage on offer—was beginning to take its inevitable toll.

Upon returning to the tent she had found, much to her horror that, if anything, the crowd had swelled in her absence, with people swirling closely around her to the point where she felt as though she were the wedding ring finger on a particularly fat person with a sodium intake problem. The presence of one too many titles was beginning to make her nervous; and in order to stave off the oral gratification vacuum created by the lack of any more whiskey, the most polite way that one could put it would be to say that she literally pounced on the circulating dessert tray.

Daisy helped herself to something that looked vaguely meringue-y and that had absolutely no odor whatsoever, and three or four more items that were most definitely chocolate by birth.

"Why, Daisy, have you no self-control at all?" Charley asked, clearly charmed.

"Zippo," she replied, popping some more chocolate into her mouth. All previous resolutions cast haphazardly to the four winds, she was once again eating in front of the Prince. "I can always run tomorrow," she added, thankful that the twisted ankle had long since healed. She considered for a moment, postulating a new personal theorem. "And besides, even if I don't use them myself, I'm a definite product of the credit card age. Why pay in advance, when you may not live long enough to enjoy the prize?"

"Well," he replied, "it would appear that, at the moment, my prize has got herself all covered in chocolate."

He removed the silk handkerchief from his pocket and wiped her hands with it.

Well, it's a good thing that one of us is always prepared, she thought. Although it did seem, at times, that she compelled him to spend an awful lot of time cleaning her up. Still…

Quite suddenly, it occurred to her that the ordeal of meeting his mother still lay in wait in her immediate future, and that there was a residue of whiskey sloshing about in her brain, and, for all she knew, chocolate stains on her dress. How in the world was he ever going to get her cleaned up in time for *that?*

Daisy felt as though an arctic wind had just blown through her entire being.

Seeing her shiver, and believing its source to be the combined effects of a summer dress with a drafty tent, he took her right hand, rubbing it between both of his for warmth.

"My, Daisy, what a rough little hand you have."

Daisy sought to retrieve it and, reflecting on all of the toilets that the hand in question had cleaned, she snatched it away. Casting about, she tried to come up with a believable alibi for why it was the way it was.

"It comes from tending my garden," was the best that she could come up with on such short mental notice. "I like to help things grow where I can."

"Never heard of gloves, then?" He shrugged. "No matter. I adore this hand. It has such character. Such a welcome change from the mashed-potato ones that one is forced to grow accustomed to."

At the mention of mashed potatoes, Daisy's feelings of dread cranked up yet another notch. The Queen would never mistake her work-roughened hands for soft vegetables. She would know right away that Daisy did not belong with her son.

Watching, as Daisy shuddered anew at the prospect of what she believed would be her certain exposure, the Prince grew concerned that she would catch a serious chill.

"Here," he offered, solicitously, "let me get you something warm to drink."

Left to her own admittedly suspect devices, Daisy tried to maintain some semblance of calm. But she grew restless in about the time that it would take to locate something warm to drink at a normal-sized party. And, as she began to wander among the crowd aimlessly—catching sight of the Queen's husband here, stumbling on a glimpse of the Queen's sister stumbling there—the level of her anticipatory anxiety grew by leaps and bounds.

"Dai-*SEE!*"

What?

As far as Daisy was concerned, the doctrine that stated "that which does not kill me makes me stronger" had only ever really applied to cockroaches. And, unless her sense of hearing had flown straight out the window—taking along all of her other faculties of reasoning with it—then the possessor of the voice that she was now being subjected to was definitely going to kill her, sinking all of her hopes dead in the water.

Miss Silverman was about to learn that it was indeed true what everybody said about these afternoon affairs: They *did* let just about anybody into them.

"Dai-*SEE!*"

Daisy considered running away, but people were jammed in too tightly: if she ever made it through the other side, she'd emerge looking like a crepe. She considered hiding under one of the food tables, but that wouldn't do either: the damp earth would undoubtedly ruin her dress, leaving her to look like a muddied American ballplayer.

It was fast becoming apparent that she couldn't run and she couldn't hide.

If only the fickle hand of fate had seen fit to introduce her to the Duke, she could have hit him up for the name of some poisons that she could employ to either do away with her problem or do away with herself (which might actually be the same thing at this point). But since that undoubtedly cataclysmic event was still sometime in her future and not yet a part of her past, there was nothing left for it but...

Slowly Daisy turned, step by step, inch by inch, as if she were expecting to find the ghost of Bela Lugosi just on the other side of her shoulder, only to be faced with...

"Why, Dai-SEE Silverman, whatever in the world are *you* doing here of all places? The last time I saw you, *you* were cleaning my toilet. But, before I even knew what was happening, that lovely Ms. McKenna that you used to work for calls *me*, and tells *me* that you won't be coming anymore and that *I* have to get used to somebody else. Well, I tell you..."

Mrs. Reichert's considerable bosom heaved against the snug fit of her Union Jack patterned silk muumuu. She flung her long blonde-from-the-bottle tresses over her shoulders, flaying the Duke, and—having fortified herself with a single sustaining breath—plowed on.

"When Dr. Reichert, my husband, told me that he had won some kind of silly award for inventing some sort of ridiculous device that would improve people's chances of surviving open-heart surgery—like such a thing would ever make *my* life any better. I mean, really, I ask you… Don't you think that it's a lot more likely that someone like me'll keel over long before I make it into the operating room?—I told him, 'That's nice, dear.' And then, when he told me that the AMA was sending him to London to give a speech before the Royal Surgeons something or other, and that they said he could bring his wife, I said, 'Even better.' But *then*, when we got to London, and Dr. Reichert told me that we would also be continuing on to Edinburgh, and that *I* was going to get to meet the Queen, who wanted to thank him for, oh, I don't know, making the world a better place with that stupid device of his or something, *well*, then I said, '*Hey.*'" She heaved some more. "But I never thought, not in my wildest anything, that I'd be running into *you* here. Why, little Daisy Silverman, whatever are you doing—"

It was getting to be high time that little Daisy nipped this muumuu-ed moron in the bud.

"I cannot tell you how pleased I am, Madam," she broke in, adopting the arch accent of a truly blue-blooded Brit, "to learn of your poor dear husband's undoubtedly well-deserved success, after what must surely have been an entire lifetime filled with trials and errors. I mean that strictly from a medical point of view, of course. But, what is most unclear to me, is why you are continually referring to this Silverman person, for I haven't a clue as to who you might be speaking of."

Mrs. Reichert examined the woman before her more closely, speed-living through the emotional triangle of disbelief, confusion, and disappointment. She was experiencing the very common feeling of social letdown that one felt when one found that the only person at a party who was their certain social inferior, for one reason or another, wasn't.

"But you're the woman who used to clean my toilets in Westport. You're Daisy Silverman from Danbury," Mrs. Reichert persisted, reluctant to let her social edge die so quickly.

"I assure you that I am not, Madam," Daisy replied, rhyming her 'not' with 'caught' to make 'naught,' so that there could be absolutely no doubt remaining as to her country of origin.

"While it is true that I have been to Westport," Daisy continued, unconsciously sensing perhaps that it would be easier later on to remember near-truths (no matter how bizarre) than one-hundred percent man-made fabrications, "I did not travel there with the express intention that you ascribe to me."

And here, Daisy was lost for a moment, unable to recall why anybody went to Westport if it wasn't to clean toilets. But then, she put herself in Charley's late ex-wife's size tens—just to see how they fit—and all of a sudden, she had no trouble at all thinking of other reasons to go to the lovely waterside town.

"I went there for the shopping," were the words that came tripping off her tongue. "They have those perfectly lovely stores on Main Street, and the prices are quite reasonable there, I think." What else might The Other One have noticed? "I also went for the bookstores."

No, Daisy shook her now very internal head like a dog at her own stupidity. The Other One wouldn't go to a town for its bookstores. But, now that Daisy had sent her there—or, more accurately, sent herself there as being someone like her—she had to quickly figure out what she might notice there.

She began pedaling as fast as she could. "The bookstores had lots of children's books, and lots of books on social issues and for helping people with their problems. Not much about clothes, really, but I did find that they had perhaps one too many books on me. But then, isn't that always the case?"

Seeing the startled look on Mrs. Reichert's face, she hastily amended, "That is to say, on us, er no, I mean on the Royal Family, er, oh you know, that's just a way of talking here: me, us, Royal Family, all of England... If it's about them, then it's about us too, right?" Daisy gave a Solomon-like shrug. "I think that it really is possible sometimes for people to carry an obsession much too far." She was hoping that the very silent Mrs. Reichert was not by this point mistaking her for either an impostor Royal or a complete royal ass.

"And as for your mention of the city of Danbury before... I mean, Hat City, *really*..." And here, Daisy bestowed upon Mrs. Reichert a most condescending look, as she indicated the perfectly made summer hat that she was wearing on her own head. "As anyone can very well see, we are quite capable of coming up with our own perfectly good creations right here."

Heaving a great sigh of relief, and feeling that she had juggled all of that quite well, Daisy was grateful that Bonita was not in a position to see her. Because the un-whiskeyed portion of her brain was emitting distant signals that warned that Miss Chance might not take too kindly to this denial of her previous position.

And besides, she really didn't mean to be misleading anybody, but rather, it was more that she was growing so used to being this Sills person.

"I do not know any Silvermans now, nor have I ever," she added, putting the final kibosh on even the most stubborn of suspicions. "My family name is Sills."

Daisy experienced a wave of gratitude, Part II, that Bonita was tied up elsewhere with whatever it was that Bonita did when nobody could see her, because Miss Chance had definitely "naught" caught on to the whole name thing yet either.

Mrs. Reichert took in Daisy's auburn hair that, while still the same color that she evidently associated with her former cleaning lady, was now combed to perfection and sans its distinguishing baseball cap. She took in the tasteful, brightly colored summer dress, the one that fit into this place so much more than her own—however well-intentioned—red-, white-and-blue attire. She took in the pumps that could spectate through life with the best of them. And then she reassembled all of these pieces into the framework of all of the things that Daisy had just said.

"No, of course, *she* could never be *you*, and *you* couldn't possibly be the person that I was mistaking you for. *She* would never be invited to something like this." Mrs. Reichert sighed her heaviest sigh yet. "I don't know what I could have been thinking. Must be all of that Prozac that Dr. Reichert has me taking." She started to turn away, dejected.

Daisy, who only intended to save her own skin, had not meant to push the other woman to the brink, where she would begin to question the workings of what passed as her own sanity. Feeling a wave of sympathy, Daisy impulsively reached out and grabbed Mrs. Reichert by the sleeve.

"Oh, my dear woman, haven't you heard?" she asked in her most reassuring voice. "It is so easy for one to make the kind of mistake that you have just made. Why, everybody who is anybody, these days, has one of those—what does one call them? Ah, yes—*doppelgängers* crawling around somewhere on the face of the planet. In fact, speaking of which," she added, lowering her tone to a more confiding sotto voce level. "I do believe that the Duke of Edinburgh—what with that eternally retro hairstyle and such—is quite frequently mistaken, by a number of Ladies of the Bedchamber, for the Kim Hunter character in *Planet of the Apes.*"

There, Daisy thought, feeling most satisfied with herself, *that ought to make this sad woman feel better about herself.*

Mrs. Reichert, for her part, shivered, as she bestowed upon Daisy a look of absolute, abject terror. Taking as much care as possible, so as not to offend this strange woman, she extricated herself from Miss Sills's grasp, before hurriedly disappearing into the crowd.

For just a moment there, and in spite of that accent that was so preposterous that it just had to be real, Miss Sills had reminded Mrs. Reichert exactly of Daisy. The good doctor's wife had briefly recognized in her the person who had predated the act of forgery that Daisy's life had become, and just that smidgen of a glimpse was enough to wake her up to the fact that she should have reacted more appropriately with *joy* when that lovely Ms. McKenna had informed her that Daisy would no longer be coming to do her house.

No matter what Dr. Reichert had to say about it, the time had definitely come to wean herself off of that even lovelier Prozac.

And, as she burrowed deeper into the throng, screwing her way back into the woodwork, hoping to escape all Silvermans for all time, she found that she no longer minded so much the notion of occupying the lowest rung on the Garden Party ladder; no, not if that meant that she could finally rest, assured by the implicit knowledge that Daisy Silverman was safely off somewhere else, tormenting other people's minds on some other unsuspecting continent.

* * *

"Daisy," the Prince asked with evident amusement, "was that you I just heard speaking English to that sad-looking American woman?"

Daisy had been so preoccupied, what with observing the squirming retreat of Mrs. Reichert's surprisingly agile form—not to mention, wondering how things had managed to become so badly botched, when they had seemed to be going so well—that she had not heard the Prince come up behind her, bearing a cup of tepid tea. Startled, she whirled to face him.

"Veddy much so," she replied, her hands clasped firmly behind her back. She determined to continue—at least, for a time—in the manner in which she had begun. "I am considering going native."

But, in spite of her outward air of calm, her run-in with Mrs. Reichert had produced the undeniable effect of sobering up Miss Sills, nee Silverman. Considerably.

* * *

Daisy was back in the attack mode.

"You can't be serious," she was saying.

Charley had just informed her that being a Royal was pretty much like any other job.

"Oh, yes, very much so," he said. "We call it the Family Firm."

"I hardly think that it's the same thing as your average mom-and-pop business. And besides, when have you ever had to worry about money? After all, it's your mum's mug that's on the change in everyone else's pockets."

The Prince sighed for the very first time in her presence. Ever since schooling days, he had been quite regularly blamed for situations that he'd had no hand in creating. And it was particularly galling that such an accusatory tone should come now from this quarter, from the one place where he wanted so badly to impress.

He sought to explain. "It is all part of what is expected of one. Everything is tied up with some tradition or another."

"*Everything* that you do is dictated by tradition?" she asked, incredulously.

"Pretty much," he shrugged, not really seeing what she was getting so worked up about.

From where Daisy was standing, it seemed that tradition encompassed the things that people did because they always did them, and that, after a certain point, evolved into activities that people could explain using no other line of reasoning.

"Tradition should be something more than merely doing something the same way, just because it's always been done that way or because your father did it. I mean, what about that school that you were telling me about, the one that you hated so much?"

A part of her hoped that she wasn't beginning to sound too preachy, but she found that, once launched, she had difficulty maintaining much concern over that.

"Life isn't meant to be lived as a dress rehearsal for the first fifty-something years, Charley. This is it. And as for all of that tradition stuff that you're always going on about, well… If it's not good or satisfying or productive somehow, then it's just so much meaningless activity, like gerbils on those pointless wheels that people put in those cages, patting themselves on the backs that they've provided their pets with a full lifetime's entertainments. If there's no reason for something…"

She paused, trying to come up with a more straightforward

manner in which to state her case.

"Put it this way: back home, ballplayers—on national television, mind you—play with their own balls all the time, just because they can and because they always have. You might say that *that's* an American tradition. But personally, that's one tradition where it would be just fine with me if the next generation were to put an end to it."

The Future King of England was thoroughly perplexed. His new friend might be attractive and more fun than polo, but she would come up with these notions that could strike one as being passing odd at times.

"But, Daisy, who else's balls should they be playing with, if not their own? Surely, you cannot be proposing that they should cop somebody else's. Why, one would think that such behavior would be considered theft or, at the very least, bad sportsmanship. No?"

For the first time Daisy was conscious of the gulf that separated their two worlds. And this sudden awareness of the yawning crevasse, just gaping right there at her feet, was making her feel as though she had to shout across it—at the top of her lungs—just to make him hear her. And the sensation of *that* was making her testy.

"So, that's it?" she asked. "Everything with you is just a job or tradition?"

He didn't know what to say to that.

"What about the role of a wife?" she pressed, not caring if she sounded irascible. "Is that just another job too?"

He should have seen the red warning lights flashing. A wiser man might have known enough to get the heck off of the tracks at this juncture, that there was a good chance that there was a freight train coming.

But, instead, the Prince gave a confused shrug and a slight nod. Even without having said anything, it was, clearly, the absolutely wrong thing to say.

"And I suppose you always get full satisfaction from your butcher?" she asked, icily.

The Prince startled her, by suddenly taking her hand in his and asking, "Daisy, why are you being like this?"

She put her other hand to her head, massaging her temple for all she was worth.

"Oh, I don't know," she said. "I guess I'm just not myself today."

"Who are you, then?" he asked softly, bending down to receive her answer.

But, before she could give it to him, he suddenly straightened to full height.

"Oh, look," he said, eyeing the procession as it drew near. "I do believe that Mother is finally ready for you now."

Somehow, one kinda doubted that.

• • •

If Daisy was daunted by the prospect of meeting the Queen, if she was behaving in any way out of character, then she was perhaps deserving of personality amnesty. Sure, she had managed to remain blasé about meeting Charley. But, really, when you think about it, anybody could handle that neat top hat trick if they only thought about it first.

But his mother?

Now, that was a horse of a more royally red color.

One must keep in mind that this woman had personally represented the apex of the greatest pyramid scam of all time for nearly fifty years, the absolute pinnacle of all royal Everests; that she had made enough money at it to take on God at the tables at Vegas, a Windsor Fats; that others who had previously been presented— among them other royalty, presidents, Elton John, and assorted power-brokers ad nauseum—had quaked in awe at the vastly superior wealth and power embodied by that one little woman in the hat with the mysterious handbag draped over her arm. (Yes, down to a Duke and Duchess, they had all invariably wondered about The Bag.) Why, it was enough to give a sultan an inferiority complex, make a sheik feel like a nomad.

Was it then surprising that one other little woman, herself a

toilet bowl cleaner by trade from Danbury, Connecticut, should fall
into line at the last? After all, and special as she was, even Daisy, after
a full year of resisting the media onslaught of tragedy transformed
into entertainment and inanity, had finally given in and watched
the O.J. verdict along with everyone else in her frequently cuckoo
country. Did you really believe that this heretofore insignificant
individual was going to meet with and—oh, who knows? Topple?
Tip? Let's just agree to say *trample* all over the Royal Family. One
means to say, really, darling, who was *Daisy* at that point to buck
against all of that tradition?

Generally considered to be something of a force majeure in her
own right, the naturally indomitable Daisy caved.

Rejecting the technical edicts of her religion of birth, Daisy
bowed her form before another mortal being, executing a perfect
curtsey. Odd, the things—that one had found unimaginable
before—that one found oneself doing when finally confronted with
the end product of over nine hundred years of monarchic rule.

"Your Majesty..."

Shahs, Michael Jackson, other queens, all had fallen into line
and had all acted and reacted in pretty much the same fashion.
When you got right down to it, there really were only just so many
possible variations on the theme of presentation, their range limited
by the appropriate laws of protocol and human nature. One bowed
and then, reminiscing afterwards, one might say that the Queen had
been lovely. One might say that she had been as kind as one could
want her to be. But, one did not go around saying that she seemed
a trifle too full of herself. *That* was simply just not done. Restricted
stimulus: circumscribed response latitude.

"Ma'am..."

Princess Margaret, listing at the Queen's side, cocked a scathingly
sardonic brow at Daisy's genuflecting form. She was thinking that
her sister would devour This One like just so many tiny kippers.

Oh, shut up, Daisy thought silently, testily, considering how all of
her own life—until the advent of Bonita—she had longed for some
form of female companionship. *Be grateful that you even have a sister.*

"Do you have any embarrassing eating disorders that we should be advised of at this juncture in time?" the Defender of the Faith was asking Daisy.

"No, Ma'am," came the stunned reply.

"And," continued the undisputed Talking Hat of the Commonwealth, "concerning the topic of frontal nudity: are you given to baring your breasts in public places in front of businessmen other than my son?"

"No, Ma'am," Daisy again demurred, by now thoroughly baffled. Perhaps it was true what they said about inbreeding.

"Then you'll probably do," the Queen said, taking the startled Daisy's hand and grasping it within one of her own gloved ones.

The Queen had decided that she liked Daisy.

Daisy, for her part, failed to attend to the Queen's mood, having become subdued by dawning horror when she had noticed that she had inadvertently transferred a chocolate stain from her own person onto the Queen's otherwise pristinely white glove.

Damn Charley! He'd missed a spot. Maybe if she held onto the Queen's hand a while longer, she could subtly rub that damned spot out with her own hand.

But, then, if the Queen twigged to what she was doing, might she not think that Daisy was coming on to her or, at best, just a tad bit too weird for her son?

Oh! Why were these things always happening to her? And where the heck was Charley, with that damned silk handkerchief of his, when you really needed him?

• • •

Sturgess had been too occupied with reading Daisy's lips to note the stain that she had left upon the glove. Standing off to one side behind the Prince, he had observed Daisy's performance with at first grudging, and then proud, approval. At least, she hadn't called the Queen 'Liz' to her face. And, clearly, the hours of drudgery spent in the butler's pantry at Holyrood, brushing up on their curtsies, had really paid off.

Bonita, on the other hand, frowned slightly upon the proceedings, having put in a side bet for 'Betsy.' But she, herself placing far more of a stress on Daisy's actions than upon her words, deemed that to be a relatively minor disappointment, outside of which it would appear that her charge had acquitted herself quite well. She particularly relished the notion of Daisy having left her mark upon the Queen, much in the same way as a cat—one who should have been fixed—spraying the corner of your house, and you not sniffing it out until later.

Bonita, unfortunately, had come upon the tableau just in time for the windup, and so she was a witness to the glory, but not the lack of guts.

Proving, once and for all, that you could fool all of the Royalty some of the time; some of the Americans all of the time; and Miss Chance, well, maybe just once.

* * *

As for Daisy, lost in all of her efforts to—for once—get things right, she had never even sniffed out the fact that the Queen smelled of neither Beef Wellington nor of tea roses, as one might expect, but, rather, she gave off absolutely no odor whatsoever.

* * *

Out of sight, out of mind, or something closely related to that.

It didn't take Daisy all that long, once the Queen's procession had passed beyond view, to heed her own most typical advice. She got over herself. She recovered from her traumatic meeting, and she commenced—in Daisy-like fashion—to think of the Queen in pretty much well the same way that she would anybody else, like Mrs. Reichert or one of the other Westport matrons. Why, before you knew it, she probably *would* be telling people that the Ruling Monarch had seemed a trifle too full of herself.

You know, Charley, about your mother... was how the words were beginning to formulate themselves within the confines of her busy little mind. But, seeing the happy look on her friend's famous countenance—as he strolled by her side back towards Holyrood in the damp, taking care to match his gait to her considerably shorter one—she realized that he was quite pleased with the way the afternoon was going. Getting into the spirit of things, she decided for once to give way to the better part of valor, and so, bit down hard on her frequent nuisance of a tongue.

Instead, while her mind was exercising itself on the sure-to-be-touchy subject of his mother, her demon tongue seized upon that golden opportunity to trip her up by leading her down yet another forked path with the ultimate destination being offense.

Absently, she enquired, "So, what do you folks do around here to celebrate the Fourth?"

Just more of the same-old, same-old for the average Englishman, Daisy was about to learn, much to her chagrin. One would think that nothing out of the way had occurred on that date in the history of the world.

"Actually," the Prince replied, "we do not usually make a habit of celebrating conflicts that our country is alleged to have lost."

Daisy backpedaled. "Oh, that!" she laughed nervously. "I wasn't referring to that old thing at all! No, what I meant was that that date just happens to be my birthday."

"Now, then," he looked down upon her with an open smile, completely devoid of the air of strained tolerance that one had every reason to expect. "Why does that not surprise me?"

6

"His Highness is greatly changed," Sturgess conceded. "He seems so much less melancholy than he used to be."

"Mine's changed too. More like a Sills now."

Sturgess favored this cryptic remark by bestowing a confused smile upon the redoubtable Miss Chance. Perhaps she meant to imply that Charles had the pleasing effect of making Daisy become more herself than ever?

It was the night after the afternoon before, and the two were jointly pacing the Picture Gallery, holding their own postmortem. They were both relieved to find that, in fact, nobody had died.

"Never been so happy." Sturgess hurried along, the gleaming black tops of his leather shoes reflecting back up upon the man who moved with his hands clasped behind his back. This way of speaking, with its reliance on pure ideas and its refusal to accept the necessity for subjects in the world, was rather catching.

"Made for each other," Bonita responded in kind, as always finding that, in a world without subjects, meaning was clear if you knew what you meant. And if you didn't? Well, ambiguity could be comforting too, sort of like the intellectualized equivalent of Creole cooking.

Somewhere, in the United Kingdom, a dog conveniently chose that moment to howl at the moon.

Distracted by the sound, they each turned away from the other and, in turning simultaneously, caught sight of their side-by-side reflections in a pair of old looking glasses.

Bonita saw that the blurred quality of Sturgess's glass reflected an image of him that, while it also made him seem pudgier, had the happy effect of foreshortening his form until he was brought down to manageable size.

For Sturgess's part, he could plainly see that Miss Chance's glass had the equal and opposite fun-house effect. *Why*, he thought to himself, *she looks practically like any normal person now.*

Amazing how perfect everything can be once you distort reality, Bonita thought.

Or, maybe it was the real world that warped everything, transforming perfection into something less, was the spin that Sturgess gave to it.

Sturgess sniffed the air. And was that satay he was smelling? Why, of course it was. He'd know that scent anywhere! It was gingered beef satay over hot brown rice. Yummy.

Without taking the time to think first before speaking, they both uttered the exact same words at the exact same time:

"Make an interesting couple."

And, again:

"So do they. Maybe help?"

They turned again, so that they were now standing face-to-face.

"Make it Bonita," the shorter of the two suggested, by way of a peace offering. An abrupt bob of the topknot invited reciprocation.

"Not on your life," Sturgess laughed his refusal. He had no desire, at this late juncture, to have the world learn that his mother had saddled him with Pierpont.

"Ye really are a scary wee person, are ye not, Bonita?" Sturgess stated more than he asked, but with an attractively accepting smile.

Glint of firelight on eyeglasses; flash of teeth.

"Like to think so."

7

How absurd! Daisy thought. How ridiculous and how absolutely boring it all was. Talk about routine!

It was to be her last full day at Holyrood, and she was standing at one of that cold building's tiny windows waving to her new little friend—the Queen—as the other departed in the rain to carry on with her prescribed duties.

On the prior evening, over a private supper of plump pheasants that the Duke had not shot, the Queen had confided to Daisy about how the annual visit to Holyrood was more of a duty call, crammed full with garden parties, factory openings, and excursions to inspect the regiments. And how she hated it all.

Balmoral, which lay 150 miles to the north, was really so much nicer, she had added. That was where they all usually headed at the end of summer, extending their stay until well into the fall. It was serene there, but also ever so much fun. Less work, more play. And Philip was never a dull boy there.

In fact, during the supper, where the lights had miraculously remained on throughout, Daisy had behaved herself so well— having assumed the all-ears position—that the Queen had decided that she made for very good company indeed. And, having arrived at that relatively snap assessment of the younger woman's virtues, she had made the questionably sound gesture of extending an invitation for Daisy to join them at summer's end at Balmoral.

Poor you, Daisy thought now, sketching a last little wave at the receding grim figure in her regimental dress, as the Queen trudged off to do her duty at a jam factory opening. How pathetically tedious it all was. After all, the Little Inspectress (as Daisy had come to think of her) was Colonel-in-Chief to so many, meaning that that particular woman's work was never done. Why, there weren't enough jewels in the crown to get Daisy to do that job.

At least, Daisy thought, if the Queen had to go out into such dreary weather, *why couldn't it have been to a distillery opening?* Now, there was a cheerier prospect.

"Ah, there you are," the Prince said in a relieved tone of voice as he entered the room, coming up behind her at the window. "I have been listening for your voice everywhere, but you have been so quiet of late."

It bears mentioning here that Daisy, oddly enough for one so otherwise diminutive, was possessed of the enticingly graceful neck of a gazelle. And that, after all of these months of resisting, the Prince could restrain himself no longer.

He commenced to nuzzling her neck and, as he fell to, all thoughts of sympathy for the Queen fled from her as so much pixie dust. And, as Daisy turned from the window and into him as it were, her undeniably remarkable nose at last making contact with The Ear, which could only be termed sui generis—both in its sheer size and the intricacy of its whorls—the dicey lights at Holyrood flickered and went out.

Considering how gloomy the day had become on the outside, even the most acutely sight-advantaged fly on the wall would be hard-pressed to make out anything but mere shadows on the inside.

8

The Queen stood in the rain and gave one final backward glance at Holyrood, taking in the windows that now revealed only darkness. She could not for the life of her decide where she would be worse off: back there, or out here.

Ah, well, she sighed, adjusting her gloves just a smidgen so that no draft could get in there, and moving her handbag higher along her wrist. The Bag kept falling down onto the top of her hand, and there seemed to be no getting around it. This was just going to be one of those hopelessly dreadful days that one must merely endure; a day when The Bag would insist on behaving as though it had a mind of its own. There was simply nothing for it, but to head on off to work.

The Queen had been on the job for nearly half a century. No way was she going to let a little thing, like a spot of bad weather or the whimsically sullen nature of The Bag, stand in the way of the fulfillment of her duties.

9

What with all of Daisy's Harrods' glad rags, a case might be made that she was now looking too good.

But, could it likewise be claimed that she was talking too wise?

Only time would tell.

10

Just as Daisy was closing the door to the room behind her, on her way to gather up Bonita for their short trip to the train station, a servant hand-delivered a letter to her. Slicing through the rather Byzantine seal, it was revealed to be a message from the long-silent Pacqui:

My Dearest Daisy,

Oh, why must you insist on behaving in such an American fashion? It will soon prove most unfortunate that you have refused to pay heed to my well-intended sentiments, which spring only from the depths of my heart. But you are listening too much at the wrong times and you are not listening at all at the right times and soon the whole world will know anyway, so it will not matter anymore that you have failed to pay just attention to your most loving servant,

Pacqui

Postscript: Perhaps, I have always been the wrong person to help anyway, since falling in love usually has the crazy side effect of making me behave like a homicidal maniac. Ha-ha!

Post-postscript: The consequences of your actions will be dire.

Post-post-postscript: I would help you more if I could, but your heart-wrong spurnment of my previous efforts have left me spent. And, anyway, a person pays the paper only by going solo. Lotsa luck.

Daisy carefully folded up the page, feeling completely safe again only once its peculiarly eerie message had been forcibly sealed back into the envelope.

She thought about it and she thought about it, but she just couldn't figure Pacqui out. Had she led him on somehow? But he had seemed like such a nice man—one would even go so far as to be unimaginatively condescending, and testify that he had seemed as harmless as a mouse.

Was it possible that he was stalking her?

11

As the rest of the Holyrood holiday-makers performed last-minute personal packing preparations just prior to departure—stowing away an ermine stole here, the inevitably stray fifth of whiskey there, perhaps a less recalcitrant Bag finding its way into a third—there was seen to occur a shift in the skies over Edinburgh. And, as they each boarded their various transportation forms of choice, with the intention of scattering to their several destinations—Clarence House for the Q.M., Kensington Palace for Princess Margaret, and Buckingham Palace for the Queen and Duke—for the first time in a week, the sun chose to finally put in an appearance.

As for Prince Charles, so far as anybody could make out, all that could be stated with any degree of certainty about his ultimate spatial goal at this point in time was that he now had his very own agenda.

12

When she and Bonita disembarked the train at Euston Station, not far from the Hotel Russell, Daisy noted from the clock on the wall that not even ten hours had passed. The vehicles serving under the Queen were performing as though they believed that Mussolini was running the show. And, as they emerged from the building, they found that the breath of fresh air that they had been waiting for did not last for very long. For, before they even knew what they were about, the two were engulfed within a sea of reporters.

That cruel stepsister, the press, was doing its level best to transform Daisy's previously unimportant existence into a living hell.

But Miss Chance, rising to her full lack of height, silenced them all by obscurely saying that "Miss Silverman" did not "consider her identity as being that of Prince Charles's girlfriend," but rather, that of "a devoted reader of fictions." And, seeing as how the Prince had been known to crack the occasional spine, they'd had a thing or two to discuss from time to time.

Once it was firmly established that Daisy refused to gossip about her relationship with the Prince, the members of the Fourth Estate resolved to settle for what they could get, and allowed Daisy to field a couple of ridiculously easy questions concerning her favorite topic of conversation: reading.

13

Prince Andrew had rarely found either occasion or inclination to phone his brother, but he found himself moved to do so now.

"Is it true that your girlfriend said those things to the press?" he asked.

"I have no idea," the elder of the two replied. "What are they saying she said?"

"Let me see, I'll read it to you. Now, what paper was it in? Ah, yes. Here it is, the *Times*:

> *When asked her opinion of the trend of books-on-tape, Miss Sills replied, 'I find them to be the literary equivalent to the vibrator. It's just not nearly as fulfilling as the real thing.' When pressed for further details, she added with an obvious display of energy, 'I prefer something that I can wrap both of my hands around!'*

"Would she really say something like that, Charles?"

"Mm." It sounded as though he might actually be smiling down the wire. "That sounds like it could be her."

For the first time in the history of their relationship, a note of respect for his elder brother crept into the voice of the one who had been formerly known as Randy Andy.

"I'd say you finally found yourself a real live wire this time." Then he paused for the briefest of moments before adding in a jealously pettish tone of voice, "Are you sure you're up for it?"

14

In fact, there was only one person who was disturbed by Daisy's comments.

There would have been two, but the man who was a Prince of Corfu by birth, but a Prince of England merely by error, had elected to take a slower form of transport, riding the Royal yacht down the coast back towards London. Once there, he would finish out the month at Buckingham Palace and attend the Royal Regatta at Henley-on-Thames, Oxfordshire being *the* place to go for Pimms. Aside from being at sea while Daisy was fending off the reporters, he was also far too busy with two books—that he had requisitioned from the British Library, and which they had promptly shipped up— to pay any heed to the daily wags. One of the books was entitled *Bagging Your Bird Every Time*, while the other was a book on hard-to-trace poisons, with a view towards doing away with his wife's wretched bagpiper once he had arrived safely back at the palace.

That left only one person to be disturbed by it.

And that person just happened to be Daisy's newest friend, the one who chose to sign much of her correspondence: *E II R.*

15

Everyone was in agreement, however, down to a queen, that it was distinctly odd that the *Times* should be so far off the mark in regard to their quoting of Miss Chance, re: Daisy's family name. It was further agreed upon, by one and all, that something really must be done about those sloppy copyeditors of theirs.

16

That evening, the BBC aired a new radio program, called "The Bloke on the Corner." An experiment, it was designed to provide the man in the street with a forum for their opinions. The first question ever to be placed by the program for the due consideration of the general populace was, what do you make of Prince Charles's new so-called friend?

Freddie Crumpet, age 96, from Dover, who was only in the city to visit his granddaughter, had the following trenchant observations to make: "Looked nice enough, though you can't always tell sod all from a picture in the paper. Looked a little shell-shocked, maybe. Reminded me of some of the men in my regiment during the Great War. At any rate, I like the idea of anybody associated with the Royal Family reading something other than the racing column."

To which, Erika Swythe, 33, identified as a working mother of three from Liverpool, added: "Wha's all o' this here *friends* nonsense? They're not foolin' anyone, ya know? I mean, the woman said *vibrators* right there in print for cryin' out loud... Mus' be noice bein' a toff. Yeah, I loik that. Why, how'd it be iffin' I was to be doin' jus' wha'ever I bloomin' well pleased all o' the time? Me husband'd 'ave me locked away for nutters, 'e would. Jus' the excuse he needed! An' whydja hafta call this program 'The Bloke on the Corner' anyway? I mean, tha' seems right sexist, it does. Now then, iffin' you're askin' me, a much better name'd be 'The Blokette on the Corner,' yeah, that'd be better. Or even maybe 'The Bitch in the Street.' An' wha's all o' this man on the street bullshit? Never 'eard o' the woman on the street then, hmm? Why, next thing ya know, you'll be askin' us ta pee standin' up."

Being only the second person whose opinion was ever solicited for "The Bloke on the Corner," and having once obtained possession of the microphone, it seemed a distinct possibility that Mrs. Swythe had no intention of relinquishing it ever again. In point of fact, as the nation listened (or, maybe not), she maintained her grip for the remainder of the half hour.

One week later, needless to say, this experiment in broadcasting was not replicated.

August

1

In August, even the persistently (some might say, disgustingly) perky Dr. Johnson might be hard-pressed to find London anything other than dull. Traditionally speaking, nothing much happened there during that month. The annual invasion of tourists having, like ants, already descended upon the city in droves, the residents—not to mention, psychotherapists the world over—had reacted by fleeing in droves, like lemmings. The elitist tedium that was embodied by Wimbledon was in the past for the one, while increased suicide rates—whether for one's patients or for one's self was really anybody's coin toss—still lay in wait in the post-holiday future of the other. Everybody was biding their time between Pimms cups and, once again, those same everybodies—or, at least, the ones who were anybodies—were on vacation. In fact, if you swung a stick around London now, the only people of import that you were likely to hit would be the Statue of Nelson in Trafalgar Square and your own Aunt Tillie from Gary, Indiana.

For excitement and psychotherapy, then, one was forced to seek them out in less conventional venues.

2

Tap, tap, tap. Stop.

Tap, tap, tap. Stop.

Daisy, taking the roundabout way home to the Hotel Russell from the British Museum, paused in front of the frozen yogurt shop. The day was hopelessly overcast, and the relentless drizzle made the umbrella that Bonita had forced upon her a necessity, as she cupped one hand around her eyes, pressing her face against the window to see if she could discern any welcoming lights from within, inviting refuge from the encroaching gloom.

Emerging a few moments later, having secured an extra-large serving of chocolate, she proceeded to juggle both the umbrella and the dish with her left hand, while manipulating the plastic spoon with her right. The mechanics involved in this hampered her progress somewhat, but that was all to the good. Charley having left for Scotland a little early on his own in order to attend to some pressing affairs that he had claimed would only bore her, she was faced with her first Friday evening alone in a long time, and she was at a dead loss as to what to do with herself.

Tap, tap, tap. Stop.

Tap, tap, tap. Stop.

Daisy paused again, feeling herself being tugged by a series of indescribable smells that were wafting out onto the evening air through the propped-open door of a Chinese restaurant. Steamed dumplings, cashew chicken. She walked backwards a couple of paces, peering in. Garlic shrimp and fortune cookies? Damn! Maybe she should have had some dinner instead of leapfrogging straight for dessert.

Oh, well, she sighed philosophically. Extensive past experience had taught her that while frozen yogurt and garlic went together just fine if you ate the garlic first, somehow, when you tried to reverse the process, the resulting combination was just plain icky.

Tap, tap, tap. Stop.

Tap, tap, tap. Stop.

Hey, wait a second. Was there an echo out there?

For quite some time now, every time that Daisy had moved a few paces along the glistening sidewalk, there had occurred an equivalent answering response from behind her. But it had taken the novel concept of dinner before dessert to yank her meandering consciousness up to a level of full awareness where she might be better equipped to deal with those threatening, dogged reverberations.

Ever since her return from Edinburgh, members of the press had been shadowing her every move, as though they were a whole roll of bad pennies waiting for something to change. And, granted, maybe it had been forgivable the other evening, when that one reporter had trailed her into the ladies' room in the tube station, peeking over the top to catch a snap of her straddling the loo. After all, he'd looked young, had a dirty job to do, probably had a whole flat full of starving kids at home, and he had to earn his living somehow.

But not even allowing a girl a moment's free time, in order to eat her dessert in peace? That really was the limit! It was the kind of gross harassment that literally shrieked for extreme measures. Or, at least, it did in Daisy's book.

Feeling herself to be justifiably and adequately armed—with righteous indignation, if nothing else—Daisy whirled to confront her pursuer.

As she was completing her turn, a figure leapt from the gathering darkness, seizing both of her wrists.

She tried to pull away, but the hold was too strong.

"Daisy!" the voice of her attacker cried, whether with malice or with something else, it was impossible to tell. *But anyway,* she thought, *it sure was loud.*

She pulled back one more time as hard as she could, and just barely succeeded in yanking the figure towards her, where she could examine his features under the lights from the Chinese restaurant.

"Blah!" she screamed, umbrella and frozen yogurt dish flying.

It was pretty safe to say that the sight of Pacqui, standing there, had scared the daylights out of her.

"Daisy, it is you!"

"Pacqui?"

"I was not certain at first, it being so unforgivably lengthy a time since we last met and your appearance having changed so somehow. My Daisy," he laughed softly, pointing at her person.

She glanced down at what his finger was indicating. The point of her umbrella had only missed impaling Mr. Wu by mere centimeters, but she had succeeded in donning her dessert, proving once and for all—and with an empirical exactitude that would never be called into question—that there was at least one other item besides a garlic chaser that chocolate did not in fact go with.

"But now I see that it is most definitely you!" he added.

"Pacqui!" she screamed again, unthinking. "Why have you been stalking me?"

"Stalking?" His brow furrowed, a hurt expression clouding his features.

"The notes," she stammered. "All of those threatening phone calls."

"But I was merely trying to advise you, as your most dear friend, that you must be discreet. The press in this country can be brutal and I did not wish to see you eaten up by them. Or spit out, for that matter."

"But what about that thing you wrote, about being a homicidal maniac?"

He roared out loud, his body shaking with laughter. "Oh! Silly Daisy! You were worried about that homicidal maniac stuff?"

She nodded dumbly.

"Why, that is just an old insider's embassy joke!"

"But I thought that you were angry with me. I thought that somehow I had led you on, but I couldn't for the life of me figure out how, or what I could do about it, seeing as how you had fallen in love with me—"

Another rather insultingly loud shriek of laughter managed to forestall her speech.

"Oh, no! Daisy! You thought that *I* was in love with *you*?" he cried with incredulity. "Oh, no! I am in love, it is true. But I am in love with Packey!"

Her confused expression begged for enlightenment.

"Remember when I told you that there are three of us at the Embassy: Paki, Packey and Pacqui?"

She nodded.

"Well, I have fallen most gloriously in love with Packey! And only as most recently as last night, he has most joyfully informed me that he completely returns my affections. So you must congratulate me."

"But, then, that means that you're not in love with me?"

"Of course not! It is not enough for you that the Future King of England has fallen rump over teakettle for you? Must the whole world likewise fall prey to your inestimable charms?"

He gave her arm a reassuring pat.

"Just remember to grant a wide berth to those leeches from the press, and you should do just fine here."

He headed off into the night, but then paused, turning.

"You know, you really must do something about that most incredible imagination of yours before it carries you off somewhere."

He continued for a few paces before calling over his shoulder, "And a ready supply of napkins might not be such a bad investment either!"

3

And just how *had* the Fleet Street scavengers learned of the existence of Daisy as a fixture in the Prince's life?

Well, nasty Court rumor had it that the Prince *had* had to put in a formal written request to the Lord Chamberlain on behalf of Daisy, in order for her to be presented to the Queen at Holyrood. The Lord Chamberlain had then passed this seemingly innocuous tidbit onto the Master of the Household, who, in an attempt to avoid a further thrashing from his wife late one drunken evening, had offered it to that gossip-loving grim person by way of an evasion tactic. She, in her turn, lording her own exalted status in life over her little sister, had passed it to her along with the tepid tea and stale scones one dismal afternoon. And Little Sis, inevitably, had parlayed the information—accompanied by her questionably intact virginity—into a romantic liaison with a fledgling stringer for the *Evening Standard*, whom she had met in a pub at closing time one evening.

The result of all of this telling tales out of school was, as they say, some idiot's idea of history.

4

Ever since the Garden Party at Holyrood, the press—that cruel stepsister—had been tripping all over itself in a panicked effort to dig up the dirt on Daisy. Although, another truth to tell, having come up with exactly zippo, they were now pathetically overdue for another shift in focus. After all, there were just so many consecutive days that even the *News of the World* could run banner headlines, screamingly proclaiming: "MYSTERY WOMAN STILL NOT SAYING MUCH!" Even they could only persist in the pursuit of the vacuous for just so long. Eventually something, of at least the slightest newsworthy value, had to give.

In fact, things had gotten so bad that, really, any minor alteration in the landscape would serve as a major scoop.

5

It was perhaps a mathematical given that in a city of London's size—with a populace numbering around seven million, combined with an annual influx of about twenty million tourists to be tossed into the equation for good measure—that This One would finally run into The Other One. It had only ever been a matter of time, really, and when that summit did occur, it happened, quite naturally, in the umbrella department at Harrods.

So what if the inevitable summit was in reality no more than just a dream? Inevitable meetings really are just *so* inevitable.

● ● ●

Before he'd died, Daisy's father, Herbert, had advised her that if a girl wanted to avoid going wrong in life, it was always a safe bet to keep her legs crossed and her mouth shut. And while she hadn't had any trouble—at least not *too* often—with the physical requirements necessitated by the first portion of his counsel, the second had on more than one occasion proven to be a mental and oral impossibility. She thought, therefore she spoke, and that was pretty much how her Descartesian personality had always dictated that she behave, and there had never seemed to be much that could be done about it. It was the nature of her beast to speak, and that she did.

Leaning on the handle of the purple umbrella she'd been holding for support, Daisy gave an ethnically inspired, self-effacing shrug of the shoulders to the blonde woman whose image towered over her own by nearly a foot in the mirror they were gazing into, standing side by side. "I didn't think you needed him anymore?" she winced, really asking more than telling.

The Other One returned with a shrug of her own, surprising This One with the dismissive gesture that backed up the most magnanimous words that Daisy had ever heard in her life.

"Oh, I don't care about all of that," the Princess pooh-poohed. "I just wanted to see what you really looked like. Oh, sure I saw those pictures in the paper; but those black and white jobs never really do one justice, do they? Color is ever so much nicer. Don't you think?"

Daisy couldn't help but stare at The Other One, marveling that even when she appeared to be trying her hardest to look tacky, The Other One just couldn't help herself: She might be wearing an outdated turquoise, mauve, and orchid Pucci babushka around her head, but those damned purple granny sunglasses accessorized perfectly.

The Other One sighed. "Sometimes, I think that it's kind of like a bad marriage. The press and one, is what I meant to say. It's as though…" She looked upwards, squinting one eye and chewing on the corner of her lip. "It's as though one feels stifled and can't wait to get away. But, then, when one finally does, and all of the attention stops, one feels as though it was the other party that had abandoned you. Don't you think?"

"I never really…"

"No, of course not. You haven't gotten to that stage yet."

Daisy, who had been about to say that it was not the kind of thing that she would ever expend even the tiniest particle of gray matter on, remained mum.

"And then of course, there's the public," The Other One sighed. "So, I guess, it really is more like a bad triangle than a one-on-one thing. But, only, with the press being the bad husband and the public being the good lover. I think. And then, I expect that even the good lover will decide to leave one day."

Daisy, being Daisy, just had to offer advice.

"You should never worry about what other people think," Daisy counseled. "You need to either learn to be pleased with the person you are, or change to become the person that would give you most pleasure to be. But, under no circumstances, should you ever worry about what the rest of the world thinks."

"What a novel concept," The Other One giggled her agreement, "just ignore what others think." As she giggled softly, an evanescent puff of perfume escaped from her person. And Daisy, dying to know what the most popular woman in the world smelled like, endeavored to chase it with her nose.

Daisy sniffed, inhaling an odor oddly reminiscent of the seventies.

Kinda "something," kinda now...

She struggled to retrieve the aroma from the banks of sense memory, snapping her mental fingers along with the catchy beat. Now, that was certainly surprising, she thought, getting a full-flavored hit from a cheap drugstore scent.

Kinda sleek, kinda "wow..."

No way!

The *Princess of Wales* smelled like *Charley*?

Nobody would ever believe it...

"You really have given me quite a lot to think about," the Princess said. "Say," she added, clearly enthused, "those are some super shops you have in your town!"

What? blinked Daisy.

"Westport, silly. The papers said that you hailed from there."

Clearly, one couldn't believe everything that one read in the papers.

"I passed through there once, when I was on a visit to the States. They have a lovely Barney's there, don't they? I thought their prices were quite reasonable. Don't you think?"

Daisy—who had long since given up on the temptation to say that she *did* think, and quite a lot actually, only not about those things—found herself thrust into the preliminary stages of déjà vu. Hadn't she had this conversation at some point before?

"Oh, and they had this really great bookstore there. Klein's was what I think they called it. Anyway," she added, reaching out to impulsively rub Daisy's forearm as though she were the person responsible for the creation of the store. "I got some great children's books there, for Harry and Wills, of course. Oh, and a new one on AIDS hospices. But, when I passed the biography section, all I could see was my own face staring out at me. Spooky, the effect that still can have when one is not expecting it."

It was this whole conversation that was spooky, Daisy thought. She found herself wondering what it must be like to suddenly find yourself famous, your image plastered on every magazine cover the world over. She shuddered at the prospect, as though she were someone living in the darkest heart of Africa, who truly believed that the photographers were trying to steal her soul.

Diana, seeing the shiver, reached out to rub the arm again, this time with reassurance. "Oh, you mustn't trouble yourself about such things. You know, I'll just bet that you're far too smart to let the press get the better of you."

And Daisy who, like most people, did truly believe that she was smarter than the average baron, found herself feeling mollified. This really was nice, she thought. Now they were both each making the other feel better.

"Say!" Diana impulsively cried. "Do you think that we might have lunch together sometime? I'll bet we could be super friends!" But then, her face clouded over at the impossibility of it all. "No, I suppose not…"

And where *were* the members of the press, while this meeting of the minds was going on right under their very noses? Why, they were covering the earth-shattering events at the bleeding London Riding Horse Parade, for goodness' sake, that's where *they* were.

Besides, the meeting between Di and Dai was, as they say back in *Dallas*, all just a dream sequence.

Still, when Daisy finally rose, wiping the leftover sleepy stardust from her eyes, she did so with a smile of contentment; somehow, now, Dai felt as though she'd been given Di's permission to proceed.

A dubious quantity of each having been achieved, excitement and psychotherapy had been temporarily placed on hold for the duration. For other cheap thrills, then, the roving eye would have to scan elsewhere.

Which shouldn't be much of a problem since, quite soon, Daisy—along with a host of royals—would be back in Scotland.

September

1

The Prince was walking in the sunken gardens, in front of the granite mansion that had been built in the Scottish baronial style by Queen Victoria's Prince Albert. He was anxiously awaiting the arrival of Daisy, whom he had not seen in well over a fortnight, and it would have taken a trained lip-reader—or one very good friend—to make out the words that he was mouthing to himself.

Sturgess bravely approached, extending before him the woman's namesake flower.

"Here, take this, Sir," he offered. "It is still the most scientific procedure devised by man for discerning the true feelings of a woman."

And so, for the remainder of the afternoon, to anyone observing from afar, Charles could be seen to be pacing up and down, the hands that were usually clasped behind his back with dignity now obsessively tearing the petals off of flowers with an Ophelia passion. And those same faraway people, had any of them been bold enough to venture nearer, would have heard the Future King of England muttering under his breath, repeatedly, and with a renewed and ceaseless devotion to his cause, "She loves me; she loves me not. She…"

2

The sight of one thousand of them, all in one place, went a long way towards making the typically perceived common-as-weeds daisy seem, oddly enough, a lot less humdrum.

And their presence in her room at Balmoral, when she arrived, made the human version feel a lot more welcome concerning her two months' stay there.

3

"I believe that it is all going quite well. Don't you?" Sturgess asked.

He and his partner in crime were holding one of their, by now, regular confabs. On this occasion, however, their eagle's-eye view was from the 100-foot Great Square Tower, where Bonita was finding the rarefied air to be gloriously clear, if just a little bit cool.

"Time, Sturgie," she advised, patting his arm, just as a strong gust of wind came along, ripping the bow off of her topknot, and sending her long gray hair loose, whipping like a standard behind her. "That's the only thing that ever tells diddly squat."

4

"I can see why you love it so much here," Daisy said, gazing straight up at the Great Square Tower, that looked oddly unbalanced somehow, as though, with just the slightest encouragement, it could be persuaded to come crashing down on top of them. Even with her hand shielding her eyes against the glare given off by the sun, she was unable to make out the identities of the two figures standing at the top of it. Daisy was finding out that she particularly liked the lonely romance of towers, the whole Rapunzel element and all of that. But then, so far, she had liked everything that she had seen of Balmoral.

Located in the Grampian region of Northeastern Scotland, its heather-covered moorlands, peaty lochs, wooded glens—not to mention, salmon-filled rivers (smoked, with bagels and cream cheese—yum!)—all appealed to Daisy. The castle itself was made out of granite, whitewashed, with numerous small turrets. It was situated on rising ground and, in addition to the sunken gardens in the front, it also had rose gardens on the side, and the River Dee flowing behind and around it.

It was the main holiday home of the Royal Family, the vast property and spartanly furnished castle providing an atmosphere where they might enjoy a well-earned respite of relaxed informality. In fact, the whole family liked going there, unlike—say—Holyrood. Balmoral was an idyllic place and, with its relatively meager and, thus, intimate size—only 250 rooms—a place where they could all play at being country bumpkins. And, if the idea of the Queen and Prince Philip in their Ma and Pa Kettle mode—ensconced in a castle that was capable of sleeping one hundred and thirty, making it the most accommodating private residence that Daisy had ever had the pleasure of being in—seemed just a trifle incongruous, she shrugged her shoulders philosophically: c'est la vie, just so long as nobody was at guerre.

"Care to go for a tramp in the woods?" Charles offered.

5

If she was having no trouble understanding his spiritual attachment to Balmoral, what with its endless possibilities for entertainment and communion with nature, in terms of hunting, fishing, and hiking—activities which, with the notable exception of the last one, were certainly forms of behavior that she had absolutely no intention of ever engaging in (although, *Field and Stream* would have a, well, a field day with it); yes, if she was having no trouble at all understanding the Prince's specific attachment, attraction, affinity— not to mention, a whole host of other words beginning with the letter "a"—to Balmoral (the region, as well as the Castle), she was having a considerably tougher time of it, concerning the subject of his spirituality in general.

They were, as promised, in the middle of an eight-mile tramp that had started at Spittal of Glenwick, northeast of Loch Muick and heading around the loch counterclockwise to the southwest corner, where they would then cross to the Dubh Loch. They were at two thousand feet and, even though there were already a few patches of ice on the water, there were still a couple of hardy bluebells that were determined to make their presence known in the woods. The subject on the table for discussion was, of course, astrology.

"Okay, okay, I get it! I get it already," Daisy was saying, grateful for her gaiters, as she picked her way with care through the boggy muck that surrounded Muick. "I mean, I can see how *some* people might attach some relevance to the fact that you're a Scorpio and

I'm a Cancer. But somehow, I get the feeling that there's a lot more going on down on Planet Earth than there are in the stars that you've dreamt of, Horatio."

As she tucked a stray auburn hair behind one ear with her left hand, she swatted at a persistent highland midge with her right. The most outstanding result of this flirtation with ambidexterity was that she succeeded in throwing herself off balance, landing tush first in the mud, and providing evidence to the argument that, perhaps, hiking was not going to prove to be her natural forte, either.

As the Prince gently helped her regain her footing, she noticed that a puzzled, hurt expression had come over his features. Startled, she wondered how to proceed without causing further offense. Pretending to be preoccupied with the removal of brambles from her Icelandic sweater, she decided on cowardice as being the best approach. Perhaps, if she were to just close her eyes and yank, she wouldn't have to see the look on the patient's face until after she'd excised the tooth.

"It's not that I don't believe that astrology has its merits, its place. But I just think that you could do so much more if you were to put your mind to it," she went on, deeming it time for the final pull, one foot braced against the doorjamb, pliers in hand, soothing brandy bottle at the ready, "by getting involved with something outside of yourself."

"Hmm," he brooded as they walked on, one forefinger placed thoughtfully to his lips, the fist of his other hand loosely clenched behind his back. "Hmm. Perhaps you might furnish one with a 'for instance'?"

She shrugged, searching the branches for divine inspiration. "Other people?" she offered haphazardly, asking more than telling. After all, she didn't want to appear too pushy. She had always thought it was an awful thing that, once having found the purported man of their dreams, women then always seemed to be intent on re-casting them in their own image. Which was fine, if you were looking for somebody with the potential for looking killingly pretty in pink, but otherwise... Perhaps, it would be best to proceed with caution.

"Outside interests?" she tried again. "Got any hobbies?"

"Well," he replied. "I have something called the Prince's Trust."

"What's that?"

"It was designed with the purpose of helping disadvantaged young people."

"Now that sounds promising."

"I am also greatly interested in the problems of the inner cities."

"Better and better."

"And then, of course, there is organic farming…"

"Mm," Daisy interrupted. "I'm not so sure I like the sound of that. It seems like something you'd do where a person might end up pompously self-absorbed or living out in Berkeley or something. Hmm." She gave the matter a few more moments' thought. "But, you know," she finally continued, "that might not be so bad. Why, between that and those other things you mentioned… There you go! You could be another Jimmy Carter!"

The Prince, after a few moments reflection, at last decided that she *did* intend this as a compliment. Feeling greatly encouraged, he continued on, filling her in on the highlights of his curriculum vitae.

"I also like opera, alternative medicine, and architecture."

"Too loud, yawn; fine, unless you're talking about covering my body with leeches; why?" came the appropriate responses.

"You see, that ties into my feelings about the inner cities," he went on, clearly warming to his subject. "I am most interested in protecting traditional British life from the rape of modern progress—"

"Whoa, whoa! Time out here."

The Prince pulled up short, though his expression revealed that, clearly, he did not understand the command.

"I'll grant you, that that *sounds* like an admirable notion," Daisy said. "*On paper*," she added, a slightly caustic tone creeping into her voice. "Still, I'm awfully glad that you weren't around when the debates over the merits of indoor plumbing versus the good old slop jar were going on."

"Perhaps you might have something there," he said thoughtfully. "But, it is hard enough, always having to try and strike the proper balance between what one thinks might be best for people and what the reality of it is. Especially when the bottom reality is that it really doesn't matter much what one thinks or does. There might be more of an incentive, if one were anything more than just a figurehead."

Daisy winced inwardly, knowing that she'd never make it as a doctor. Judging from the dejected look on her friend's face, that "first, do no harm" dictum represented a hurdle that she was unlikely ever to clear. And, when you got right down to it, she thought, it really was unfair to judge him. After all, if anyone—other than Michael Jackson—had ever had a justifiable claim of diminished responsibility, well… it was sort of as though the entire world were his co-dependent. In fact, it could be argued that he lived in a world not of his own making. But then, how many people ever did?

"I know that the concept of the future is supposed to fill one with feelings of hope," he was saying. "But, somehow, whenever I think about the one that has been intended for me, all I ever seem to feel is lonely. One would think that it would be all power and fun and games, but the reality of being a future monarch is quite different. It is all about doing everything that you do in a way that others, especially one's own family, believes that one should do things. If you see what I mean."

The problem was that Daisy did see exactly what he meant. She thought about the things that she had already observed, on such short acquaintance, concerning the general pack mentality of Charley's family; about The Firm, where personal desires always had to take a backseat to the consensual demands of group approval. She thought about it, and as she thought, a kernel of anger began to grow in the pit of her stomach, as though she were smelling a pot of chocolate that somebody had thoughtlessly left upon the stove for far too long, neglecting to stir constantly. It was anger at them, but it was also anger at him. After all, there was just so long that you could get away with complaining about the role that others had cast you in. You had to either try out for another part in the production, or you had to get out your trusty spoon, figuring on digging your way out to China. But the one thing that you couldn't do was simply sit back and continually complain. Because if you did that, then, before long, everybody would be blaming the victim.

"Father always says…"

Screw Father, was what Daisy would dearly have liked to have said, having met the Duke and having found him to be comprised of all sound and fury, signifying diddlysquat. But the better part of someone else's definition of valor managed to stay her tongue.

This taming of the tongue was a challenge that Daisy had not fully mastered yet. Having never considered herself to be a conventionally pretty girl, she had developed that bodily part to its greatest capacity relatively early on in life, and thought of it—with a certain degree of pride—as being her greatest asset. Unfortunately, it could also get her into a lot of trouble. It could pacify or, if she decided that you were a whiner, it might whip you. As it had done, on the previous evening, her first meeting with the Duke.

During an amiable after-dinner game of cards—some incomprehensible four-handed thing that they all knew the rules to, and which she did not—she had caught the Duke out sulking over losing.

"Now, don't whine about it," she'd said without thinking. "It's just a silly game."

In fact, there were a lot of things that she would have liked to have told that particular person to stop whining about.

It was patently evident, to even a Cyclops, that the Duke was jealous of his wife's superior social status. And, true, it must be galling for a man, of his unaccountable pride, to go through life with the knowledge that one would not be welcomed at anyone's table, were it not for the particular person that one happened to be married to. But, just because Daisy could understand him, it in no way meant that she wished to encourage this maladaptive form of coping behavior. Here was yet another one who she would like to shake, this time saying, "You're nearly eighty years old, for God's sake, get over it!" Perhaps adding, "And besides, I'm sure nobody had to twist your arm."

But she had deemed it best to reserve that nugget of wisdom, that free psychoanalytic character assessment, for a more opportune moment. Maybe when they got to know each other better.

"I wouldn't mind too much about what he says," was the advice that Daisy offered to Charles now.

"But he will leave such insistently huge footprints all over the place…"

Daisy gave a quick nod of sympathy. On the one hand, she had already experienced, first hand, the belligerence factor that was the Duke and, having herself been raised by the much more forbearing Harold, did not envy the more royal gentleman's descendants. But, still, on the other…

"So what? If big feet were an aphrodisiac, then Bozo the Clown would be on the cover of *GQ*."

As they had been speaking, the misty fog, which had still enshrouded the banks of the loch, had been slowly lifting. Daisy looked up at the sun, and saw a dark form silhouetted against the sky, saw the form plummet to earth at what seemed to her an incredibly high speed.

"Charley!" she cried. "What *was* that? It looked just like a shooting star, only with wings and feathers."

He shielded his eyes with his hand, studying the tree line where Daisy was indicating, although the form had already disappeared.

"Did it look to have pointy wings or splay-tipped?" he asked.

"Pointy, I think."

"A streamlined tail, perhaps?"

She nodded.

"Did you happen to notice if it was traveling at a speed of one hundred and eighty kilometers per hour?"

Daisy hurriedly performed the measurement conversion in her head, coming up with a figure of just over one hundred and ten miles an hour, before becoming exasperated.

"I didn't clock its speed, Charley," she said, spreading her arms wide. "Do you see some kind of radar gun here? All I know is, the thing was going down *fast*."

"Well," he said, "if it was indeed pointy, instead of splay-tipped, then it was probably a peregrine falcon as opposed to being, say, a golden eagle. Although they are both seen around here—the farmers abhor them—and both are designated as being protected species, the falcon is by far the quicker of the two, hitting its prey at the speed which I believe that I already happened to mention. I cannot imagine anybody being boorish enough to hunt them since they are not supposed to, and if it was going down as fast as you described, then I suspect that it was probably diving for brunch."

"It is amazing the things you see in the woods, isn't it?" Daisy said, linking her arm through his as they continued on their stroll.

"Quite," he said, smiling with pleasure at their obviously mutual appreciation concerning the wonders of nature. "In the autumn, you might even hear the sounds of the rutting of stags out here."

"My, but you do say the most charming things."

6

Later, that evening, the Duke was hosting a barbecue in the backyard at Balmoral. He found himself in the heretofore unheard-of position of wishing to impress his son's guest by showing off his knowledge of her native customs. Besides, on these September jaunts to Scotland, where the Royals endeavored to pretend that they were no different than any other Tom, Dick, or Pierpont, the Duke liked to fancy himself an outdoor chef—a Galloping Grillsman, as it were.

This typically meant that the Family was forced to rough it by dining alfresco from deep picnic hampers, stocked with provisions that had been prepared by the castle's kitchen staff. After all, the Duke had reasoned, quite sensibly, just because one wished to enjoy the reputation of a gourmet chef of the great outdoors, was certainly not reason enough for one to do any actual cooking.

But on this occasion, due in whole part to the presence of their American guest, the Duke was making the supreme culinary sacrifice, and he was thus doing the cooking himself. Deeming it most appropriate to serve a guest with cuisine prepared according to their own country's preferred methods, he had staunchly stationed his solid form behind that longtime favorite American institution, that original mass carcinogen-producing food processor long pre-dating the Cuisinart: the charcoal grill.

Over his kilt, he wore a pristinely white chef's apron and, upon his oiled hair, the highest of toques.

"Don't you eat game, Miss Sills?" he asked now, with some

asperity, as he tossed some more meat on the coals. He was experiencing a peculiarly uncharacteristic disappointment at this lack of enthusiasm shown by a guest.

Daisy thought about the fact that it was September 20th, Yom Kippur this year, as she pushed the bird around on her plate. "I guess I'm just not hungry today," she said, not noticing the veiled glance that Bonita—who was eating with gusto—shot in her direction.

"That's odd," Charles said. "I don't believe I have seen you eat a thing all day." But then he grew distracted, as his gaze traveled from the sterling silver platter on the red-and-white-checked plastic tablecloth to the man who was manning the food station. "Father," he asked, eyeing him suspiciously, "have you been shooting the falcons again? I keep telling you that they are a protected species."

Philip replied, using a twin-pronged barbecue fork to jab a number of times at the enormous-looking piece of game that lay smoldering—extending over the edges of the rather tiny grill— before he was finally successful in flipping it.

"Don't be daft all of your life, Charles," the Duke grimly replied, intent on the job at hand. "It's a pigeon."

October

1

And so, Yom Kippur had come and gone. The Braemer Highland Games, with the inevitable Scottish dancing and caber tossing, had also come and gone. At that more widely acknowledged annual event, presided over by the Royal Family, the burly Angus MacFarlane had lobbed the caber—a 125-pound tree trunk—farther than anyone had ever seen a piece of nature forcibly thrown (for no apparent reason) to make it a record-breaking third straight year. Outside of a "good show, Mr. MacFarlane" from the Queen, and a "how about another shot of Glenfiddich, Angie, you great big brute of a caber-tosser, you" from Big Mollie who lived down the lane, there hadn't been much else for anybody to say about that. September had passed gracefully into October, and the highlands were awash with and drowning under a veritable sea of heather.

So, what else was new?

In fact, time had taken on a bit of a fast forward quality to it, not that different, really, from the onset of the third trimester of a first pregnancy, what with its top of the roller coaster revelation concerning the inevitable ground rushing up to meet one. But, if the first trimester had been characterized by an anxious wake-up call concerning the future; if the second had yielded a more fatly complacent anticipation of prospective bliss; and if the third was the trite train out of control; it was then, perhaps, to be expected that the labor itself—when it finally occurred—would be one hell of an intensive exercise in deep breathing.

But that blessed event still lurked some ways off in Daisy's future as she, along with the rest of the Royals and their guests—including some five hundred friends and members of the English aristocracy—readied themselves for the annual Ghillies' Ball.

2

Daisy examined the pressed towels that lay atop the oaken bureau, right next to the ceramic ewer and washbasin that were accommodatingly situated in her sleeping quarters. The Queen's royal mark was embroidered onto the cotton and was accented with the, by now, comfortingly plaid Scottish border. She was thinking about how man's acquisition of the technological capacity to imprint three initials, onto any surface large enough to bear them, had heralded the onset of the Me Generation and had, likewise, sounded the death knell on any further idealistic hopes of human sharing.

But the very next moment found her wondering, idly, how DSW would look *right there*, on 200-thread Egyptian cotton. *Perhaps the team colors could be changed to a more Israeli-inspired blue and white?* was the thorny question that she was posing to herself, as she rifled her wardrobe for something to wear. While all of this ball nonsense that was a part and parcel of Charley's world was becoming more user-friendly to her, it could still be a fashion minefield for one who had formerly prided herself on being a classic example of *Glamour* Don'ts. She was debating the relative merits of ostentatiously mendacious, virginal white on the left, and trusty, safe-as-tramps-and-mourners black on the right—and also wondering why a woman's fashion sense, at its most stylish, always necessitated the blatant avoidance of vibrancy—when a knock came at the oversized door.

She opened it, hangered garments in hand, only to find Charley slouching against the jamb in the portal. In his arms he carried a rather large box that was tied with a big red bow, which he presented to her upon entering.

"I hope you will not mind, but I took the liberty of purchasing you a dress for this evening's festivities," he was saying, as she busily tore into the box. "I merely felt that it would give me great pride if you were to wear something that I had selected." He coughed nervously into his closed fist. "However, er, that is to say, if you are not entirely pleased—"

"Charley, it's perfect!" Daisy exclaimed, liberating the dress from its yards of crinkly packing. The more easily distracted portion of her brain considered that there were probably heads of government in the world, not to mention prostitutes, who traveled with less protection than that garment had received.

Daisy cast an appraising eye upon the article of clothing in question, and found it to be exactly the kind of thing that she would have chosen for herself, were she not of late trying to clothe herself as the kind of person that other people might wish her to be. The dress was of a filmy material, but was cut along a straightforward line, without any frills or nonsense, and so, it managed to create a mild air of femininity without giving way to the dreaded evocation of frou-frou.

But it was the color that really got to Daisy.

It was as though someone had gathered all of the colors of autumn and had managed to convince Winslow Homer to adapt them to his palette, channeling his considerable artistic talents into the creation of a watercolor dress. The dress was at once graceful and lively, and Daisy marveled at Charley's unerring sense of taste. And, while some might argue that the color spectra encompassing shades of maple, russet, and hunter's green was not everybody's definition of vibrant, anybody who had ever taken a drive through Redding, Connecticut, in the fall could tell you that there was really only one purely visual depiction of the tired phrase "riot of color."

Why, if she were to wear this dress, and what with her auburn hair, she thought, clutching the garment to her bosom and allowing herself to finally be sucked into a world where men named Ralph and Oscar and Calvin were king, she would feel like a fawn, a wood nymph; she would feel like the month of October itself, like the best part of New England; she would feel like Halloween and Thanksgiving combined in a good year, like a whole season in…

"Oh no!" she cried, having held the dress up to the light, in order to make certain that there was no obnoxious detailing around the collar area. "I can't wear it like this!"

"Whatever is the matter with it? Are there steaming spots all over it? I told them at the shop to be extra careful—"

"The spot isn't on the dress, Charley," Daisy said with an uncharacteristic whine of dismay. "It's on me."

She noted the puzzled look on his face, and held the dress up over her own clothes in order to illustrate her point. The dress, while a nonnegotiable statement of refinement in every other regard, had a shockingly low neckline. If she were to wear it as is, his mother—not to mention, the rest of his family, plus the free world—would know exactly what kind of stuff she was made of.

"You know about that birthmark of mine that I told you about…" she began, with a gesture towards the area of her collarbone.

"Oh, pooh-pooh," the Prince interrupted, pooh-poohing. "I have always been quite certain that this birthmark, which you appear to be so concerned about, is really nothing. You only imagine it as being your most salient feature when you look in the mirror—not so different, really, from a woman who is at most only one stone overweight thinking that she looks like a mountain, or one who has a nose that is slightly larger than the norm thinking that she looks like a toucan. It is all that you see in yourself, because it is all that you allow yourself *to* see, but I can assure you—based on hard-earned firsthand knowledge—that it is not what the world sees."

The Prince paused for a sustaining breath. He was unaccustomed to making such impromptu, unscripted, and non-internally uttered speeches on the spur-of-the-moment, and the sheer exhilaration of it all had left him slightly gasping. "At any rate," he concluded, "we are all marked by birth in some fashion."

He took her firmly by the shoulders, as though she were a child and, turning her around so that her backside was to him, gave her rump a friendly pat, jumpstarting her in the direction of the bathroom. "Now then, off you go. Just try it on and see how it looks. I am quite sure that, once you have seen yourself in the mirror, you will see that I am completely right and that the thing that has been giving you so much trouble is really nothing."

Feeling as though she would have made either a great slave or an adequate midget Barbie, she found herself, in spite of grave misgivings, bowing her will to that of a dubiously higher authority and following his instructions to a T.

Just the briefest movement of the big hand on the clock found her on tiptoes, studying the top half of her person before the beveled oval glass in her bathroom. And what she saw there provided proof that, much to her astonishment, the Prince did indeed have some clue as to what he was talking about. For, somehow, the multihued nature of the dress minified the visual impact of her birthmark, the autumnal theme of the one enhancing the healthy highland glow that she had achieved, and causing the slight discoloration of the raspberry to only make her seem that much more attractive by virtue of having a skin tone that was not so ordinary as to be complacently reliant on the merits of just a single color.

Why, she thought, her spirits soaring once again, she looked like a palette, a veritable equinox, a...

Now, that was certainly odd, she thought, peering at her image more closely. Perhaps it was wrong, what everybody always said, about gold going with everything. For, while the birthmark had completely passed muster, the Star of David—which she had worn daily for years—somehow didn't mesh with the Vermontish, almost Presbyterian quality of the dress, striking the only discordant note. She chewed on a nail, debating over what to do.

What to do, what to do.

She couldn't very well tuck the chain into her collar as she had done on previous occasions, the lack of collar being the central cause of her dilemma.

Just take it off? a tiny voice inside her brain suggested with a shrug. *How much harm can one night make?*

And, sucked in again by the sight of her own image (why, she looked like an arbor, like a forest princess!), Daisy's hands found their way traveling up to the base of her neck where, almost unconsciously, her own fingers undid the clasp, removing the chain. Hesitating for only an instant, her hand hovering over the marble counter surrounding the sink, she opened her fingers up one by one, and she simply let it go.

Then, she exited, intending to show Charley how perfect she looked in the present he had given her, how very much like a princess.

She was, therefore, absent from the bathroom by the time that Rachel's not-so-tiny voice—which was still strong enough to transcend time and space, making her presence felt live from the grave—managed to maternally bust through yet another dimension, ready to contribute her own two cents.

"Nu, Daisy, so my necklace isn't good enough for you anymore? Tsuh. And, you mean to tell me, for that schmatta somebody actually paid good money?"

But, by the time that she was finally able to make her thoughts heard, there was nobody left in the bathroom to hear her. Since her daughter, as Rachel herself might have put it, was already off somewhere hoity-toity; or, as Kevin Costner might have added, Daisy Silverman was now Dancing with Goys.

3

Daisy danced with Prince Andrew; she danced with Prince Edward.

At the annual Ghillies' Ball, held in mid-October, there was Scottish dancing in Grand Hall, and it was permissible on this occasion for commoners to ask Royals to dance. Needless to say, Daisy took undue advantage of this situation, adopting a Sadie Hawkins stance and pestering Charley repeatedly. And, while that besotted individual did not mind this in the slightest, Princess Anne did take umbrage, and declined the kindly offer, when Daisy invited her to cut the rug for an all-girls turn. The Queen Mother, on the other hand, was more than game and, in her light blue gown, formed quite a figure, dancing the reel with Daisy.

The Queen herself, clad in a surprisingly romantic and ethereal silvery pink number—with the inevitable tiara perched on her head—looked on from the sidelines. It was impossible to discern whether the tight smile on her face bespoke a mood of strained tolerance, or one of barely suppressed laughter.

Daisy danced with Prince Edward again; she danced with Prince Andy.

In fact, it was pretty safe to say that our girl was a hit, the belle of the ball, as it were.

Too bad, then, that Bonita's view of things seemed to have soured.

• • •

Bonita and Sturgess had stationed themselves in a room adjoining the Grand Hall. From there, they could hear the music emanating from the other room and, between dances of their own, were able to safely observe the proceedings—while remaining unobserved themselves—through a conveniently located squint in the wall.

"I believe that it's yer turn, Boni," Sturgess gasped, his face flushed from the dance that Bonita had led him on. He indicated the squint, with a flicker of his fingers, as he flopped with relief into the nearest armchair. He was coming to learn that, for every shot of exhilaration derived from the presence of Bonita in his life, there was the price to pay of a dram of exhaustion.

The tiny American made her way to the wall, her hand going to her chest as though to either still the beating of her heart or somehow try to contain the mammoth presence within her form. She obediently pressed her eye to the hole. Unfortunately, what she saw there brought her up shorter than she already was. Through the tiny hole, she saw it all.

There was Prince Charles. And there was Daisy, dancing with him, one hand on his shoulder, the other held tightly in his. Her back was to Bonita, but she could see that Daisy's head was tilted upwards, as though she were gazing raptly upon his countenance.

Well, the practical part of Bonita silently asked herself, what else could the girl do? At her height, her only choices were to either look up at the man, or find herself under house arrest for obscenely dancing cheek-to-belt buckle.

But, as the Prince gallantly swung Daisy around, the front of her form coming into view now, Bonita noticed that there was something wrong with this picture, although at first glance, she couldn't put her finger on quite what it was.

And, no, it wasn't the fact that Waldo was definitely nowhere to be found.

No, she thought, slowly rising in shock as the full realization of what she was seeing sank in, it wasn't that at all. It was that Daisy, her Daisy, was no longer wearing her necklace.

Bonita saw everything.

...

Bonita caught up with Daisy, whirling her around by the shoulder, just as the younger woman was about to hold Prince Philip to the earlier promise of a dance. The Duke, however, did not mind finding himself allowed to slip off the hook so easily, seeing as he still had quite a number of things to get over.

For example, he had to get over the fact that Daisy had refused to eat any of the meal that he had so thoughtfully prepared for her a few weeks back. He also had yet to get over the fact that he was still in a foul temper, the bagpiper having miraculously survived the summer as had the nonet of annoyingly resilient, blasted yapping corgis. Not to mention, come to think of it, that his wife was still undisputed head of a country, while he was not.

He stalked off, having forgotten his resolution to try just getting over it. No, there wasn't a whole bloody lot to be celebrating with bloody dancing in his life.

Bonita, for one, was glad to see him go.

"Don't you think you're getting carried away just a little bit, Daisy?" she asked, her desperation showing, the rare triple whammy in the realm of personal address laying naked, through verbalization, the depth of her concern.

"What are you talking about?" Daisy asked, only half paying attention. She was watching the retreating form of the Duke, sorry to see him go. She had been intending to work on his personality some more.

"Do you know who you are?" Bonita asked, trying in vain to reclaim Daisy's ear.

"Of course," Daisy said. "I'm Daisy," she added, leaving out the most important part.

"Do you know where you come from?" Bonita asked, her expression one of the gravest intensity.

"Is this some kind of a game?" Daisy asked. "I came here from my room in the castle," she said, just a trifle impatiently, indicating with a vague gesture of her hand the vast expanse of the rest of the granite structure, beyond. "Look," she continued, "I don't have time for this right now. I have to go find Charles."

And she hurried off, leaving a stunned Bonita behind.

Eventually, drastic measures would probably have to be employed. But, for now, she would merely sit back and watch.

For the time being, she really was too shocked to do anything else.

• • •

At the Ghillies' Ball, as with any truly great party, there was a second party, even better than the first, which was going on below stairs, as it were. And the Prince and Daisy had just put in an appearance.

It was an annual tradition with the servants at Balmoral, the ones whose presence was not absolutely required in the Grand Hall, to hold their own celebration of the harvest on the lanterned lawn of the grounds, just out of sight of the castle itself. In previous years, the late-night attendance of Prince Andrew had become the norm, looked forward to even as one of the highlights of the fete, especially by those partygoers with a more pro-randy mindset. But, the unexpected and unannounced arrival of his more staid elder brother, well, that was quite another thing again.

The Prince was about to learn that, if the best part of any New York City party could always be said to take place in the kitchen, then the best part of the Ghillies' Ball could be said to take place with the kitchen help. In contrast to the fairly lively, if wholly uninspired and yawningly expected, national music that was being played in the Grand Hall, here there was a much more animate—if just a tad bit raw—rock combo playing. As the Prince made good his entrance, with Daisy on his arm, the band had just swung into a rather raucous imitation of the Stones' version of an old standard, and Charles—who strived in vain for the first couple of minutes to behave in the prescribed, wire-hanger-still-in-the-jacket form— found that he could no longer resist the toe-tapping beat. Before he even knew what he was about, he found himself leading a greatly surprised Daisy on a merry dance.

"Shall we show them how it is done, DeeDee?" he enquired, taking her in his arms.

DeeDee? Daisy thought.

"This chap does a fine Jagger. Don't you think?"

> *I'm gonna tell ya how it's gonna be;*
> *You're gonna give your love to me...*

If this whole second party business impressed Daisy as being just a little bit Alex Haley's *Roots* on tartan steroids, complete with tribal kilts, she didn't let on. In fact, the impression that was made on those present was not what one would normally have expected.

> *Ashes, ashes and all fall down...*

It was agreed upon later, by one and all, that the Prince was really quite a fun sort of guy, much more free-spirited than one would have been led to believe, and one hell of a good dancer. His little friend, on the other hand, had seemed nice enough, though she did seem—by comparison with His Royal Highness—to suffer just a wee bit from a case of the old stuffed shirt.

> *Love to love ya, not fade away.*

4

The following morning found Daisy—or, DeeDee, as her larger friend was now intent on calling her—feeling a little bit under the weather, not herself at all, really. On the previous evening, she had plied herself with one too many glasses of the local Rhenish, and had allowed herself to be sung to and had danced to more songs from the seventies than her sore brain cared to remember. It would appear that she, the Prince, and the little people had partied long into the night.

All things taken into consideration, then, it hardly seemed surprising that, while preparing to dress for a day's salmon fishing on the River Dee with Charles—to be accompanied by the Q.M., who had muscled an invite for herself, under the guise of there being a grave necessity for a chaperone; and, to be followed by a go at grouse hunting with Phil; afterwards to return to the castle, for a final intimate dinner with the immediate family and an evening of games—that, in her haste, Daisy never even noticed the discarded Star of David where it lay, offering mute accusation, still upon the counter of the bathroom sink.

"Coming, Charles!" she shouted through the door when summoned, hurrying out to meet him.

In fact, our girl was so busy now—on the verge of becoming such a social centerpiece, really—that her failure to see the chain is perhaps to be understood and forgiven.

Or perhaps not.

November

1

November had finally come to the city of London. Along with the naturally inevitable maturation of the seasonal calendar, the time came for rolling up the shirtsleeves and getting down to brass tacks, for acting one's age, for getting serious.

Well, sort of.

Elizabeth II, Queen of England, Defender of the Faith (what did that mean exactly?), Leader of the Commonwealth, blah, blah, blah, was on her way to the House of Lords in Westminster. She had a date with Parliament.

She was traveling by state coach, clip-clopping along the Mall, doing the equine version of the proverbial snail's pace, in order that the faithful (perhaps those whose fullness, her job description demanded that she defend?) who had come out early to line the roads might be rewarded with a glimpse of Her Majesty in all of her glory. This was the only time of the year that the Queen had occasion to wear the monarch's traditional robes and crown, and those who still held the monarchy dear to their hearts, as being a viable and even essential part of British life—not to mention, those who liked to play with color, or those with a fondness for black leather and metal spikes on Saturday night would never miss the chance of witnessing this ultimate display of THEM finery. If the United Kingdom could be said to represent one united Us (with the exception of THEM) – as opposed to a divided Us and Them, then it could likewise be argued that that Us was clinically described best as a schizoid personality.

But why quibble? Besides, there were really only a couple of rabidly anti-monarchist bad seeds who actually threw things at the passing carriage, the tomato (pronounced with a distinctly long American "a" sound) being the favored weapon of revolutionary fervor.

All dysfunctional relationships aside, the Queen's planned route had been designed in advance. Like Orion in winter, or the anal retentive itinerary of a cheap Caribbean cruise, her course had long been carved in stone. Her path would take her along the Mall, escorted by the household Cavalry. It would convey her to parliament, there to be greeted by the fanfare of trumpets. Her ultimate goal, of course, was the reopening of that august governing body, which, inbreeding the House of Commons with the House of Lords, liked to go under the single, more simplified—if no less unified—heading of Parliament. Thus, it had always been, and thus, it should always be. Ho-hum.

Contentious bills, infighting, filibustering, snoozing M.P.s bored out of their faithfully elected skulls—all could be safely expected to appear upon the docket within the coming year.

But what of change, what of progress, what of flies in the ointment?

Undoubtedly, these would crop up as well, although no mention was made of such possibilities in the Queen's restrainedly upbeat opening speech. But, then, when christening a ship—even the *Titanic*—it was customary to employ Champagne, as opposed to, say, Raspberry Vinaigrette. Suffice to say that, in the year to come, it was to be expected that there would be a healthy dose of cynical idealism and childish rumor-mongering as well; all the better to ensure that the wheels of government did not grind too smoothly, nor lead the populace to believe that its leaders might be relied upon to act their ages.

In the interests of keeping awake 650 M.P.s in the House of Commons—not to mention, all of those dukes, archbishops, barons, etcetera, ad nauseum, and that stick that kept coming into contact within the House of Lords—who knew what new and titillating names would have to be bandied about within the debating chambers? Who knew what scandals would need to be unearthed? Who knew what lengths these individuals might go to in their collective relief that it wasn't themselves who were caught out "dropping trou" this time?

All that one could indeed be certain of was that Daisy Silverman's second, soon-to-be cruel stepsister had finally reawakened following its summer slumber, its perversely reverse hibernation. And that, before long, the roused beast, stretching its arms out and yawning a hungry hello to the world, would once again need to be fed.

2

The Second and Third in Line to the British Throne were enjoying a rare tramp around the grounds of the palace in the company of their father, the man who—through genetic entitlement and the purported will of God, if not through personal inclination—was still referred to in some circles as being the Next in Line.

"So," the Next began, drawing an enormous breath for fortification, and almost swallowing a bee, which had absolutely no business being around the flowers at B.P. this late in the season but, what with the unseasonably warm weather—what with all of the global warming and ice caps melting and all of that other terrifying rot—what was a future monarch to do?

"What do you boys make of Daisy?" was the question that the Next finally succeeded in spitting out, placing the issue squarely on the table.

"Well," replied the Second, hesitating, one eye on some sort of ground animal that had just scampered off under the bushes, the other eye, as ever, firmly focused on a diplomatic future. "She's not exactly like our mother, now, is she?"

"Nor will she ever be," put in the Third, crossing his arms, his fists clenched in a decidedly obstinate fashion. His own training, regarding the fine art of verbal finesse, had been, unfortunately, sorely neglected in favor of his elder brother. "We already had one of those. Ya know?"

"Yes, of course you did," hurriedly soothed the Next. "And

that is eminently fair of you to point that out to me."

The Next paused as his ears registered what sounded like a gunshot coming from the general direction of the Duke's quarters, a man who had only ever been in line for the loo.

"When *will* Father learn not to play with his guns out of doors?" the Next wondered, grasping his earlobe between his thumb and forefinger, and shaking it, in order to silence the ringing.

Turning his attention back to the boys, he decided that it would be most positive to proceed with the negative, crossing his fingers that the worst-case scenario did not, in fact, prevail. "But, it's not as though you *hated* her, or anything drastic like that, is it?"

"Oh, no," relaxed the Second, vastly relieved that "not hating" was all that was going to be required here. "As a matter of fact," he waxed expansive, "one is rather impressed with the way she never seems to mind falling off a horse."

"Yeah," snickered the Third, just a smidgen nastily.

"Ya know" and *"Yeah"*? thought the Next. And there ensued a lengthy lecture on the hazards of viewing too much American television via the palace satellite dish.

"And *I* like the way she never minds making an ass out of herself either," finished the Third, at last receiving the opportunity to complete a thought.

The Next proceeded to tick off the points made, using his fingers to count them, while aloud he verbalized the salient features. "So, what we have here, then, is: 'doesn't seem to mind falling off of a horse'; and, for you," he said, indicating the Third, "'never minds making an ass out of herself either.'"

The Third nodded his head once, decisively.

"Hmm," mused the Next, clearly puzzled by it all as he unconsciously gave his lower lip a chew.

But then his eyebrows lifted, his outlook seeming to brighten considerably. "Well, I suppose that'll have to do then. How about those fireworks tomorrow evening—probably be a simply stupendous show, what?"

3

Like a misguidedly ethnocentric anthropologist, Daisy was
experiencing some degree of difficulty in understanding the British
traditional celebration of November 5 as being Guy Fawkes Day.
After all, she hailed from a country where just cause for a holiday
tended to be more black and white. You waved flags on the Fourth,
because you *had* won the war; you marked December 7 off as a day
of remembrance because the Japanese *had* bombed Pearl Harbor. It
therefore seemed downright peculiar to be commemorating a day by,
in effect, magnifying the positive within a potential negative; hard to
credit one of the most rained upon and reigned upon cultures in the
history of the world being possessed of a more optimistic outlook
than their American counterparts. But then, there you had it.

Guy Fawkes Day, for the uninitiated, represented the national
observance of the 1605 failure of the eponymous malcontent to
blow up the Houses of Parliament. This accentuation on the bright
side, with its insistently upbeat focus on an event that did *not* in
fact occur, impressed one as being something akin to the Americans
creating a Squeakie Fromme Day ("Thank God that little twerp *didn't*
succeed in shootin' Ford. Maw, let's all have us a weenie roast!") or,
perhaps, a Day of Bay of Pigs (what with the American propensity
for creating acronyms everywhere, it could become known as Do-
BoP, which could be kind of cool). Could the Benedict Arnold
White Sale be so very far behind?

Yet, if Daisy was having a tough time figuring out how the

supposedly grim, stiff-upper-lip Brits had managed to outpace her own people in the lightheartedness department—through their blithely incisive appreciation of the fine art of barely averted disaster—she was finding that she was experiencing zippo trouble in reaping the rewards of the celebratory fallout. For, if the temporarily distant and wholly irrelevant fact that some overzealous sniveler with a bad aim had failed to level, through lobbing as opposed to lobbying, an entire legislative body—and this, some three hundred and ninety years previous—meant that on *this* day Daisy would be able to stand amid the protective camouflaging of an arbor of trees, while fireworks exploded overhead and her favorite beau stood with his arms about her, nuzzling her neck and snugly holding her from behind, then she was all for it. Damn the torpedoes and try not to drown.

"Fuvrthawtf mm mm mm eed?" enquired the Future King of England, almost drowsily.

"What?" Daisy giggled, shrugging a shiver as he nibbled on one of her earlobes.

"Fsowoodu mm mm mm mm mm mm mm me?"

"What?" she asked a second time, as he proceeded to attack the other ear. It would appear that elocution and romance made for a strange stew. Daisy wriggled out of his embrace and, turning, faced him. "I can't hear a word you're saying when your nose is in my ear," she laughed. "What did you say?"

"I said, or rather, asked, 'Have you ever thought of getting married?'"

"Oh, Charles," Daisy whisper-sighed, supporting her elbow with one hand, while the other hand covered her mouth, in an attempt to either keep the flies from coming in through that orifice or to prevent anything truly idiotic from flying out. "Are you nuts?"

Eschewing military advice, the Prince decided to ignore the question of his temporary sanity for the time being, choosing to proceed without caution instead.

"And then, DeeDee," he hurried on in a rush, as though intent on spitting it out before his nerve had a chance to desert him, "I asked, 'If so, would you consider doing it with me?'"

"Oh, Charles," she almost whispered the words this time. "*Are you nuts?*"

"Quite, er, possibly, hmm, perhaps. That is to say, still and all…" and as he was pronouncing this eloquent speech, a velvet jeweler's box materialized in his hand. He extended the box to Daisy.

She opened the lid to reveal a ring that, while some might call it a tasteful setting, had a rock on it that was nearly the size of her head.

"I can't… We can't… How can we… *Can* we?" she stammered in confusion, proving, once and for all, that the art of rhetoric had indeed fared no better on the other side of the Atlantic.

"There are a few minor details to work out, of course," he allowed, with an expansively dismissive wave of the hand. "But, details…"

This was all getting to be too much too fast for Daisy. While a part of her was more than willing to be swept away by the emotional forces that were tugging at her heartstrings, a more rational voice in her head was pleading for just a little more time on terra firma.

She cast about for a temporary stopgap, hoping to pull a parliamentary action, and thus, avert potential disaster, or at least for the time being. With that noble aspiration in mind, she located a loophole and through it she leapt.

"How 'bout we just live together for a while?" she suggested, with an apologetically wincing shrug. "Maybe see how we like it first?" Then she waved the velvet jeweler's box in the air. "And do you think that, just maybe, we might keep *this* between the two of us as well? Just keep it under our hats until we're both sure of what we're doing?"

"Fine," he smiled, the victorious crack of fireworks and the visual sparkle of Daisy combining to produce an aura of confidence. "Whatever it takes."

• • •

In a strictly humanitarian sense, all men had always counted with Daisy, but it was fast becoming increasingly safe to say that, now, there was one man who counted far too much.

4

Daisy spent her last night at the Hotel Russell staring out the window, in the direction of the British Museum. She was wondering if, before the car came to collect her tomorrow, she'd have time to go across and perform some zero-hour research. She had remembered reading in a history book, once upon a time, in a different life—while cramming for a hoped for, but never to materialize, appearance on *Jeopardy!*— that there was something loose in the world that was referred to as the 1701 Act of Settlement. She recalled that this document, while hardly fodder for scintillating cocktail party conversation, ensured that the Future King of England could not marry a Roman Catholic. What she was desperately hoping to learn was if there was any fine print on the damned thing. Did it, for example, *say* anywhere that he was likewise prohibited from marrying a Jew?

As the evening hours ticked by, what with nowhere to do her research and Bonita being out on what she described as—hold the phones!—a date, Daisy found herself growing antsy. Feeling as though she were living out something akin to teetering on the cusp, the dividing line between the Before and After pictures in a scam weight-loss ad—but not feeling sure which side she was starting from or which side she was transcending to—she decided to take a walk about town, enjoy the bracing London night air, revel in her final moments of freedom.

Her footsteps took her down past Oxford and Regent Streets, where she noted that the Christmas lights had already been turned on in anticipation of the coming season. As she wandered the streets aimlessly, she sought to breathe in as many of the city smells as possible, in order to store them up in her memory, for she had the feeling that the place where she would soon be going would be another world complete unto itself. But as she hurried along the pavement, pitter-pattering, her heavy sweater bundled snugly about her, she found that a curious thing was occurring: the scents, which at first were quite vivid, were beginning to fade. And as she scurried, trying to catch up with them, she found her frustration growing along with her sense of the cold.

In desperation, she finally sought refuge in the very first welcoming place that she saw, the only place that she could think to turn to on a bitter, odorless night. Like her father before her, on the eve of a cataclysmic event in her life, Daisy Silverman sought refuge in a church.

As she entered at the portals to St. Martin-in-the-Fields, opposite the National Gallery and overlooking Trafalgar Square, her thoughts went back to a nervous Herbert Silverman, ants filling his pants on the eve of his wedding day to Rachel. Unable to sleep, and cursed with having been born in a generation before the advent of 24-hour everything, he had wandered the streets, looking for someplace—anyplace—to kill some time. Finally, unable to stand the cold anymore, he had found that, in a pinch, a Catholic church could serve as a haven for a nice young Jewish boy from the Bronx pretty much as well as anything else could, and the priest there had proven surprisingly sympathetic on the topic of jittering self-doubt. When God gave you lemons, as Herbert became so fond of saying in later years, only a schlemazel would fail to make a glass of lemonade.

And, if the environment that Daisy now found herself in impressed her as being just a touch hermetical, at least she was safe there. But as she gazed up at the cross, hanging there above the altar, she couldn't help but wonder just what in the world she was letting herself in for.

5

A Maxfield Parrish sky hung over the city of London on the morning that Daisy made good her approach, the sound of the team of six's hooves clip-clopping merrily along the Mall, the metallic clang of shoe against pavement making her advancement evidently audible to anyone with sense enough to open up their ears and just shut up and listen for a change. Sunbeams shot through the trees that lined the lane, creating the kind of light that granted one the belief that otherworldly things might be possible on a given day.

• • •

"But a horse-drawn carriage?" Daisy had asked, her eyes gone wide with disbelief, when Charles had come to collect her earlier. "Isn't that maybe just a wee bit excessive?"

"But, my dear DeeDee," Charles had said, tucking her hand inside the crook of his arm and giving it a reassuring pat, "I *want* to give you the royal treatment."

Uh-oh.

• • •

Now Daisy watched the outer world pass by as though viewing it from the center of a dream. Admiralty Arch, St. James's Palace, Clarence House (home to Daisy's good buddy, the Q.M.): all seemed to whiz by her as she sat, bouncing along at Charles's side, her hand clasped tightly in his. Something suspiciously furry had been thrown across her lap to prevent a chill, something fuzzy and soft and whose origins she had best not enquire about lest she be told that it had once been a living thing. As she looked out the window, she was finding that the phrase "going to the Mall" didn't mean quite the same thing over here as it had back home. And, as the horses neared the end of the drive, she felt the knot in the pit of her stomach expanding as she recognized the full impact of the fact that, having approached by the eastern front, she would soon be at the portals of a one-of-a-kind kind of place; that rushing up to meet her was the supreme architectural expression of the British Monarchy; or, to put it more simply, in words of two, Buckingham Palace. And the royal standard flapping proudly overhead could mean only one thing: the Queen was in residence.

Halberd-bearers. The sounds of trumpets blaring.

The carriage rode through the forecourt now, seeming oddly to be going faster. Through the main gates of the Principal entrance, past the Superintendent's Flat and the Housekeeper's Flat—with their residences capitalized on the architect's sheets, as though they really mattered; still, it *was* nice to have a title—and disappearing from public view into the quadrangle.

It was like being sucked into the air hose of a laundry dryer, like tripping and finding that one had fallen into a great big hole smack in the center of a rabbit warren, like waking up and finding that it wasn't all a bad dream and your life really did exist now within the confines of *Watership Down*, like a frog on a lab slide. It was like...

Well, you *do* get the picture, don't you?

Perhaps it was only a product of her imagination but, as the side of the carriage drew parallel with the Grand Entrance, Daisy could have sworn that she heard the unmistakable sound of a portcullis, the immense black metal spikes slamming shut behind her.

In a state of mild panic, she inhaled deeply, but she found that, now, her sense of smell had completely deserted her; the Nose was on the fritz.

But, then, did it really matter so much anymore?

Daisy was in the palace.

Part Three

"Send Lawyers, Guns and Money..."

December

1

Daisy was running through the corridors of the palace.

And it wasn't even a dream.

"No running in the hallways!" her second-grade teacher had shouted at her, predictably if unoriginally, during her formative years some thirty-one calendar selections previous.

"No running in the house!" Herbert Silverman had yelled, trying to make a threatening impression, as he waved his wife's rubber spatula in the air, Rachel having quite often been just in the middle of the process of icing a chocolate cake. "You'll give your poor mother a heart attack with all this noise, all this running here and this running there."

"Nu, Daisy," Rachel asked, not long before she'd died of a heart attack, "what's the big rush? I don't see anybody with guns chasing after you. Slow down; you'll live longer," she'd advised. "Besides, if the good Lord had meant for you to run around so much, he wouldn't have given your father such a fancy-schmancy car." Spatula in hand, she had wiped one flour-covered arm across her brow. "Now, come and help me lick this bowl," she had finished up, the full weight of Eastern Europe behind her (and we do mean behind). "I made too much frosting again."

But Daisy's personality and behavior had proved to be entirely unbowed, her nature impervious to any and all attempts to form and impress. In fact, the phrase "child-resistant" had originally been coined to describe her, and it hadn't been until a number of years later when an overworked pharmacist, on the brink of yet another malpractice suite, had overheard Herbert attempting to reprimand a chocolate-smeared Daisy and had appropriated the phrase for his own lawsuit-resistant invention.

And, as for advice, well... As far as our girl was concerned, heeding the conventional wisdoms spouted by others was for unimaginative weenies and following advice was strictly for idiots and anyone who had ever appeared on Oprah as part of a panel, which included a member of the psychiatric profession. This systematic weeding-out of those who believed that someone else had to know better than they did left the world with a short list, containing fewer names than last year's Booker. And, surprisingly enough, Martin Amis did not appear on this one either. The List, then, in its entirety, included Daisy, the Queen Mother, and two clockmakers in Switzerland—whose timepieces didn't say "cuckoo," didn't sell as well as the competition, did say the phonetically similar (but the semantically quite different) "caca," and provided its inventors, through a goodly number of sales to the legally deaf tourists who came through town, with enough to cover the mortgage of their modest chalet plus a few good belly laughs to carry them through the slow season.

From a practical standpoint, then, what all of this meant was that it should hardly seem surprising that, when faced with the Principal Corridor, outside of the doors to her suite at Buckingham Palace, Daisy should feel inspired to go for her daily run. At 240 feet in length, divided in three by double glass doors—and with mirrors on either end, reflecting startling and seemingly incessant shrinking rectangular images—one could hardly have expected her to behave any differently. The red carpet, crimson specifically, appeared to roll out before her indefinitely.

Daisy had been placed in the Yellow Suite, next to the Balcony Room on one side, and with the aptly named Blue Suite on the other. And, while the titles of the rooms might have impressed Daisy as being a trifle banal—the unrelieved coloring of the décor just a tad too unicolor—she could at least discern the practicality behind such naming, from the maid's view anyway. In fact, with over six hundred rooms in the palace, it probably would have made life a whole lot easier for all concerned, if the whole bloody thing had been color-coded. Instead, with just the possible dining rooms alone—the short list including the State Supper Room, the Household Dining Room, the Chinese Luncheon Room—Daisy was frequently finding herself confused, arriving to empty rooms; or arriving after everyone else had been seated and were impatiently awaiting her entrance so that they could commence with the watercress soup; or, oddly enough, entering a room only to learn that, for some strange reason, on that night she had been assigned to eat with the hired help.

Located diagonally across from the Throne Room, on the opposite side of the quadrangle on the Principal Floor, Daisy's accommodations could have been a lot better but they could also have been a lot worse. She could, for just one example, have been placed in the Belgian Suite, the suite reserved for the grandest visitors to the palace. This was the place where world dignitaries like, say, the Clintons, would be put up were they to come to call. But then, Daisy admitted reasonably, were she to be in the more prestigious Belgian Suite, she would be situated on the Ground Floor. The Yellow Suite, on the other hand, meant that she was on the same floor as the Queen's and the Duke's apartments, making it easy to just pop in or out should her presence be required. And, if her rooms were not the best, at least they were not the worst. Why, she could have been wrongly—or, rightly, depending on your perspective—placed in the Housekeeper's Flat. And then she would have had to figure out, all over again, how the heck a person was supposed to get by in life with just one toilet for just one person.

And when she thought about it, there were some things about the Yellow Suite that weren't bad at all. Why, the amenities alone! What with the little soaps and the writing paper embossed with the Royal Crest, this was better than the Hotel Russell. The staff here was even instructed to lay out reading material, appropriate to each guest's individual tastes. In Daisy's case, the selection, fanned out on the canary night table, had included *Chocolatier* and—with a nod towards her progenitor's reputed investing acumen—a copy of *Morningstar 500* and the closing figures of the Dow Jones Index, updated on a daily basis. Clearly, they knew exactly whom they were dealing with. Then again, clearly they did not.

Unfortunately, however, in spite of the sunny hues and her given name, yellow was not Daisy's primary color of choice. Thus, she found herself seeking out any excuse to escape the maddeningly cheerful confines of her Regency-style suite. What with bedrooms, bathrooms, a dressing room and a writing room, all designed in unmitigated shades of jasmine, she was beginning to feel as though an LSD flashback was imminent. It was only a matter of time before she began seeing those annoying seventies happy faces plastered all over the world. In order to obtain release from the odious color a run through the vivid, vibrantly carpeted halls had fast become a daily requirement. Besides, there was so much to see here!

The palace may have sat on over eight hundred acres of land, but it was the interior that could keep a person busy for an entire lifetime. It made Daisy feel as though she were in training for something. For starters, there were so many inanimate objects that one had to learn the names of. It may have been old hat for some, but who would have ever dreamed that she would be leading a life in which the distinction between ceramic and porcelain had become such a vital thing? Not to mention ormolu, gilt-edged, Regency style... Oh! And the architectural terms specific to castles alone! Postern; wall-walk; yelt. And just what the heck was bric-a-brac anyway? And was it something that the Royals would go in for heavily; or was it something better left behind on Coney Island, abandoned along with orange shag carpets and beanbag chairs?

There were also a seemingly endless number of seemingly uninhabited rooms to explore. There was the Chinese Dining-Room, which only seated a meager twenty, and where the R.F. (as she was coming to collectively think of the Family) liked to hold intimate dinners for themselves, with only occasional visitors. This room had enough of that porcelain and gilt stuff to choke a Shar Pei, along with blue walls and red carpets that she thought clashed terribly, but that no one else seemed to mind. Then there was the blue-columned Music Room, which overlooked the gardens and in which Charley had been baptized once upon a time. But, most of all, she liked to explore the Belgian Suite, which, at present, showed no signs of residents, with neither a Clinton stirring nor a Republican mouse. She couldn't say what it was that drew her there so strongly, really, whether it was the Orleans bedroom, the Spanish dressing room, or the Caernarvon Room, the Suite's own private Dining Room. Maybe it was simply the sense that Heads of State, or other individuals, who had actually done something for their countries had slept there; maybe it was the fact that the Queen had given birth to Prince Edward there, the bathroom done up as a sort of make-do delivery room, that drew her more morbid curiosity.

Best to just shake that vivid image off.

Finally, there were all the people to learn about, the so-called little people who did things around here that one had never known to be real jobs before, some with descriptions that did not appear in the *United States Statistical Job Abstract*, many with titles that were peculiar at best and which therefore bore remembering.

There were some 350 workers all together.

Phew! Talk about the vast potential for attitude problems!

There was the Lord Chamberlain (the highest-ranking Court official, whose duties of office she had encountered before), the Master of the Household, the Deputy (of what, she hadn't a clue, but somehow she was absolutely sure that it had nothing to do with John Wayne), the Steward (supervising indoor menservants), the Housekeeper (their female counterparts).

There was the Private Secretary (who handled the press, among other things), the Keeper of the Privy Purse and Treasurer to the Queen, the Crown Equerry (who sounded as though he should have something to do with horse racing, but instead—or, at least, she thought—seemed to have something to do with all of the vehicles, both motorized and non-, that were housed over in the Royal Mews, which sounded an awful lot like something noble that the cat might have oh-so innocently—some claimed insolently?—dragged in, just prior to winking at the Queen and thereby ensuring that he would be transformed by the Master Chef into kibble for the finger-pointing Corgis... but wasn't).

There were individual Yeomen (?) of the Gold, Silver, Glass Pantries and Wine Cellars, Under-butlers, Pages, Page of the Backstairs (the Queen's personal servant), the Queen's dressers and Phil's valets.

There were four Women of the Bedchamber, which sounded like a cush job, but was, in fact, of not quite as grand a stature as being one of the two *Ladies* of the Bedchamber. (Talk about splitting hairs, a nasty voice in Daisy's head was beginning to say. Did Marilyn French know about this? But then, the *People* magazine-reading voice in her brain took over again and, anyway, at least the Nasty Voice hadn't been telling her to go out and shoot anybody.)

And, of course, there was only one—count them, one— Mistress of the Robes.

There were 35-40 maids, 8 male telephone operators for over 300 phones and extensions (what, no EOE?—what was wrong with letting ladies talk on the horn?), some fulltime window cleaners who lived at home ("Well, dearie, I'm off. We're doing the Ballroom again today. Thanks for the spam sandwiches. No, tell the kiddies not to wait up; you know what a bitch all those blasted long windows can be."), and two men who spent their entire careers caring for the 300+ clocks.

Out of the "some 350" workers (so, more people than clocks, then), about eighty of the staff actually slept in the palace, so call it an even hundred. (Daisy was already finding that it was ever-so-much easier to measure the little details of the day-to-day life around the palace, if one were mathematically daring enough to round up to the nearest hundred.) These lucky, close to a hundred, individuals were housed in attic bedrooms. And while that might not seem quite cricket, what with all of the unused spaces that seemed to be lying around the place, one could hardly put them in—oh, say—the Belgian Suite, Daisy managed to concur.

Yes, there certainly was a lot to learn around here! Daisy told herself again, as she continued with her run up and down the red lined carpet of the Principal Corridor, already experiencing the beginning stages of the disorder that any one of the palace's 350 staff could readily diagnose as Red Carpet Fever. She thought for sure that she was feeling enchanted by it all.

Yes, as anybody with any sense could see, there was enough here—why, the sheer statistics of it all alone!—to keep even an actuary interested for quite some time.

So, how long then, do you suppose, would it hold Daisy?

2

Like a complimentary fruitcake, shipped under separate cover by a Midwestern factory specializing in the mass production of taste-free thirteen-layer Dobosch tortes, Bonita had safely arrived at the palace having traveled there under the considerable powers of her own steam. And while, like the much-maligned fruitcake, she might never put in an appearance in the number-one slot on anybody's holiday wish list, her advent did represent a welcome change of pace. At least to Daisy's way of thinking.

The two Americans were at the Tower of London, queuing to see the Crown Jewels. The idea for the pilgrimage had been Bonita's brainstorm. Thinking that it was high time that her "charge" got a load of what she was letting herself in for, she also thought it best that Daisy get her glimpse of the heights that her future now held from the perspective of the rest of the little people. Thankfully, there were only now about a hundred people left ahead of them in line.

"How goes tricks for *vous* in the Big Place?" she asked, in an attempt to draw out her peculiarly silent companion. Bonita had taken the initials from the acronym, transforming them into something else again.

"*Comme ci, comme ca,*" Daisy said with an ennui-propelled shrug. Sturgess had apparently been helping her brush up on her language skills in anticipation of all of the travel she would probably be doing in the near future. "We shall see. *Ca va?*" The fine art of rhyming had also obviously been rearing its ugly head during those early morning tête-à-tête tutorials, although it seemed that—for now—the Bard had nothing to worry about. Except, perhaps, figuring out a way to roll some 383-year-old ashes over in one's grave.

They were finally at the entrance to the first room that housed some of the royal trinkets. A mere prelude to the more serious stuff, as they snaked around the displays here, they saw that it was mostly just a lot of large, solid gold junk: scepters that looked as though the only king that might be physically strong enough to heft them would be a Budweiser Clydesdale, enormous platters (perhaps for serving heads on), and other stuff like that. An unbelievable show of wealth was on exhibit in that one room and it wasn't even the main attraction. This was just bijoux foreplay as it were.

And while it was all kind of fascinating in its own useless, lifeless way, a part of Daisy couldn't help but think of…

"World hunger?" Bonita provided, with an innocent raise of her eyebrows, as they paused in front of another solid gold platter, this one as big as a sideboard.

"Oh, shut up," Daisy responded, testily, hastening on to the next feature.

Considering how many people had been ahead of them when they arrived, it really was amazing how quickly they were flying through this place. Daisy kind of felt like she was being processed. Back at the palace, she was one of a handful of people whose every need was attended to by a staff of 350. Here she was one of several thousand who had paid an admission fee, all waiting to spend their fifteen seconds ogling the wardrobe accessories of one of those handful of people back at B.P.. Kind of made you think.

"Sardines, anyone?" Bonita offered loudly, magnanimously, to all those around them.

"Will you please shut up?" Daisy pleaded in desperation, her voice equally loud.

"Fine way to talk to her own mum," an older woman behind them said huffily to her own younger companion.

Bonita? The two Americans looked at one another quizzically. *Daisy's mum?*

They both turned to face the woman at the same time. "Oh, shut up," they said in unison.

The woman, who was actually a very nice woman in someone else's life—and who had taken the day off from the factory where she worked in order to take her daughter to this place, to see these magnificent things that neither of them had ever seen, to bond amongst the bountiful baubles—performed an uncharacteristically rude act. Grabbing her daughter by one wool-covered elbow, she brushed past Daisy and Bonita, muttering all the while. "Well, I never…"

"Liar," Bonita accused with a happy grin.

"Had to have at least once," Daisy added with a helplessly apologetic shrug, an open palm indicating the daughter, who the mother was now tugging even faster.

"Why do we always seem to have that effect on people?" Daisy pondered aloud.

Bonita compressed her lips, her shoulders rising so high that they almost touched her ears. She shook her head in agreeably wondering concession. "Damned," she said, as they trailed the mother and daughter into the main room.

The room was circular, dark, and cold, with the thickest set of reinforced vaulted doors that Daisy had ever seen; and which also kind of made you think, only this time, Miss Chance wasn't providing any clues. With only the barest pinpoints of ceiling lighting to guide them, the real illumination in the room came from the cases displaying the jewels.

Oh, great, Daisy thought, feeling like something of a Druid. *Now we're all going round in circles.*

"Oh, look, dear!" cried the older woman from earlier, now in line ahead of them. She tugged on her daughter's sleeve, pointing. "It's the Queen's hat!"

And Daisy, bumping her from behind, found herself face-to-bulletproof-shield with the Imperial State Crown, the Star of Africa—a diamond as big as a post-Apartheid raised fist—being the dominant feature in the jewel-encrusted setting.

"However does she hold it up on her head?" the older woman, who was from Woking (might as well learn everything about her while we can) was asking. "Why, you'd think it would fall straight down onto her nose!"

Daisy could no longer help herself. A feeling of hysteria had quite overtaken her and, as it bubbled up from her stomach, she doubled over laughing.

"What's so funny, you?" the woman from Woking asked accusingly as she whirled round, hands on her impressive hips. Clearly, she'd had enough. "There's no cause to be laughin' at the Royal Nose."

"I wasn't laughing at that," Daisy sputtered, endeavoring to recover herself.

Woking Woman waited, rather impatiently.

"It was that thing you said before," Daisy tried again. "About it being 'the Queen's hat.' It was as though... as though..." Daisy was briefly overcome by a second wave of laughter. "As though you thought you might be able to pick one up for yourself at Harrods' January Sale!" she finally finished, before going off again.

Woking Woman and Woking Daughter simply stared at her for a very long time, their joint expressions one of perplexity.

"Well, dear," the older woman said, just prior to leading her very patient daughter away one last time, "I always say that *they* may think that they won the war, but any country that produces that many lunatics, well, they might as well all call themselves Australia and have done with it. Convicts, lunatics; it's all the same thing, really, when you get right down to it. If you're one, then chances are you're probably the other. And if you're the other, then you most certainly ought to be the one. That's what I always say. Australia, America. If only they could all be trained to just stay at home."

"Do you think it might be us?" Daisy asked in genuine puzzlement, as she watched their retreating forms.

"Damned," Bonita concurred a second time.

"Where the hell is Klosters, anyway?" Daisy asked, as they neared the exit. Her mood was beginning to sour.

Charles had recently advised her that, once the holiday rounds of parties were finished up with, he should like to take her skiing there in January. Great, Daisy had thought, herself a latent control freak who had never relished any sport that removed both feet from direct contact with the earth. She had always thought that even the dentist's drill wouldn't be such a big deal, if they would only allow you to keep one foot on the ground. And, as for childbirth or jumping out of planes, well...

Bonita shrugged. "Damned," she reiterated her main point, making it an even three.

"Damned if I know either," Daisy echoed, testily, as she booted the exit door open.

This touristy display of violent and maladaptive disregard—more typical of her fellow countrymen than of herself—succeeded in proving the Woking Woman right and causing the security guard (who was also really a nice man, named Bob, in another life) to frisk her for weapons; whereupon, at Daisy's urging, he phoned the palace, only to learn that she indeed was—as she had claimed—practically One of Them.

Which was, somehow, hardly surprising.

3

"What do you *mean* that the Mistress of the Robes has absolutely nothing to do with the Queen's wardrobe?" Daisy was practically screeching, as she trailed Sturgess into the palace's estate-sized kitchen.

"Ah, Mr. Sturgess, you've arroived jest in the nick o' time," greeted the Master Chef, a man of reputedly limited culinary skills, who had at least managed to get the Child/Prudhomme girth right. "Oi've been 'opin you'd pop in."

Up until very recently, the Master Chef would have rather been eviscerated with a shrimp deveiner than be heard to have spoken such words out loud. But, in the past few months, he had noted a slow change coming about in the formerly starched-shirt valet—a loosening up of his taste buds, if you will—that was downright endearing. Having previously only shown any real depth of interest in satay, the sensitivity of Sturgess's palate had been increasing by leaps and bounds, until now his presence had become a welcome addition to the Kitchen. Were it not for the fact that the Master Chef's own abilities to discern gustatory nuances of flavor had been dulled by the lifelong, daily, ingestion of three-fifths of Port, two packages of cigarettes—causing him to flick ashes onto the partridge and piss under the pear tree, before serving holiday dinners—Sturgess's help might not have been quite so necessary. But such was the stuff that the palace staff was made up of, and there seemed to be nothing else for it but to pitch in where and when one was needed.

"Wot do you think?" the M.C. asked, stirring a stainless-steel pot that was easily large enough to accommodate Daisy. "A little garlic, maybe?"

Sturgess accepted the wooden spoon from the tottering gourmet. "Mm, sorrel soup," he said. "Lovely." He tried some more. "But you cannot put garlic in it, you know."

"Whyever not?"

"Because the Queen hates garlic. How many times do I have to tell you? She cannot eat anything that will make her smell like anything."

"Well, Oi don't see wot the big bloody deal is. Oi've read those arteecles too, you know. Oi know that when she goes to those less-civilized places, down underneath the world, that she has to eat wotever they bleedin' well give 'er. If hippo tartare is on the menu at the Pygmy Pub, then tha's wot Ol' Lizzie eats." The MC was getting hot under his stained collar, waving a large knife in one hand and a head of elephant garlic in the other. Through his purple alcoholic haze, he was beginning to remember why he had never liked Sturgess in the first place. Bleedin' sot was always thinkin' 'e knew better'n anybody else.

"You can't tell me differen', cause Oi knows—"

"Yes, of course," Sturgess soothed. "You are absolutely right. When Her Majesty is on the road, she must behave as custom demands. But when at home, well… she cannot very well have guests saying that the Queen seemed nice enough but that her breath stank. I mean to say that, surely a man of your vast intellectual powers can plainly see…"

The M.C. wasn't quite sure if his leg was being pulled, but what he did in fact see was the day's third fifth, gaping a seductive invitation from the counter. His bloodshot left eye beginning to droop somnolently in its general direction, he decided to let bygones be. "Well, tha's awright then. Just so long as you know 'oo knows wot aroun' 'ere."

"Yes, by all means have some more to drink, my good man," Sturgess placated, reasoning that it was far better to have the meat be basted in liquids of questionable origin than to be carved up himself.

"Sturgess," Daisy implored, stamping her little foot. "You're not paying any attention to me!"

"Did you say something, dear?"

"Stop guzzling soup and look at me!"

"Oh, all right," he said, turning to face her. "What seems to be the problem now?"

"I want to know what you meant before, when you said that the Mistress of the Robes had nothing to do with the Queen's wardrobe."

"Her having something to do with the Queen's wardrobe? What peculiar ideas you Americans will insist on having. The Mistress's job is that of most senior Lady-in-Waiting."

"But, I don't get it," Daisy said. This "waiting" stuff, especially, had really thrown her for a loop. Having herself lived a life where it took every fiber of her being, at times, not to rail out loud at the tyranny of the unforgiving minute, it was impossible for her to understand how anybody could simply wait for a living.

"There is nothing to get, Daisy," Sturgess responded tiredly. Sometimes he found himself experiencing an almost sacrilegious longing for The Other One. At least *she* hadn't needed to have every little thing spelled out for her. Oh, well, he sighed, they could probably do a lot worse than Daisy.

"The Mistress is in charge of Waiting. Now, then, the Queen's wardrobe, which I take it is the main thrust of all of this, is attended to by Dressers."

"Not a Mistress."

"No."

"And Charles...?"

"... is the Prince of Wales."

"I know that," Daisy said, exasperated. "I mean, Charles doesn't need a Mistress to dress him either?"

"No. His Highness has me."

"Then, if I needed—"

"Ah! I get it! The day of that State Banquet will be arriving before you know it, and you don't have a clue as to what to wear! Not to mention, the trip to Klosters…" Sturgess began ticking off the upcoming events, using his fingers. "Oh, and riding clothes, of course. Why, we need to get you your very own Dresser, someone to fit you out with clothes. Come along," he beckoned, striding briskly from the kitchen.

But I don't want *to be part of a costume party*, the increasingly naggy voice inside of Daisy's head whined, as she struggled to keep up.

Sturgess turned to her, on his face a look of excitement. "I don't know why I never thought of this before, but you're going to need so very many things now." And he proceeded to describe, in detail, the contents of the Queen's wardrobe: the medals, the badges, the orders, etcetera, ad nauseum; and what was entailed, in the way of excess baggage, for even a short journey to another country. The picture that he painted led Daisy to believe that, shortly, she would definitely no longer be able to fit it all into one carry-on bag.

"And that's just the beginning," Sturgess went on, envisioning the future for the first time, for he was, of course, in on everything. "Why, if you are going to be Queen someday—"

Here Daisy shrieked out loud, causing Sturgess to clamp one large hand over her mouth. She was beginning to feel like the malcontent heir in an old Monty Python routine.

"But, Sturgess," she pleaded, once he had removed the muzzling hand. She strived to keep her voice down and the whine out, but the latter proved to be too much to ask of her. "I don't *want* to be Queen."

"Want to be Queen?" he asked incredulously. "What an absurd notion." He was looking at her as though she were starkers. "Of course you don't. Nobody in their right mind ever does." He shook his head in dismay. Those silly Americans. What would they think of next?

4

"*La-ta-ta-ti; la-ta-ta-ta.*" The Prince of Wales was singing Daffy Duck's theme song as he did up the cravat on his suit. Or maybe it was the bow tie on his tux? At any rate, it was some article of clothing, some accessory that required manual dexterity in putting it on if one did not wish to make a complete ass of one's self. But Sturgess, for once, was too caught up in the knot of his own thoughts to pay any heed to the fashion quagmire that his Lord and Master was rapidly looping himself into.

Sturgess was concerned about the little American.

"I'm concerned about the little American," he said, speaking his thoughts out loud.

"Miss Chance?" the Prince asked, absentmindedly, as he went practically en pointe in front of the high mirror, trying to get a glimpse of what kind of visual effect his handiwork had created.

"No. The other one."

Nope, that definitely would not do. The tie had about as much to do with symmetry as a Kandinsky nude or as England did with Ireland.

"You cannot possibly mean The Other One," the Prince said, unraveling the whole thing with a surprising degree of equanimity and seeming, really, quite eager to give it another go. "Surely, you must mean This One."

"Whatever," came the rather flip response. There really was no point in trying to discuss anything of a serious nature with

His Highness when he was in one of his ridiculously precise semantic modes.

Sturgess had been growing concerned, of late, with Daisy's seemingly sudden shift in attitude. She had appeared so enthusiastic at first, so Yankee gung-ho about everything. *Well,* he thought with a heavy inward sigh, *that worm hasn't taken very long to turn.* But, then, everybody knew that the Americans had the attention spans of hyperactive children. Why, hadn't they, in point of fact, actually invented some disease called ADD? To him, it had always sounded like a bunch of poppycock, really; just another excuse for ignoring your teacher or your boss or your own mum even ("Go greet Uncle George with the news? *I* thought you said I should pee on his shoes"). But still…

"How do you think that it is going?" the Prince asked, jumping up and down in front of the highly placed mirror. Really, integrity in interior design was one thing, and all very well and good, but it would be nice, if only for a change of pace, to have a shop-style dressing-room glass so that one could have some idea of what one really looked like.

"I think that it would be best, at this juncture, to proceed with caution, Sir." Sturgess's mind was still on Daisy. Had he known that the advice that he was dispensing was, almost down to the exact word, that which was being handed out as commonly as tea and crumpets at the Pakistani Embassy these days, he might have chosen his own phrasing more carefully. But as it was…

"Yes, I think I see what you mean," Charles conceded ruefully, endeavoring to gracefully extricate his forefinger from the central knot. "Tricky things, aren't they?"

Sturgess noticed the Prince's fashion impasse for the first time. He sighed more heavily still. "Do you need some help with that, Sir?"

"Well, perhaps, if you would just… er, that is to say, mm…"

The Royal chin was lifted, regally, skyward and the valet commenced to straightening the bow.

"*La-ta-ta-ti; la-ta-ta-ta.*" The theme song was being whistled now. Badly. "*La-ta*... Was there something that you wished to talk to me about before?"

The valet finished his duties and, bestowing upon the Prince of Wales an unprofessional—yet astoundingly comforting and encouraging—paternal pat on the arm, made the decision to give it all up as a bad job.

"Never mind about that now, Sir. Ye just do the very best ye can. It's all that anyone's really ever wanted from ye anyway."

5

Daisy Silverman was dressing in camouflage.

She, too, had an important date to get ready for, a momentous occasion to look forward to, some enchanted evening in her imminent future.

Too bad, then, that she was feeling so thoroughly disenchanted.

But, if it was indeed true that the Queen ate hippo tartare when she had to take the show on the road, and if there were still people on the face of the planet who were silly enough and energetic enough to try to act like Romans when in that foolishly passionate and passionately foolish country, then Daisy could certainly learn to do her share of adapting too. Although it did seem highly probable that, when Darwin had been postulating his theories on natural selection, he had not necessarily had the Royal Family and their entourage of hangers-on in mind.

In an effort to blend in with her surroundings, then, she was wearing a red evening gown. And, while that color had speedily been transformed, to her eyes, from vivid to vapid—in about the same amount of time it would take one to say "No more John Major for me" three times fast—through the sheer overwhelming proliferation of it around her, she was hoping it would prove to be just the ticket. For she was filled with an odd mixture of trepidation and boredom at the prospect of the evening ahead. How strange to feel so concerned about the impression that one created while, at the same instant, not really caring what anybody thought at all. If she could just get through it without making a complete and utter ass out of herself...

Sheathed in flaming red satin—from thin shoulder straps, through heart-shaped neckline and waist snug enough to please Scarlett O'Hara, all the way down to flared skirt above restlessly tapping foot encased in pinching heels, that were not dyed to match but had actually been created in that color for her alone, she was hoping that, if she could no longer pass for a wallflower, perhaps she might be taken for an original cabbage rose: a relief from the endless, expected expanse of plush red carpeting that seemed to extend as far as the eye could see.

Daisy's disenchantment with everything had really all started on the previous day, during a private little luncheon with the Queen.

Oh, the food had been fine, of course, never anything to worry about there. True, it was a bit on the blandly rich side, as always—all cream and no garlic—but there was certainly plenty of it. No, one would have to really work at it to starve to death around here.

No, the problem had been with The Bag.

Right after the Queen had issued the invitation to Daisy, but prior to her attendance there, Sturgess had briefed Daisy on protocol. "The most important thing to remember," he had advised, "is that, when Her Majesty places her bag upon the table, it means that the interview is at an end, and that the time has come for the guest to graciously, but rapidly, make their exit."

And Daisy had relished this information, reveling in the knowledge that she was now "in the know," had the inside scoop, finally knew what the true purpose of The Bag was: like one of those variety programs from the early days of television, it was the hook for removing acts from the stage who had either failed to or no longer entertained. Rude, perhaps, but effective. And besides, Daisy realized quite sensibly, the Queen—if she wished to maintain her reputation as being "as gracious as you would want her to be, a real lady"—could hardly say to her guests, "Please get out of my house. You are giving me a headache and, worse, you are a bore."

But, when it had come time for the luncheon, things hadn't

gone quite the way that Sturgess had described. Right in the middle of the soup course, the Queen had abruptly risen, exiting the room without a word. Perhaps the heavy cream base had proven too much, and a visit to the Throne Room was in order?

But no, Daisy had thought. The Queen had left The Bag behind. *Surely, a lady always brings her bag with her to the Ladies'. No?*

So, there was Daisy, alone in the Chinese Luncheon Room with The Bag.

Ayup. There was The Bag, and there was Daisy.

Well, what would *you* do?

Of course, she couldn't resist. Of course, she had to look inside of it.

Feeling like a thief in the night—or a palace intruder, circa 1982—she cautiously reached under the Queen's chair, and very quietly, very carefully, undid the heavy gold clasp on the old-fashioned purse. Looking over both shoulders first, as if expecting a counterspy to attack from behind, she gently pried open the rather stiff sides and, placing one eye to the opening, peered inside.

She drew away, startled.

She peered again, both eyes shifting back and forth now, to make absolutely certain that she had seen correctly the first time.

But, no. There had been no sensual deception.

It was the cleanest, most pristine, handbag interior that Daisy had ever peered into in her life. No gum wrappers. No outdated shades of lipstick. Not a condom in sight. Not even any lint, for crying out loud.

The Bag was empty.

Having wanted for so very long to find out what was contained therein, this exposure of the emptiness of The Bag filled Daisy with dismay. And, when the Queen at last returned—offering no explanation for her absence, of course—and began to brief Daisy on the importance of the State Banquet that was to take place on the following evening (who would be there, and what was expected of Royalty on such occasions), she was surprised at how little interest Daisy showed. Surely, one would have thought that even this relatively even-tempered Colonist might show some more enthusiasm at the prospect of sitting down to dinner with her own country's president. And while one might admit that, sometimes, one might be wrong about these things, one never did.

Still, one would have thought that at least the mention of the Archbishop of Canterbury's expected presence would have elicited more of a rise. It certainly had that effect on most people.

Well, one sighed, taking a healthy swig from the luncheon claret. One's son certainly knew how to pick them.

6

Following the luncheon—and The Exposure of The Bag, of course—the day had only gone from bad to worse.

Daisy had been in a disenchanted panic. And Charley, well meaning though misguided as his intentions were, had been trying to calm her down while being yet another person attempting to brief her on events in her near future. It was fortunate for him, in a way, that, for once, *she* was not listening to *him*; had she been, she might have brained him with the nearest scepter, having quite quickly gone from a state of being eager to learn, to one in which she was heartily disgusted with the entire process of others trying to mold her behavior.

"Do you ever just, like, completely forget what's inside some of these?"

While in the process of opening and shutting doors at mad random, she had also gone a trifle retro Valley Girl.

"And, like, I can't believe that you people actually number these rooms somewhere for ease, as though this were a hotel instead of somebody's home. I mean, what is this? Just what exactly is in Room 222 anyway?"

Charley lifted his empty hands and shook his head, proving that chewing gum while walking just might be in his future after all.

Daisy, in B.P., was feeling like Alice in Wonderland. "No wonder you always look so lost, Charles," she stated, projecting her own feelings just a wee bit. "It's like the red-carpet version of Dante or something."

Really, she was quite lucky that he was not a very easy person to offend.

"Don't you ever find this all—oh, I don't know—just a tad ridiculous? And, what about your mother? Do you ever think that she gets overtaken by the urge to laugh out loud at the sheer absurdity of it all? And—"

"What are you talking about, DeeDee?"

"And the Mistress of the Robes—I mean, what is that? What does she do? I still don't get it."

"Hush, hush, DeeDee," he soothed, drawing her into his arms. "Now, tell me, what is this all about?"

Daisy felt the wind deflating from out of her sails. She stood like a wet noodle in his arms. "Skip it."

7

Protocol. Ceremony. Splendour with a "u" on loan from grandeur.

Bleagh, Daisy thought, as she paced the East Gallery now. Where had the real world gone?

She was just getting the lay of the land and possibly burning off a little steam, before she was due to meet the others in the Queen's Audience Room, prior to the group's joint entrance. She was perhaps not in an appropriately State Banquet frame of mind.

She passed under a lighted Renoir, a Van Dyck, another Renoir. *Well, really, once you've seen a half-dozen Renoirs…* she thought, in a Philistine-like fashion that made her hard to recognize as the same girl who used to haunt the Reading Room at the British Library.

In fact, with all of her finery, it was becoming increasingly difficult to recognize our girl at all.

But, when you get right down to it, you can take the jacket of *War and Peace* and slam it around a Jackie Collins—or vice versa, though why one would want to do that, one doesn't wish to hazard a guess—and the only people who would be fooled forever would be those who never actually read the books, but only looked at the jackets. Or something like that.

At any rate, Daisy, still being Herbert's daughter down to the minute hand on her new diamond watch, was impossibly early.

Which meant that there were still quite a few other individuals of interest, some of who probably considered themselves to be Daisy's equal in importance, who were still readying themselves for the festivities that lay ahead. One could only hope that they had come prepared.

8

Someone was singing in the shower.

"God, I love this place," he shouted out, gleefully, as he turned off the gold faucets. "They think of everything around here."

The rather tall man emerged from the bathroom in the Belgian Suite—the very same bathroom where the Queen had once birthed her youngest son—a plush towel wrapped around his waist, still glistening from the shower, a toothbrush jammed into the corner of his mouth. His head didn't even come close to touching the top of the doorway, as he passed from the bathroom into the bedroom. In fact, that was one of the really cool things about being President that Mr. Clinton had never quite really gotten over. For, what with all of the really big places that they got to stay in when they traveled—with the possible exception of China—he never had to worry about clearance or about bumping his head anymore.

"Hny? Ers mm frit ux?"

In the bedroom, a woman—who was smartly attired in a rather slimming midnight-blue velvet gown—was wearing a disturbed expression upon her face, as she laid out clothing upon the bed. His wife was prepared, as always: already dressed herself, one step ahead of him, as always, natch.

"I never can quite understand what you're saying, when you've got that toothbrush in your mouth," she said, trying her best not to sound like an annoyed schoolmistress. "What was that about an ux?"

"I *said*," came the familiar Arkansas twang, as he removed the brush from his mouth, his lips flecked with tiny bits of toothpaste foam, "Where's my favorite tux? You know the one I mean. Did they remember to pack it?"

His wife bit her lip, studying the garments on the bed. She sincerely hoped that what she was seeing wasn't going to completely spoil her husband's and, therefore, her evening, for she had so been looking forward to it. And, while she knew that it might not necessarily be the politically correct mindset to have, you couldn't help but be in awe of Them, she thought, shaking her top a little in order to better redistribute the wealth of her breasts within the snug confines of the designer gown. No matter how determinedly democratic you intended to appear, this, after all, was Royalty.

But, before she got the chance to say something, anything soothing that might avert the coming storm, her husband caught a glimpse of the distinctly "uh-oh" expression on her face, and his eyes shot to the bed, where he saw exactly what she was seeing.

"Oh, man!" the Leader of the Free World whined aloud, smacking himself in the head with the palm of his hand. It was a blow that might very well have knocked a man of less strength unconscious but, luckily for him, his head was hard.

"Now, Bill," his wife cautioned, "don't let it spoil the whole evening."

"But, Hillary…"

"Bill," she warned, "now just stop it. I think you look… fine in this one. Very handsome. Original."

"Shit, shit, *shit*."

He crossed to one of the many windows of the Belgian Suite, valiantly trying to keep his temper in check, to put a brave front on things. Drawing back the curtain, he placed his forehead against the pane, looking out at the stunning view of the twilit gardens and the moon-shadowed lake beyond. He tried. (He really did.) But it was no use.

"*Shit*. I mean… just… *shit*, Hillary. A man gets to be President of the United States, and you'd think that he could at least not have to look like a royal asshole in front of the whole world all the time. I mean… shit. They sent the goddamned white one again. Now I'm going to look like a waiter in a Chinese restaurant. *Again*. Shit."

9

The Duke of Edinburgh paused for a moment, in the midst of his posturing, admiring the triptych of full-length reflections that looked back at him. Perhaps, if Charles was a very good boy, the Duke might let his son have one of these for his very own one day. He studied the cut of the robes with a critical eye, squinting at the effect of the gilded tassels that befitted his station as a Knight of the Garter.

Nope, as Charles's friend was always saying. Nope, this wouldn't do at all. He was going to need a much bigger kick than this, if he was going to get through the entire evening.

Exiting his own dressing room and suite, he hurried down the King's Corridor to his wife's dressing room. He knocked at the door and, when there was no answer, quickly looked both ways to see if the coast was clear before turning the handle. A moment later, he reemerged, one of *her* robes now thrown about his shoulders, and looked both ways again before crossing the Corridor to achieve his ultimate destination.

Once safely ensconced in the Throne Room, he sat in his favorite chair—HERS—his robes arranged around him, his long legs draped over the gilded arm. He felt free now to engage in one of his pet pre-State Banquet fantasies: the one in which *he* were the King, and *she* had to walk the requisite three paces behind *him*.

In spite of the lift that such a daydream usually gave him, however, he found that, oddly enough, on this occasion he was not amused. He kept hearing the voice of that annoying little American, the words echoing in his head over and over again. "Just get over it, Phil!" she had said to him, yet again, in exasperation the evening before.

He looked down at his present attire, experiencing a novel feeling of dismay. Was it just barely possible that the little tramp had something there?

He hurried back along the King's Corridor, hoping to replace his wife's things before she and her own Dressers appeared and found them missing. It would never do for her to catch him out. He would never hear the end of it.

And as he hurried along, his black-booted feet silently causing tiny dents to appear in the crimson carpeting, a rather strange thought occurred to him: for the very first time, in his entire married life, he felt as though he had figured out something important before anybody else had had a chance to catch on.

Now, if only he could figure out just what that something was that he had figured out, why, he would be sitting very pretty indeed. Right in the catbird seat, as it were.

10

The Archbishop of Canterbury was hoping, yet again, that the theories that he had espoused from the pulpit were indeed true, and that there really was a hereafter. For, surely, there must be some greater reward for the pains that one was forced to endure in the course of this vale of tears that some termed "life."

Take this placard, for instance. This item, this *thing* of protocol issued by the Master of the Household to announce the proper processional to the evening's State Banquet. The Queen and President Bill Clinton—not even William, mind you! Must they always familiarize everything?—were to lead, followed at the requisite three paces by the Duke of Edinburgh, squiring that political distraction that some liked to call Hillary. If not all well and good, at least that was as it should be. Then they were to be followed by the Queen Mother on the arm of her inevitable escort, Prince Charles. Nope, as any Colonist might tediously say, nothing out of the ordinary there.

And the Colonies certainly were of relevance here, because the problem with which he was faced was a decidedly American-inspired one. For, after the Queen Mother and the Prince, there was to follow the Archbishop of Canterbury, the Primate of the Church of England—him—who was to have as his companion… Daisy Sills?

What the Archbishop could not know, was that Charles had lobbied for, and won, the right to have Daisy escorted into dinner by him. It paid to know people in high places, and the Lord Chamberlain—following a more than gracious contribution to his own personal Fresh Air Fund—had been more than willing to jockey others around so that Daisy might have the position opposite Charles at dinner. And nobody else had seemed to mind this highly irregular state of affairs in the least. Nobody, that is, except for the A. of C., of course.

What that man did know was that he had been forced to suffer many indignities in his time, but that this really was the limit! To be saddled with an unknown American quantity, and not even a Royal one at that! Never mind a Princess, nobody had ever heard of her before. She wasn't even a politician's daughter. Why, at least when he had had the job of waltzing into dinner with The Other One...

Oh, he waved the past away with his hand, thinking that tonight might not be as awful as he had previously let his mind run away with imaginings that it would be. Fie on the Lord Chamberlain's Byzantine seating arrangements for dinner, his exacting charts that followed a pecking order that only he knew the secret behind. And maybe the L.C. had something there, maybe it was necessary to have all of the earls and dukes put in their right places. For, elsewise, anarchy might reign, and then how would a Field Marshall ever be able to prove that he was more important than an Air Chief Marshall? One means, really...

In fact, he told himself with a grin, as he studied the chart again, an evening spent with the American nothing, Sills, might afford him a rather pleasant change of pace. Nope, nothing awful there at all.

But, try as he might, it was impossible for the A. of C. to maintain such a Pollyanna-ish worldview for very long.

Of course it would be awful, he finally decided, letting the grin die away like a Briton under a Saxon siege. The whole night was going to suck.

11

Elsewhere, the ladies were having their own set of problems.

In a flat in Dolphin Square, a Princess could be heard to be knocking on the loo. If the Archbishop thought that he had problems with his designated escort, they were as nothing when compared with Princess Anne's.

"You must come out!" shouted Anne, as she pounded on the door with one closed fist, while she tried, single-handedly, to insert an earbob into her hole. The bordered flounce on the bodice of her pink dress betrayed it as being a few years out of date, but then, she thought, who the hell really cared? Besides, pink was such an insipid color anyway.

She knocked again, harder. It was almost time to go. He *would* make them late.

"I'm not going," came the muffled masculine voice from the other side of the locked door.

"You must." She paused briefly, trying to come up with a good reason why he must. "People expect it. And besides, Mother is heartily sick of dysfunctions among the family. I was hoping that we might... oh, I don't know... present a united front or something."

"Well," said the voice, "I'm sick of these functions, too."

"Yes, I know, dear. But it's much worse for her, you know. After all, it's her noggin that's always on the block. It seems that the very least we can do is help her out now and again..." Her own voice trailed off for want of enthusiasm.

"Well, it's tough on the rest of us, too. Besides..." The voice paused, an embarrassed note beginning to creep in. "My tummy hurts."

"Oh, no! It must have been all that pickled herring for lunch!"

"Perhaps."

"Well, then, I guess there's nothing for it. You must stay home. I certainly wouldn't want to sit next to you at dinner in the condition you must be in."

"Quite. Understandable."

Anne briskly grabbed her bag and rather roughly straightened the skirt of her gown without looking in the mirror. "Well, alright then, I'm off. Stiff upper lip."

"Yes, yes," came the tired voice.

As she shut the door behind her, she thought that she'd probably have a better time without him. He was always such a dreadful whiner about these things anyway. Not even noticing the sound of breaking crockery—knocked off the wall display due to the sheer force of her slam—she thought that it would be a welcome change to only have to worry about her own miserable time, as opposed to having to worry about another person's as well.

Little did the Princess realize, as she stalked off in search of a cab, just how much she had in common with Daisy. For, as we all know, Daisy hated whiners too. And, for the record, as to the odor of pickled herring, well... suffice to say that, as far as certain scents were concerned, it was possible to take the well-intentioned notion of recycling a tad too far. Or, as Rachel Silverman had been so fond of saying, "When you forget the soap, so shall ye reek."

12

Bonita studied her image in the mirror, pleased with the effect created by the scarlet and gold livery. Worn just loosely enough, it was virtually impossible to guess the sex of the individual beneath the clothes. And while the white breeches were a shade uncomfortable, she thought, as she bent down to adjust her stockings, it was probably just because it was such an unfamiliar garment for her to be wearing. And she did so like the nice shiny buckles on those chunky shoes.

Straightening, she donned the white powdered wig with shoulder-length queue. With considerable effort, she was able to successfully rein in her own willful tresses, tucking the straggly ends up under the sides of their synthetic camouflage. She surveyed the final effect.

"Spiffy," she pronounced.

"Slut," her reflection winked back.

"Showtime," they concurred.

13

"Here, let me get that for you, Ma'am."

"I'll get it, I'll *get* it," the Queen stated, shooing the startled Dresser aside. The queen rarely got pettish about her wardrobe like this, but when she did...

"Must you all hover about One so? One would think that you thought that One was incapable of dressing Oneself."

The Dressers raised quizzical eyebrows at one another, behind the Monarch's back. Just what exactly were they supposed to be doing then?

"Out! Out!" the Queen commanded. "We are not in the mood to be fussed at this evening."

The Dressers beat a hasty retreat, as she shut the door firmly behind them.

Enjoying a rare moment of solitude, she turned her attention to the pleasant matter of her jewelry. One might think—the "one" in question being we general, garden-variety "ones," as opposed to the far more imperial "One"—that the Queen would be somewhat jaded on the subject of gems. But one, being heir to the vulgar ignorance of the common man, would be way off the money. For, the one and only One took great pride in her jewelry collection.

She selected a Family Order, worn on a ribbon on her left shoulder, and reserved solely for State occasions. It contained pictures of her father and grandfather, the miniature portraits encircled with brilliant diamonds.

Checking out the robe situation, she could have sworn that the velvet crimson pleats on one of them was off-kilter, aligned in a funny way on its hanger. Had one of the Dressers been into the Sherry too early? Or had old what's-his-name been rooting around in here again?

Ah well, she thought. Neither situation really bore thinking about. It was ever so much nicer to concentrate on her jewelry.

What next? Hmm, let's see... bracelet, earrings, Family Order, necklace; alphabetically speaking, so far everybody was present and accounted for. But, surely, with all of those idle letters following the "n" in the alphabet, there must be some other shirker still lurking out there somewhere. No?

"Oh, no," the Defender of the Faith groaned aloud, remembering. "Not the letter 'T.'" Usually, there was a Dresser present to help her out with that alphabetic straggler. Where the bloody hell had they all disappeared to? None of them were ever around when you needed them anyway.

Selecting a diamond and emerald tiara and grabbing some pins, she proceeded to attempt to screw the wretched thing onto her own head.

Talk about a crown of thorns!

If there was one thing that could foul her mood even quicker than old what's-his-name messing around in her robes, it was the diamond and emerald tiara. The blasted thing was giving her a headache already. There ought to be a law...

Go ahead and laugh, if you will, but people who thought that wearing tiaras was all fun and games clearly didn't know the half of it.

14

And then, of course, there was the problem of Pacqui and Packey.

"But *why* must you walk in with one of the horse women?" Pacqui asked Packey for the eleventh time, stamping his little foot.

"Hold still, hold still! How many times do I have to tell you that this bondage stuff is never a success when you insist on moving about so? You are creating a situation where it is quite impossible for me to tie you up."

"Fine," said Pacqui. "I'll make for you a deal: I will stop moving around long enough for you to tie me up, if you will explain to me about the horse woman."

"Fine, yourself," said Packey. "Deal."

"Shake?" offered Pacqui.

"Done," said Packey, as they shook hands, each accenting their pact with a brief gentlemanly bow of the head.

"You know, don't you," said Pacqui, as he endeavored to stand still, tilting his chin upwards so that Packey could create a bow with the tie of his tux, "if somebody ever decides to write the story of our romance—perhaps a gay Pakistani *Gone With the Wind?* Sounds good, no?—the agent will never be able to sell the rights to the audiobook people. Too confusing. Or, at least," he added, craftily, "not unless one of us is willing to change his name."

"Would that that were the least of our problems," said Packey, giving the tie a final perfectionist tweak.

"You know I love it when you say things that sound as though

you are quoting Shakespeare to me. It gives me goose bumps…
so stop it already, a deal being a deal. I stood still, *so*… the horse
woman?" Pacqui looked at Packey expectantly, at first, then
warningly. "Now, don't be a welch jelly…"

"Alright, all *right*. But I don't see why we have to go through this
every single time. For a man who considers himself to be a high-
ranking member of the embassy—now don't look at me like that!
Yes, yes, of course you are right, it is true. Stop giving me the hairy
eyeball!—and is considered by *others* to be a high-ranking member as
well, you never seem to grasp these finer points of court protocol."

"Stop walling my stones. The horse woman…?"

"You know I only have eyes for you, but I must walk into the
dinner with whomever the Lord Chamberlain says that I must. He
is the man who holds everyone's short hairs in his hot little hands.
Besides, dearest," Packey soothed, "you know that nobody is ever
allowed to escort the person that they love the most into dinner.
Togetherness just is not done. Why, a person should consider himself
lucky if he does not actively detest the person he is paired with."

Pacqui thrust out his lower lip in a pout.

"Dearest," said Packey, "you know I would rather eat with you
than with anybody else in the world."

Hearing the ring of truth in this assertion (and it really was
there), Pacqui began to brighten, his mustache beginning to twitch
upwards in an irrepressible smile.

Seeing this, Packey decided to press his suit. Placing his hands
on the other man's shoulders, he added, "Much better to be with
Pacqui than with whatever watery tart the Lord Chamberlain has
selected for me this time. Now, then: kiss-kiss. Let's go see how we
look in the mirror.

"So, what do you think?" he asked, placing a proudly possessive
arm around Pacqui's shoulders. "We are perfect, no? Quite the
Queen's fleas' knees."

Pacqui looked carefully, just to be certain that he was seeing
exactly what his lover was seeing. Let's see… identical height, weight,
shape; same coloring, haircut, mustache; and the fashion sense of

a pasha with a lifelong subscription to *GQ*. Packey was right. They were perfect, Pacqui thought, a matched pair. They stood like that for a long contented moment, arms about one another's shoulders, looking as though they were posing for a portrait.

They decided that it never bothered them that racists used their exterior similarities as ratification for the claim that they all looked alike. Seeing their individual selves reflected in the other at all times, they merely took it as being the highest of compliments. For who else would either of them rather look like most in the world?

Pacqui was, of course, the first to break the spell.

"You know, I really do not mind at all the *Patty Duke Show* quality of our life, if only it weren't for the problem of audiobooks…"

"Stop with that already. Sometimes, I swear, you are just like a dog with a boner."

"Speaking of animals, about that horse woman: which one of them did you say that the Lord Chamberlain has stuck you with this time?"

"Bowwow, I didn't. As a matter of fact, I never even checked myself. Now let me see… I must have left that placard he sent me around here somewhere… Did you check the wastebasket yet, dearest?"

15

Zee; omega; zed.

The Last Picture Show; The Last Hurrah; The Last Tycoon.

Tsar Nicholas; Pluto (the planet, *not* the dog); that Mohican character.

Not to mention, of course, the Littlest Piggy: cultural icon, known far and wide for its innate—learned?—ability for crying all the way home.

Over in Kensington Palace, the Queen's little sis was stewing in her own juices, as it were. Princess Margaret had her very own little thing to be heartily sick of. *As if anybody really cared*, she sulked, taking something larger than a sip—but smaller than a breadbox—from her glass of wine.

She was tired, fed up, sick unto death, with being the last on any and every list that had ever been made up in the history of the world. So, maybe things weren't quite as dire as she was making them out, but you try telling her that. From where she was sitting, the situation was quite... that is to say, when one thought about... oh, bloody hell. Suffice to say, that it just plain sucked.

And, as she poured herself just one more glass of wine, she sincerely hoped that they would at least remember to send the car for her this time.

Ye-es, she drew out the thought, while staring into the wisdom-filled bottom of her glass. Anybody who actually believed that being last was not synonymous with being least probably also thought that wearing tiaras all of the time sounded like a keen idea.

If she ever found such an individual, she would sell them a nice, healthy chunk of London Bridge. Or, maybe she would just shove it down their throats.

Buckingham Palace
State Banquet
December, 1999

Queen Elizabeth II	President Bill Clinton
Prince Philip	Hillary Rodham Clinton
Queen Mother	Prince of Wales
Archbishop of Canterbury	Daisy Sills
Princess Anne	British Prime Minister
Prince Andrew	Mrs. BPM
Jodie Foster	Prince Edward
Ambassador Packey Packel	Princess Margaret

(and approximately 484 other distinguished guests)

16

Like the nucleus of an atom, the fetus of a hippo, or the quaking tremors brought about by creatures in the Jurassic Period—who hadn't a clue as to how to tread gently on the Earth—the mostly Royal procession began, appropriately enough, from the Queen's Closet. Situated between the Queen's Audience Room and the White-Drawing Room, and all such things being relative, the Royal Closet was not what you might expect. In fact, contrary to its innocuous title, which made it sound as though it might be a narrow receptacle for storing dirty gaiters, it represented a rather good-sized drawing-room in its own right—complete with the appropriate marble, crystal, and heavy damask design features. Traditionally, it was the place from which any important evening's festivities usually began for the R.F.. And, as Rachel used to prompt Daisy—being the youngest Silverman branch on their particular family tree—to recite each and every Passover: "So, nu? God? Why should this night be different from any other night?"

Considering how much earlier than everybody else Daisy had been ready, it was somehow fitting then, that she should be the last one to make it into the Closet. Even Prince Edward—often tardy himself—was already in there with Jodie when Daisy arrived, breathless, just in time to make the fast acquaintance of her escort.

She barely had time to shake his hand, but sometimes, first impressions forming hastily and hard, that is all it takes. The rather recently appointed Archbishop of Canterbury's hand hung like a limp codfish in her own, a species of handshake that Herbert had always taught her to avoid at all costs. Not to mention, that the Primate was possessed of a profile even more severe than that of the Duke's, making him a much stronger candidate for being somebody's cruel stepmother.

And, how nice, Daisy thought, upon being presented to that smug visage, *to be able to be so absolutely certain that one's own poop didn't stink.*

But she really had no time to dwell on notions theological; or to attend to the very pertinent fact that her olfactory sense had just put in a brief reappearance; or to even properly appreciate that the President of the United States, in person, failed to disappoint a bit and that he was, in fact, just as tall in real life as he appeared to be on TV (even if he obviously didn't have a clue as to how to dress for a black-tie affair). For, before she knew what she was about, she was being whisked along on her merry way, carried on the surging tide of veddy important people.

At the entrance to the White Drawing-Room—a room with no visible lines for a door—the Queen gave a sovereign nod of the head and the wall swung forward, as if by sorcery. It was sometimes tough on her, striving to maintain that imperiously impervious smile, when the Batman-like effect that this entrance had on other people always filled her with such pleasure. She often wondered, just what would happen if any guests on the other side were to stand too close to the outwardly swinging wall. Perhaps knocking one's guests on their hindquarters, or flattening them like pancakes, was not the done thing in polite company but, thankfully, this hairsplitting point of etiquette had never been tested to date.

Meanwhile—as Daisy played with the notorious swinging door, idly attempting to figure out how the trick was done—the other 484 invitees were arriving downstairs, beginning their inevitable progress towards the Music Room, just on the other side of the White-Drawing Room, there to rendezvous with the sixteen more important (in whose minds?) people already waiting upstairs.

They entered by singles, by pairs, and by clusters. They came through the Ambassador's Entrance; they came through the Grand

Entrance. After a brief stop, in order to deposit their coats and things on the bed in the guest room (only kidding!), they, each and every one, found themselves in the Grand Hall.

Those accustomed to such things as a part of everyday life gave it all the old ho-hum treatment. The rest, in an attempt to maintain a mien of outward urbanity, strained not to rubberneck. This set of circumstances left the world, briefly, with one very harried butler who couldn't carry a tune, and 484 dignified souls who would need to seek chiropractic assistance come the morrow for self-inflicted whiplash.

The Grand Hall was, for lack of an adequate adjective, impressive. What with its crimson carpets, its soaring marble pillars with gilded Corinthian columns, its gold, its mahogany, its Sevres, its... you name it. If it represented a superlative item on the individual spectra of the decorative arts, it was there. It was everything and more that one could require from a foyer. The Grand Hall was, quite simply, the most.

Having thus been relieved of their splendour virginity, they made their hushed and bustling way towards the Grand Staircase. There, spit-and-polished black shoes ascended the double staircase, soundlessly passing over the crimson carpet, studiously avoiding the cold marble. There, gloved hands reached out to grasp the heavily gilt bronze balustrade, maintaining a precarious balance on heels, as they gave into temptation, craning their swans' necks heavenward, at the domed skylight overhead. All came finally together at the top, the twin sides curving upwards in a bow, deposited in front of the doors of the Guard Chamber and the appropriately named Green Drawing-Room beyond.

The crimson and gold carpeting of the Green Drawing-Room had already impressed Daisy, on her previous visits there, as being a little bit too far over the St. Nick top for her own tastes. Thankfully for the guests who passed through—before crossing the Picture Gallery and entering the Music Room, there to see the waiting Queen—Daisy Silverman was not piloting the tour bus.

Of course, just because Daisy wasn't piloting the bus, didn't necessarily mean that one could prevent her from obsessing about poor interior design choices—at least, not at this stirringly stimulating juncture in her life. And so, as she sat in the Music Room, listening to some somnolent musical interlude or other, she found her mind drifting across the hall and into the Green Drawing-Room; found herself thinking that the décor choices expressed there represented a clear case of overkill, as though someone had slipped The Russian Tea Room a whole handful of 'ludes. True, the effect of the complementary colors was striking, but, then again, while the odor of horse manure was striking too, that didn't necessarily make it something worth aspiring to. As Daisy leaned across to Princess Anne, however, thinking to pass a whispered comment to this effect, she caught a strong whiff of that Royal personage, and found herself biting her own tongue, having formed a lightning-quick reversal of opinion. Obviously, for some people, certain odors *were* worth aspiring to.

Sitting there, her own tongue firmly held between her teeth as Anne looked back at her, patiently waiting for word or thought to emerge, Daisy took in the full effect of the Princess's chosen attire. Clad entirely in pink frou-frou, it occurred to Daisy that she looked more like a confection than a person, like marzipan only with walnuts, or a giant petit fours. Thinking to offer some advice—something perhaps along the lines of women of a certain type not being temperamentally suited to certain styles—she opened her mouth, and began the process of unleashing her tongue. Thankfully, before she got the opportunity to find out if she could, in fact, fit her entire foot into her own mouth, the doors to the Music Room were flung open, the hordes began to descend, and it was time for the Royal Party to rise and greet its guests.

A few moments later—as she stood as part of the official receiving line, shaking hands, and using the kind of warmly firm grip that would have made Herbert Silverman proud, at any rate—Jodie was wondering just how one would go about shooting the scene before her; how to convey the idea of hundreds of potentially interesting people, all doing potentially interesting things, all having lives outside of this room where events were (potentially) constantly occurring; how to, finally, convey all of that, while keeping the real focus of the cameras, and, thus, her audience, firmly on the activities of a very small handful of a few of the (crazier than most) characters. When she got back home, she resolved, she would check to see if Joseph Manckiewitz had left any liner notes from *Cleopatra*. And then she would divide by twenty.

Jodie was, in fact, as she stood at Prince Edward's side—her ruby-red lips looking as though nature had painted them that color; as she parted them regularly and with ease, only to reveal the perfect smile beyond—proof positive of woman's (and man's, one *guesses* you might say) ability to go on to achieve great success as an adult— in spite of *and* because of the occurrences in one's youth—and that life was sustainable inside of the fishbowl, if one only had the right set of gills. (As a matter of record, the only other individual that Hollywood had managed to raise successfully to majority, without throwing it out with the bathwater, was Ron Howard. But, unfortunately, the former Opie was already otherwise engaged when Edward rang him up, leaving the Prince with no other recourse but to resort to the second choice on his list.)

Jodie was also proof positive that one could express, in one's wardrobe, the dizzying heights of impeccable taste—tonight being clad in a money green satin sheathe, and, thus, refinedly combining wealth and sex in such a way that no man present, including Edward (who usually did not let himself become bothered over such things), would get a wink that night—while, at the same instant, conducting oneself with such an air that it was impossible for the world to ever accuse you of caring a fig about such a banal thing as the world's impression of one.

Meanwhile, a few paces up the line, the Queen Mother reached into the folds of her ermine-trimmed robe, producing a flask from which she took a surreptitious slug. Replacing it in her pocket, she reached up a hand, dearly hoping that she was straightening her tiara as opposed to knocking it further off-kilter.

The Q.M. looked around the room with a slightly skewed vision, taking in the twin chandeliers, the eighteen columns, the candelabra ringing the room. In its present capacity as Music Room, there were few furnishings to be found in the oval room, the domed ceiling being its neatest architectural trick, and the red-and-gold curtains providing its strongest splashes of color. In fact, as far as the Q.M. was concerned, the Music Room still *was* the Grand Saloon, as it had been called in Victorian times.

Shaking hands with some pasha or another, she took another furtive swig. As she attended with one ear to the fascinating problem of the falling price of palm products, she cast an eye across the room at the brass-inlaid walnut piano. Perhaps, if they were lucky— or, not, depending on one's perspective—Princess Margaret might be prevailed upon, following dinner and a few nice glasses of wine, to give them all a treat by tickling the old ivories.

And, speaking of dinner, the Q.M. wondered, *where the hell is it, anyway?* The rumbling noise in her stomach chimed off the hours like clockwork. *Surely, it must be drawing nigh on nine o'clock. No?*

• • •

The entire party had bypassed the State Dining-Room, making a beeline for the much larger Ballroom instead.

Which was something of a pity, Daisy thought, herself preferring the smaller room, what with its string of Gainsborough portraits lining the walls. It was always fun when gazing at these to attempt a chicken-and-egg analysis: had the artist left off painting horses just long enough to do these portraits of the Queen's ancestors? Or had the inspiration process been worked the other way around? Either way, Daisy liked the Spanish mahogany table at the room's center, liked its relative intimacy when compared with some of the others in the palace. Unfortunately, however, the room only seated sixty comfortably and the Ballroom, being far more spacious and crowd-friendly, was the only answer for it.

Over one hundred feet in length, sixty in width, and having a ceiling that rose a full five stories overhead, there would indeed be ample arm space at the table such that Edward needn't worry about Mrs. B.P.M. poking him in the eye with her shrimp fork, or his aunt engineering a moat around his foie gras if she chanced to knock over her wineglass.

The room contained six chandeliers, each the size of a planet, and was entirely decorated in crimson, gold, and white, with the inevitable red carpeting covering the parquet floor. In honor of the holiday season, however, slight alterations had been made. The room was festooned with faux snowflakes, suspended—through the artful use of carefully placed wires and by even more carefully managed lighting—as though by magic. This created the impression that the party was taking place inside of a snow globe.

Of course, there had to be a Musician's Gallery in the room. Not to mention, enough Footmen—attired in scarlet and gold livery, white breeches, stockings and buckled shoes—to populate a whole book of fairy stories. And, since tight and short ponytails for men had sprung back into fashion after about two hundred years, a number of these Footmen were sporting appropriate queues. In fact, the whole scene put the President—who, quite naturally enough, was seated at the top table, in front of the throne dais, which stood out in bas-relief against a background of red hangings—uncomfortably in mind of indentured servitude, the single word "slavery" not being very far behind it in his thoughts, as the word began to flash on and off in his brain like the red "petrol low" warning light on an Aston Martin.

A few places down from where the President was seated, and on the opposite side of the table, the Q.M. winked at Mr. Clinton as though to reassure him that things were not as politically dire as they seemed or, at the very least, to goose him into lightening up. Under normal circumstances, the Q.M. would have been seated to the left of the President, her and her daughter forming a Windsor sandwich around the American leader. But Charles, just prior to the onset of the evening's festivities, had pulled her aside, convincing her that he needed her by his side at dinner for moral support.

Her assent, which had evinced the trademark equanimity that

she liked to bring to all of life's little curveballs, had thus left Charles free to gaze across the table into the eyes of his beloved. It also left him free—if he could only find a way to slouch down in his seat low enough—to stretch his piggies out under the table, and play footsies with her as well.

From a more practical standpoint, however, what this playing of musical chairs meant was that Daisy was seated smack between the President of the United States of America and the Archbishop of Canterbury, Primate of the Church of England. This positioning, placing her as the woman to the right closest to the Queen, was quite an honor. It also meant that—since everybody who was anybody was in attendance, as well as everybody who wasn't—she would be on such conspicuous display for the entire evening, her prominence impossible to ignore or deny, and that anybody who wished to, or anybody with eyes in their head to see, might bear witness to The Beginning of The End.

• • •

The Leader of the Free World and the Leader of the Commonwealth (kindly note the layers of meaning—like a peeled onion, blah, blah, blah—that a mere comparison of titles can take on) had already raised their traditional toasts to one another.

The Queen—resisting the temptation to reach up and adjust her diamond tiara, which was digging a ridge into her forehead—had toasted the President on his performance, saying how nice it was to have them there, and commenting on how equally nice it must be to "always be able to feel so certain concerning one's support from the public," to which he had responded with a quizzical, if gracious, smile.

He, in his turn, trying to maintain status quo or achieve quid pro quo or some such thing, had said how nice it was to be there, and returned her other compliment by stating that, "It must be just as nice *not* to have to worry about the public's support."

And it really *was* nice, having the Clintons over for dinner, the

Queen thought to herself, as she took a healthy serving of the first course. From the options that the Master Chef had presented her with, she had elected to serve the forty-second President of the United States and his wife Quail Vol-au-Vent; and, for the main course, a dish that she had recently christened Braised Bush Stag.

Whenever possible, the Queen liked to inject her own brand of mischievous wit into what might otherwise be tedious proceedings, and sometimes, the nightly menu was really the only place where she could exercise a free hand to do so. Little did the ninth President to dine at the palace under the Queen's reign suspect—for, while there would always be more presidents, there would only be but one Queen—as he enjoyed eating his quail, that someday (if she lived long enough, God willing), the Queen already planned on serving *his* successor a preposterous dish called either Gored Game Bills or Bill-less Gored Game Birds. She couldn't quite make up her mind yet on which.

Yes, it certainly was nice having them, in spite of all of that Irish stuff a few years back. And why, if The Other Man had won, then someday they would have all been subjected to some odious dish using tinned pineapples as a base. (The Master Chef, on the other hand, had secretly been hoping that The Other Other Man would change his mind and run. There were ever so many—no longer called for—recipes for newts that he would have liked to try out: Newt Stew, Boiled Newt Legs, Newt en Croute… the list of the ways in which one could cook that particular goose were seemingly endless.)

And the President, for his part, really *was* glad to be there. If one needed to run to a monarchy for a pre-holiday retreat from getting relentlessly bashed by Republicans back home, so be it: hold the fries and pass the tea. A boy from Arkansas could certainly do a lot worse.

. . .

Meanwhile, at the President's right elbow, Daisy had thus far been successful in heeding Herbert's old edict: her legs were crossed and her mouth remained shut. And, if this meant that Charles's evening was not turning out to be quite the rip-roaring good time that he had dreamt about, at least nobody had been offended. Yet.

As a matter of fact, Daisy was too busy listening to the voices in her own head, as she pushed her food around her plate with her fork, idly wondering if she was using the one that Sturgess had taught her to; too busy trying to figure out just how in heck life had managed to pick her up at Point A and deposit her at Point B; too worried about being caught out as being the fraud that she was, to be able to string two words together out loud. It was all she could do to keep up with who was who, never mind what was what. Why, the complicated structure of the workers at the Court alone was enough to give one mental pause.

Take the Yeomen of the Guard, for instance, the men in funny costumes who were lining the room. What was the difference between one of these guys and the Warders of the Tower? For their supposedly different Tudor uniforms looked remarkably the same to Daisy's untrained eye. Her head was beginning to spin. And what were the differences, in duties, between the Lord Chamberlain and the Air Marshall—and who really cared? She would never get this stuff straight.

"But... does it matter?" was what she would have liked to cry out. She was stopped, however, by her most recent recurring waking nightmare, the one in which she was walking through a forest and somebody drops a pin—not only does it make a sound loud enough for the entire world to hear, but it also manages, though being only one of those skinny straight pins that come back with your shirts from the dry cleaners, to drive a hole in her head like a stake. Vivid, maybe, but to each her own flirtation with psychosis. So, instead, as she continued to listen to the voices, she merely kept smiling and nodding idiotically at all that was being said around her—all the while hoping that she wasn't smiling about famine, or agreeing to go eat hippo in Australia.

In all of her readings about the R.F., she had never given the matter any serious thought, not along the lines of walking around in the other guy's shoes for a bit, Daisy realized, as she smiled idiotically at the British Prime Minister, who neglected to smile back. (*Oh, dear,* Daisy thought, *perhaps he* was *shouting up the table to Hillary something about a national health program for the poor.*) As she took in the scene around her—the plumes, helmets, the tiaras, swords— she had to ask herself: *Were any of these people for real? Was this the product of a modern country keeping pace with the rest of civilization? And,* the most burning question of all, as she returned Andrew's half-leer with an idiotic half-leer of her own, *why? Why any of it?* As the much-maligned daughter of Lear—the King, not the American TV producer—had quite rightly said: *What need you one?*

Why pay any attention at all to who was who? Daisy thought, raising a goblet of wine to her lips, thankful that the color was a match to her dress, so that when she undoubtedly spilled some wine on her person, nobody would be the wiser.

And was that Bonita over there, hiding out under that ridiculous Tudor costume and fraternizing with the Yeomen?

No, it couldn't be. Surely, it was a trick of the wine.

Oh, yeah, she suddenly remembered, seeing everybody around her at once, as if pulled by strings, swivel their heads to one side. She was supposed to be doing this left/right conversation trick. She turned her head decidedly to the left, gazing up into the eyes of the President of the United States. You'd think that somebody would have realized ahead of time just how short she was, and given her a cushion or a dictionary to sit on. But *nooo.* She felt positively Lilliputian. So she opted for overcompensation, injecting an extra dose of personality into her words. Coals? Newcastle? Ayup, but somebody had to do it.

"Great job you did with Ireland!" she gushed, raising an approving toast to the Leader of the Free World, thereby earning a glower from the Duke. "(Hic!) My parents (hic!) (hic!)," she hiccupped, "they *definitely* would have voted to reelect. And while they both might have (hic!) (hic!) reservations—oh, you know—

(hic!) Paula, (hic!) Monica and a couple of other minor details, they were uncategorically post-Nixon in their political mindset."

Mr. Clinton, whom Rachel would have deemed "such a handsome man," really did cut a fine figure in his tux (although Rachel's daughter would have amended that he needed to see Sturgess before making all fashion choices with regard to color in the future). He slouched, in a politically correct fashion, towards his dinner companion, the better to see the world from her perspective. "You know, Miss Sills, I do believe that you're right. We, as Americans, must take responsibility for the drinking problems that exist on our fine reservations…"

(?)

"…and that are going on, probably, even as we speak." Then, perhaps deciding that he had been serious for long enough, he allowed what was intended to be an evanescent smile to flash across his face, but then second-guessed himself, thus granting it the hang-time of a Michael Jordan hook shot or the aft play of a first-term election victory. "Still, it is always nice to feel that I have the support of our older citizens."

And Daisy, of course, failed to fill him in on the fact that both of her parents—staunch constituents though they might have been—were now dead.

What she couldn't quite bring herself to overlook, however, was his evident decline in fashion savvy.

"You know, you really should see Sturgess before you head for home."

"Excuse me?" came the polite response, accompanied by a cautiously puzzled frown. It wouldn't do to let on too heavily that he wasn't completely up on all the doings of every single M.P. that they had in that Parliament of theirs.

"About your wardrobe?" the newest advisor advised. "You see, I have this pet theory? Everybody in the world has one sense that they're better at than all of their others, and that they're better at than, oh, say, other people who are better at other senses." And here, she bent her head conspiratorially to whisper. "Personally, since I did vote for you, I'm hoping that with you it's vision, and not smell. Otherwise, we're all screwed." Then she straightened in her chair, rising to her full height and arranging the folds of her red gown around her, as she finished up in a normal voice. "Well, see, with Sturgess, it's a matter of taste. The man has just got *the* most impeccable taste. Any questions?"

Oh, my gosh! she thought, clamping a gloved hand over her own mouth. Had all of that just been said in a way in which... other people could actually hear it? Were the Voices beginning to come out now?

• • •

"... Yes, I do agree... But, don't you find, that it is a great difficulty at times, the reconciliation of a traditional nature with an environmentally conscious one? Why, just the other day, I was suggesting to Mother that we really should try out one of those artificial trees here, sort of set an example, start the kingdom moving in the right direction. Oh, of course I have heard the arguments all about how the trees are planted for that purpose. But isn't that a little bit like saying that baby seals are bred to be clubbed to death for fur, so that it makes no never mind? Why, then, you might as well make the leap and go the whole route and say that you can do the same thing with people... So, what do you think? Perhaps you and Bill might consider one of those lovely synthetic trees—perhaps one of those silver ones with the blue balls, thereby taking care of the old Hanukah quadrant as well, hmm?—for the White House next year...?"

Daisy was gazing raptly across the table at Charles who, catching her eye, gave a smile and raised his glass in salute, before continuing his most engrossing discussion with Mrs. Clinton.

A few place settings down from Charles, Jodie listened with intent, while Packey pitched an idea for a new sitcom that would involve two identical cousins who just happened to be gay, and which was tentatively to be titled *The Packey Dick Show*. And while Jodie's initial reaction seemed to be that the idea was maybe too derivative, a quick conversational insert by Packey concerning the critical and popular success of *The Brady Bunch* movies served as a reminder of just how lucrative derivative could be. America loved derivative. Why try something new when you could have more of the same? Why take the chance on the potentially more interesting, but risky, caramel turtle ice cream, when you could play it safe with vanilla? *The Packey Dick Show*, Packey was saying, would simply be yet more vanilla—of a slightly different flavor, of course.

To the left of Daisy, the Queen and the President were still quite busily telling one another how good it was to have the other there and how good it was to be there, respectively.

And to Daisy's right, just on the other side of the bulk of the Archbishop, Anne had drawn Andrew into a heated debate of whose childhood had been worse, to which Charles—leaving his new friend, Hillary, hanging in mid-sentence—decided to jump into feet first, just for the fun of it. Of course, when Edward tried to join in he was quickly shouted down. Why, all he had ever had to do was show up when the pictures were being taken.

Daisy listened to the conversations that were swirling all about her. Then she looked at Charles, seated across the table from her. *He* looked so relaxed, and getting more so every day. Why then did *she* feel like such a pretentious ass of late?

She was, of course, still reeling from The Exposure of The Bag. She was torn between her love of Charles, her wish to remain the dazzling woman that she had become, and her dawning realization that there was a lot more around here that was empty than just The Bag. Section off one more piece of her, and she'd be a Picasso.

Following the exemplary behavior of the Queen Mother, Daisy took another slug from the excellent wine, wiping the excess from the corner of her mouth, using the back of her hand. (Too bad the gloves went better with the fish dish.) Seeing heads swerving to the right, all the way down the table, as dessert was served, Daisy went with the conversational flow. And so, turning the full force of her own considerable attentions to the right and thus to the Archbishop, she formed a resolution to take matters into her own hands.

Daisy had frequently thought that it was a good thing that she didn't believe in heaven, a concept that she thought of as The Promising Lure of the Ultimate Carrot. This way, she figured, she could expend her abundant endowment of energy on simply "getting it right" this time.

Too bad then, that—lately, at least—she had been getting it all wrong. Although, perhaps, from her clinically theoretical standpoint, her own batting average was neither here nor there.

True, there were some people who claimed that if you only lived for and in the present, that it necessarily implied a selfish nature. But, the way she figured it, if she was ever going to do something for the poor of the world, then she was going to do it now or shut up about it, as opposed to relying on some other being to attend to things at some unspecified later date.

And, of course, The Promising Lure of the Ultimate Carrot flowed rather neatly into The Doctrine of the Barest Minimum.

It seemed to Daisy that there were an awful lot of people these days, who were just gliding through their lives, operating under the absurd notion that it was okay to spend seventy-two years playing video games and surfing the Internet, because something much more important was going to be happening to them in the future, and that the real fun show was going to start… in another life. She, on the other hand, preferred to believe that this life—for what it was worth—was all she was ever going to get. You couldn't spend *all* of your life waiting for something big to happen later. *Well, actually,* she thought, *you could. But what was the point?*

Sometimes it seemed as though, all around her, people were treating God as though He/She were the greatest enabler of all time, and that most people's personal relationship with what they all liked to refer to as "their" God (as though there could, quite possibly, be billions of different ones) was, if not the most fulfilling, then certainly the single most co-dependent relationship in their lives.

When you began life with the erroneous—to her—premise

that someone else had already died for your sins, there was not a whole lot of incentive left to do more than just scrape by. You kind of grew up with the misguided inkling that, surely, someone else would *always* have to pay, your own fare being the responsibility of some other—possibly nebulous—being.

"What *is* this 'heaven' stuff that you people are always going on about?" she could distinctly hear herself asking the Archbishop now, as she started the motor running and listened to the engine rev, gearing up towards pontificating like a pontiff. She reached for the dessert wine, hoping the nervous tremor in her hand were not as obvious to others.

Oh, God, she groaned inwardly, how much of what she thought that she had only thought had she actually said? For, now not only was she thinking these dreadful things, but she was actually saying them out loud.

• • •

No need to go into all of the gories; suffice to say that, from the crème brulee onwards, matters went from bad to worse, the Voices just popping out of Daisy right and left, like a popcorn air popper run amok, gone kompletely kaplooie; and that, by the time the Queen had led the after-dinner procession through the East Gallery, Silk Tapestry Room and Picture Gallery, and into the sitting-rooms beyond—there to enjoy coffee and after-dinner drinks, with the Queen's favorite bagpipers providing a subtle musical backdrop— Daisy had pretty much well been a success in saying something that she would later regret, something that she herself would think of as offensive, to everybody who was anybody and everybody who wasn't. She really was very equal-opportunity-minded, our girl.

The Royal Family—mercifully—exited first, thus freeing up the rest of their guests to draw the evening to a relatively early close. Which worked just as well for just about everybody, but especially for the poor Archbishop, who just might be in need of some medical attention.

Having overheard a conversation between a Miss Ruby Plyte-Twyse and a Ms. Hortense Spengle-Splyce, he had choked on his wine when he learned that Daisy Sills was to be Charles's next wife. This—the news, not the spewing up of Chateau Lafitte—made him regret, for all time, the haste of his predecessor in declaring that the Prince might marry again. Better that the previous A. of C. had bitten off his own tongue, the present A. of C. thought—as he bit stoically down on his own, thereby creating the minor medical emergency that would later require care—than to have ever uttered such words aloud.

And it was a pretty safe bet to make, that if Miss Ruby Plyte-Twyse, Ms. Hortense Spengle-Splyce, and the A. of C. all knew a thing, then, chances were that the Royal Family—if they did not know already—would very soon as well. And before long, so would the world. Daisy had finally opened up her own personal bag of tricks and, with The Bag part deux now gaping wide open, all kinds of pussies had popped out, soon to be scampering freely all over the palace.

Just about everybody else having been put to sleep, there was not much left but the crying, the last to go to bed being the cleanup staff whose bedrooms were in the east wing attic and who all thought that they either smelled something fishy or saw something that was not quite right.

Which was really neither here nor there either since, by this point, nobody's senses were working right anymore.

* * *

At every slumber party, at every summer camp, at every boarding school, there are always at least one or two dirty stay-ups that refuse to go to sleep when the last call is made for lights out. And, having already established that things at the palace were run pretty much like a Jewish Seder, there was really no reason why things here should be any different.

Long after the last maid had climbed the staircase to the attic, there was still one home fire burning, still one golden light that could be seen blazing, if one were to peer in at the right squint.

"I still canna' put my finger on what it is about that wig that excites me so. Maybe, it's just that, seein' as ye're always such a dominatrix, it makes for something' of a wee change, havin' ya looking' more like ya might be good at takin' orders. There's a certain air of servitude about—"

"Shut up and pass that cold quail... Starving. Criminal for people to have to stand around for hours and hours just watching other people eating. Like being a waiter, but with no action and no tips."

Sturgess inhaled deeply. Mm. Tonight she smelled like 100-percent cotton. So maybe it wasn't a smell that you could eat but, still, there was something reassuring about...

"There were quite a few glitches tonight, weren't there, Boni?"

"Mustn't talk with such a full mouth... Ooh!... So much for the wig... Mm... Maybe things have gone on long enough."

17

It was the morning after the night before, and the Queen was thinking that it was a pretty good thing that she wasn't one of these silly fools—like The Other One, for example—who bought into her own press. *The New York Times*—having stringers all over the world, of course—had quoted the President as saying that Her Majesty was "lovely" and "gracious" in every way. The Queen had survived the presidencies of nine Americans, and these were the two adjectives that they had all invariably and unimaginatively used. Was this a surprising coincidence to anyone? After all, they could hardly report that they had found the Monarch to be a colossal bitch, now, could they?

She patted her dogs, listening to her own personal bagpiper playing underneath her window. It really was a lucky thing for him that he seemed to be so impervious to the cold, for it was turning out to be quite a chilly December.

Fifteen minutes later, her private musical entertainment complete for another day, she summoned her personal Footman. She had written a message for Daisy, demanding that the younger woman join her for lunch. Cocktails in the Orleans Room at 12:30. Lunch in the Bow Room at 1:00 sharp. Be there. Aloha.

18

Elsewhere on the Principal Floor, diagonally across from the Queen's apartments, somebody else was stirring. The only problem was, that this person—the current resident of the Yellow Suite—was not feeling quite as chipper as the Queen.

Daisy groaned, clutching her head as though it might help matters. What had she done?

She had a vague recollection of not being able to keep her mouth closed but, outside of that, there was no way that she could say with absolute certainty just what exactly she had said, or to whom. So, just to be on the safe side, she formed the blanket assumption that she had offended everybody. The way she figured it, there was a good reason why the same phoneme was used for the word "dumb," and for the horror movie sound, as in "Dum ta dum dum... *Dum*!!!"

All of this theorizing was confirmed when—as she sat on the floor of the jasmine bathroom, her head hanging over the toilet—Footmen came, bearing notes on silver salvers. The Queen was demanding her presence later at lunch but, first, the Queen Mother wished for Daisy to join her for breakfast. So, she was being called on the carpet by all of the biggies. She was right: she had been insulting and she had been dumb and now she would probably be booted out on her keester, tossed like Dino the Dog on the *Flintstones*. She really had made a pathetic mess of things, and there was just no way that she was ever going to get out of this one.

"I should have just stayed in last night with a good book," she declared to the empty room at large.

Charles, of course, had also sent a note, a cheerful missive requesting her presence at dinner, but that didn't necessarily mean anything. He was always cheerfully oblivious these days.

And, anyway, where in the world was she going to find the stamina or the antacid necessary to complete all of the food consumption that others expected of her on this dark day?

19

"Believe it or not," the Queen Mother was saying, as she banged on the heel end of the bottle, finally managing to shoot a stream of Louisiana hot sauce across her plate of fried eggs. "Now what was I saying? Ah, yes. Believe it or not, people are *supposed* to enjoy parties. You must try not to beat yourself up so much, dear."

So far, except for having to watch another human being eating kippers, breakfast was not going as badly as Daisy had envisioned. So far, she hadn't had to actually eat anything, and speaking didn't appear to be required either.

"In fact, people are supposed to enjoy life. Oh, I know it's not considered the 'done' thing these days, for people to have a good time with drink anymore," the Q.M. went on, taking a healthy swig from her glass of tomato juice. "People all over the world go home at the end of the evening, congratulating themselves on their own scintillating sobriety, patting themselves on the backs for how little fun they had. But, take it from me: life is just the merest of blinks..." and here the Q.M. performed a demonstration, going slightly cross-eyed for a second, behind the cerulean netting of her hat's veil, "And then you die. Mind you, I do know from whence I speak. I did, after all, survive the Blitz. And *I* say, to borrow some words from that late young Beatle boy, 'whatever gets you through the night.'"

She paused for a long moment, considering, her face lost in the philosophical contemplation of some elusive and profound thought. "Ye-es, John always was the most intelligent, but it was

George that I never would have been able to kick out of bed for eating chips. And of course, Ringo was the most fun. As for Paul, well... one does not like to be nasty, but... what does he have to whine about all the time? After all, the man owns more of Scotland than we do."

The Q.M. retrieved her cane from where it had been leaning against a chair and, banging it resoundingly on the floor for emphasis, managed to bring her companion—who had been beginning to doze off in her chair—back to a blinking state of wakefulness.

"I think that you are absolutely right, Daisy," came the pronouncement. "I think that Paul should *just get over it.*" She helped herself to some more tomato juice. "Besides, dear, I think they all rather liked you."

• • •

Now, Daisy thought, closing the door gently on the breakfast room, *all I have to do is get through a measly old lunch, without getting myself beheaded, and I should be home free.*

20

For the very first time in her life, the Queen found herself nervously fingering the double row of pearls around her neck, as she waited in the Orleans Room for Daisy. Thankfully, the younger woman did not keep her waiting, and, after a brief discussion, in which it was stated that nobody would be requiring anything alcoholic for quite some time, they adjourned to the Bow Room. It was in this room that the Queen and Philip hosted four or five luncheons over the course of the year, each for six to eight lucky men and women. Compared to the Garden Parties, it was a unique way of bestowing recognition on people for jobs well done, sort of like the difference between the Last Supper grouping and the loaves and fishes mob scene. Although, somehow, neither metaphor seemed apt for Daisy's predicament, unless, of course, one were to point out that she was about to be fed, or that she had been—like Judas, perhaps—talking too much among the wrong circles.

Once inside the Bow Room, Daisy found herself squidgeeing around in her seat, involuntarily wincing as she waited for the axe to fall. She guessed that it was kind of nice for the Queen to want to feed her before killing her.

It came as some surprise then, when, upon raising her glass in Daisy's direction, the Queen toasted, "To you, my dear. Now, then, perhaps it is best that we get right down to business. Have you and Charles discussed a date yet?"

Had Daisy been in a physical state where she could have stood the consumption of food or beverage, it would be a safe bet to place that she would have spewed it all over the Monarch at this juncture. This day was not going at all as she had anticipated. Not only was the Queen not indicting her for her bad display of behavior, but she also actually seemed to be rather joyfully awaiting the announcement of Daisy's future intentions. And, somehow, the implications of it all was far more disturbing than if she had been set out on the cold curb with the empty milk bottles and yesterday's news. She found herself thrust into a blind panic.

"Where shall the wedding take place?" was the Queen's next item on the agenda. "Westminster? Hm? After all, it certainly cannot be St. Paul's. Charles has already 'been there' and 'done that' as you might so aptly put it."

One might think that Daisy would be still swimming about in a state of shock, perhaps in total awe of the situation that she found herself thrust into. But, one would think wrong. It is surprising how resilient one's personality can become when, all around you, people are losing their heads, and they all seemed to be blaming it on you; to a .monarch, assuming that you *would* marry the future King, and having the gall to presuppose that it should all be on the groom's family's terms.

"How about an intimate ceremony in a small synagogue?" Daisy found herself muttering under her breath.

"Excuse me, dear?"

"I merely said, 'How about a Primate-conducted teensy ceremony in Prague?'"

"Yes, you might have something there with the 'teensy' part. Perhaps it would not be in our best interests to make such a great big show of this one. It is refreshing to see you grasp, so early on in the game, how important it is that one's individual needs always play second fiddle to the institution. Still and all… Prague, dear? One is not quite sure what you mean by that. Perhaps you might elucidate…"

As talk of Eastern Europe and of Daisy's impending nuptials flowed on, Daisy found her mind irresistibly drawn to the Glass

Coach, which she had seen once upon a time while strolling through the Royal Mews.

Would she get to ride to her wedding in Prague in it? She wondered. Or was that to be one other thing that Charles had already 'been' and 'done'?

Only time would tell.

• • •

Thus, extraordinarily, Daisy began to learn that, not only was her life not in the state of ruins that she would have imagined based on the runaway behavior of her mouth at the State Banquet the evening before, but that the Queen Mother was—as always—right in her assessment of the situation: Daisy Sills was a hit.

21

Princess Anne was once again speaking to the voice through the closed bathroom door. "Yes, it went a lot better last night than I had thought it would, actually."

She smiled. She was thinking of how much she had indeed enjoyed her brief, yet energetic, dance with Daisy on the evening before. She did *so* hope that, one day, the younger woman might fulfill her heartfelt promise, accompanying the Princess on a Save the Children mission to Africa. She smiled at the prospect.

"Stomach still wonky, is it?" she shouted through the door now.

"Well, you know," cried the voice, pitifully, "I did eat that herring…"

"Yes, but that was *yesterday*." She paused, remembering something before speaking. "Haven't you heard of a thing called 'antacids'? I suggest that you take some and then *just get over it*."

And, with that, she grabbed her bag and trounced out, slamming the door behind her, more china crashing to the floor in her wake. She carried on, however, not having heard a thing.

She had places to go and good deeds to perform.

She would not wear pink anymore, but she *would* go to Africa.

• • •

In the early hours of the dawn, Pacqui had promised Packey that he would not make a fuss about any future escorting of horse women in the future, and that, if any name-changing ever needed to be done—for clarity's sake—he would gladly bite the bullet, thus becoming Rudolpho.

. . .

Mrs. B.P.M., over her morning tea, had resolved that, in future, she *would* find something interesting to say to someone at all of these dreary functions that her husband's career demanded that she attend. Either that, or she would *just get over it.*

. . .

Edward and Andrew decided that it was quite all right that neither of them would ever be King of England.

. . .

Hillary Clinton swore that she wasn't going to let a little thing like a few extra pounds trouble her anymore, as she boarded Air Force One, also in the wee hours of that morning. Daisy was right: women *could* rule the world, if they were only brave enough to throw out their bathroom scales and *just get over it.* There was certainly no law, Hillary thought, stating that *she* couldn't run next time.

Her husband, striding confidently and unsuspectingly at her side, didn't really have very much to get over himself, having already gotten over so much. But, perhaps, when he got back to the States, he might tell a few other people—Paula, all of the Republicans, Al, Buddy the Dog—to *just get over it*, and just see what they had to say about *that!*

. . .

Princess Margaret would have gotten over quite a lot of things, if she could only figure out where to start.

. . .

As for the Duke, Daisy's words had become a mantra for him, a rallying cry around which his future life was to be formed. As he repeated the words over and over to himself, while standing in front of his bathroom mirror, he resolved to throw out the new batch of poison that he had recently concocted for the dogs and the bagpiper, and to stay out of his wife's closet as best he could.

He couldn't wait to see Daisy again at dinner, he decided, grinning widely at his own image. Perhaps she had some more sage advice on how he could improve his personality.

. . .

In fact, the only people who weren't singing Daisy's praises were the Archbishop of Canterbury and the British Prime Minister, both of whom could smell an ill wind, boding nothing but disaster for the nation's future, and the Queen Mother and Jodie Foster, neither of whom had ever had anything at all to get over in the first place.

. . .

Daisy was finding that her adopted life had taken on a decidedly surreal quality and that, all of a sudden, *she* was doing the talking and everyone else was listening. The world was following her advice, the universe was singing the Daisy song, the British Empire was doing the Daisy shuffle. Although the image of La Belle Monde, all marching to Daisy's own personal drummer—for the very first time in her life—does kinda make ya think, huh?

Or, as the French Ambassador might have put it—or, perhaps, maybe it was Pepe Le Pew— *"Quelle idee horrible, non?"* (English translation: "There really is no accounting for people's tastes, is there?")

And, finally, the Yiddish: "So, nu? How long could such a crazy circus go on?"

22

"'Deck the halls with balls of..."'

It was 10:30 on Monday morning, and the Queen had already been hard at work for a full fifteen minutes. She was in her sitting room, the one with the serenely painted blue-green walls and curtains, surrounded by photos of family and friends, as she sat in her voluminous mahogany chair, slicing open the day's correspondence.

"'Tis the Queen's right to be... "' The Queen's voice broke off, mid-song, when the interruption came. "Yes?" she enquired, still in a jolly mood.

The Master of the Household would later concur with his wife that it was a good thing that Her Majesty was in her sitting room when the news came. For this meant that, not only was she probably already sitting, but that she was doing so in that huge chair which was rather difficult to hoist oneself out of, and also, there was that monstrous desk separating the two of them, making it impossible for her to reach him when she attempted to swat him with the racing column for being the messenger of bad tidings.

The President of the United States had the little red button, Batman had his utility belt, and the Queen of England had her boxes. From such common items are made the trappings and responsibilities of all great power. And, had Daisy in her ignorant innocence but known it, just as a working pen was mightier than an empty page, so a box was much more to be feared than The Bag.

Warnings of impending crisis often came to the Monarch in the form of highly confidential documents, delivered by the Master of the Household in a red box, portentously covered in black Moroccan leather. Scandals, and other fun gossip from abroad, might also be reported inside one of the boxes—for there were, of course, several different boxes, the theory being that one can never be too rich or too thin or have too many designer-approved ways in which to receive bad news. These boxes followed her everywhere, apprising her of delicate "situations."

In theory, then, the Queen might be in Borneo when a box—the ornamental equivalent of the other shoe dropping—happened to land on her desk, hunting her down with the juicy information that a distant cousin was having it off with one of the stable boys. Or, likewise, she might be seated in the relative comfort and safety of her own home, when the news finally reached her that, perhaps, her son's future bride was not all that she was cracked up to be.

Having read the distressing contents contained therein, she had allowed her glasses to fall so that they hung, suspended, on the chain around her neck. Oh, dear. Did this mean that she would have to spend the rest of her days, doomed to a constant waking existence of nostalgia for The Other One? How dreary.

In her later years, the Queen rarely entertained herself with fantasies of beheadings, but this was proving to be one of those times. Unfortunately—or, fortunately, depending on your perspective—as she studied the quaking Master of the Household, she realized that she hadn't a clue as to who best to start with.

Oh, double "oh dear," she thought. If the Houses of P. ever got wind of this, next year's Civil List would be reduced to zippo. As that now wretched American girl might say.

> *Deck the halls with balls of Daisy,*
> *Fa la la la la, la la la la.*
> *She will make the Monarch crazy…*

It really was enough to put One off One's kippers.

23

It was Tuesday morning, and the Prime Minister had come to call. This, in and of itself, was in no way out of the ordinary. Traditionally, every British Prime Minister—whether liked or, in some cases (MaGGIE) disliked by her—had a standing Tuesday morning meeting with the Queen, whenever she was in residence and Parliament was in session.

And oh boy, was she in residence that morning.

As the P.M. cooled his heels outside of the 1844 Room, he reflected upon the fact that this was to be no ordinary weekly audience. He would neither be giving the standard report on the state of the nation, nor would he be offering up little tidbits of gossip concerning the waywardness of M.P.s. Instead, he would be addressing his attentions to a discussion of The Crisis.

Finally granted admittance, the Prime Minister entered, striding purposely across the white-and-gold room, only to be stopped dead in his tracks by the Negress head clock. A rather ornately over-the-top timepiece, it utilized one eye for counting the hours, while the other marked off the minutes. The damned frightful thing always gave him the willies, as if he might somehow be personally responsible for Kenya. Eerie witch. Be that as it may…

He shook it off.

"We cannot have this," he pronounced magisterially, or at least as magisterially as a man with a large forelock—that no amount of hairspray could contain—could muster. Not even giving proper salutations to the Queen who had stood in half-profile waiting for him, still as a postage stamp, in the center of the room, he barreled on. "She must be stopped. The American simply must go."

The Queen of England turned fully forward, drawing herself up to military posture, as she returned the P.M.'s steely-eyed stare.

"I shall look into it," she said grimly.

Clearly, the shit had hit the fan.

. . .

So, obviously, Parliament knew all about Daisy. And, if one cruel stepsister knew about her, it could only be because of one reason: the press, being the other cruel stepsister, had told them. The two stepsisters having reared their ugly heads simultaneously, like two sea creatures—journalism and government being the Scylla and Charybdis of the modern world—one could say that the gloves were finally about to come off.

This, of course, left one burning question still loose out there in the world: who was the cruel stepmother?

Okay, so maybe two. (And the second one kind of has two parts, but the answer is the same, so you shouldn't quibble.)

Who had narced on Daisy? Who sent the message in A Box?

. . .

Ars longus; vita brevis.

Death even more *brevis.*

Get the message... Daisy?

24

Fleet Street had finally gotten ahold of Daisy.

And the resultant experience had left our girl feeling as though she had undergone an invasive procedure, quite possibly at the perfection-seeking hands of an anal-retentive proctologist.

The press was lying about Daisy on a regular basis now, the slander coming fast and furious, like spitballs when teacher's back is turned. This made it increasingly difficult not to give way to hating, and, it certainly was a Herculean expectation, to demand that our girl no longer deal in lies of her own.

• • •

"DOES THIS WOMAN HAVE WHAT IT TAKES TO TOPPLE THE MONARCHY?!" screamed the headlines on *People* magazine.

Beneath the banner was a photo of Daisy's startled face. Snapped as she ran from the press—the gates of Buckingham Palace separating her from them—the black iron bars made her look as though she were in prison, the bags under her eyes giving her that distinctly raccoon-ish air.

And, in the lower right hand corner of the cover, there was a smaller shot of Bonita, looking rather like a Medici in profile. The smaller banner whisperingly screamed: "The Mysterious Miss Chance: Governess to the Tidy Bowl Cleaner… OR… Procurer of Verboten Imports for a Prince???"

News of Daisy's exposure had obviously hit the other side of the Atlantic as well and, in a beautifully appointed and completely unused kitchen in Westport, Connecticut, a large blonde woman in a red and green holiday muumuu sat at the butcher block table—heavy elbows on table, pinky thoughtfully inserted into mouth, bulk precariously balanced on a too-narrow stool—as she pored over the contents of her favorite 'zine.

"I knew it, I knew it!" she cried, seeing the jailbird face gazing out at her from the cover.

"Knew what, dear?" came the perfunctory response from the breakfast nook, where Dr. Reichert sat, stirring his coffee as he read the newspaper. Well, he thought, you had to give her some form of encouragement. Sometimes.

"Daisy Silverman! Remember that girl that I said that I saw in Scotland? You remember the one—at the Queen's Garden Party? And I told you how she was really our cleaning lady but that she told me this out*landish* story about only being a double banger or something like that? And, anyway, that girl was with the Prince of Wales, and sure, I thought it was strange. I mean, what could little Daisy Silverman be doing with the future king? But then I remembered that she didn't work for that cleaning company that we use—what's their name again? Kwality Kleaning? It'll come to me. Anyway, I remembered that she didn't work for them anymore, and that nobody there could tell me where she'd gone when I tried to hunt her down, after that new girl that they sent over made such a mess with the toilets. Anyway, I got to thinking and, when I put two plus two together, I realized that the crazy girl that I saw in Scotland just *had* to be Daisy... and here it is! Right in *People* magazine! You see, it's true: I was right. Oh, I know you sometimes think I'm crazy myself, but—"

"Oh, give it a rest, dear," came the mutter from the beleaguered Dr. Reichert. Nope, on second thought, he realized, it never did do anybody any good to give the old girl any encouragement at all. Ever since their return from that Scotland trip, his wife had been seeing phantom cleaning ladies everywhere she looked. And it was beginning to drive *him* crazy.

More Prozac. He'd definitely have to up that Prozac dosage.

25

At the northeastern end of Hyde Park, near the Marble Arch and on the ancient site of Tiburon gallows, exists the Speaker's Corner. On this geographical spot, where those condemned were once allowed to freely speak their minds, grew a tradition in more modern times. On Sunday mornings, and on evenings during the summer months, basically any Tom, Dick, or Erika was allowed to mount the soapbox, so to speak, there to air their personal views on just about anything to anybody who might care to pay them heed. The events in London, of late, causing some people to feel even more opinionated than usual, this public pontificating was now taking place on a weekday, even though the city happened to be in the midst of its winter season.

Oil and water; Nancy and Raisa; monarchy and democracy. Well, if you were going to grant people the basic democratic right to free speech, then you were going to have to expect a little insurrection every now and again.

The topic open for discussion would appear to be the Future King of England's engagement to a commoner, a foreigner, a Jew, and a cleaning lady—all rolled into one.

Erika Swythe was speaking now, but that was nothing new. Erika Swythe had been addressing the topic, heartily, for some two hours now.

"Now, then, the ways I understands it, is that this Archbishop character says that this is all hunky dory. And it's a fine thing to say that wot people be doin' behin' closed doors is their own business, but that only holds true if wot they're doin' isn't everyone else's business. If you take my meaning. Why, just the other day, I tol' my son, Bernie, I says: 'Bernie, don't you dare put your filthy drawers out on the line without puttin' some soap on 'em first, or I'll whack you with my fist.' Those were my exact words, yes, they were. And he did, too. If you ask me, the whole world would be a much better place if corporals were punished. And that goes double for some o' them wot think they're better'n the rest o' us. If they had to bend over and take it every now and again like we do, well, you can bet they'd think twice first, they would. You'd better believe it…"

26

The Queen's own private dick, who operated under the title of Chief of Security, wasn't having a very good afternoon. He quaked before his boss, as she stood there, holding the damning sheets with both hands.

"You were responsible for vetting Ms. Sills—or, perhaps One should say Miss Silverman? The toilet bowl cleaner?— HOW COULD YOU NOT HAVE KNOWN? Was there not any information on her passport—like her NAME, for instance—that might have tipped the hand? The report of your initial investigation stated nothing about the fact that she is JEWISH. Was your snooping so lackadaisical that it failed to turn up this rather salient tidbit of information?"

"Actually, it... it did, Ma'am."

"It WHAT?"

"The information was there."

"It was there and you failed to mention it? Why?"

The Chief of Security cleared his throat nervously, coughing into a fist that was clenched tightly enough to strangle a plover.

"It, er, didn't, er, seem worth mentioning at the time."

"My son, Heir to the Throne, has been escorting this... this... *woman* all over the Kingdom, with the intent of marrying her, and you didn't think it was worth mentioning to Us that she just happened to be of the Jewish faith, or that her chosen field of economic endeavor just happened to include PLUNGING HER ARM IN

AND SCRUBBING UNDER THE RIM OF TOILET BOWLS?"

The Chief of Security squirmed. "But she seemed like such a nice girl, Ma'am. And, you know yourself, the Prince hasn't looked so happy in years. If ever, come to think of it. And, besides, Ma'am," he added hastily, "it wasn't as though I'd found out that she was an axe murderess or anything drastic like that. Now that, you can be certain, I definitely would have reported." The Chief of Security thrust back his shoulders, pretending an indignant response to the perceived offense to his dignity that even he could not quite convince himself that he felt.

This was the worst day in the history of Palace Security since that scandal in the early '80s, when those idiots had fallen asleep at the switch, allowing that nut Michael Fagan free entrée into the Queen's boudoir, compounding their colossal boner by refusing to respond promptly when summoned by their Monarch for assistance in the removal of the intruder. Why, they'd all but turned down Her Majesty's sheets for the man. Surprisingly, the Queen had taken that entire episode quite well. Considering.

Her reaction to this, on the other hand, was much stronger— not to say, angrier, in a very Henry VIII sort of way. And the entire matter was being laid at his feet.

"Not an axe murderess? Oh, my, We *are* grateful," his boss was saying now.

The Chief of Security breathed a sigh of relief. Perhaps this wasn't going to be so bad after all.

"We must content Ourselves with THAT, must We? Not an AXE MURDERESS? The next thing One knows, there will be strange men IN OUR BED AGAIN!"

The injustice of it all! he thought to himself, as he shifted his bulk from one bunioned foot to the other.

His mother was right: he should have become a bobby instead. Might as well serve the common good. For all of the gratitude he was getting around here.

27

If the episode involving Fleet Street had shared similar characteristics with an unpleasantly thorough rectal exam, the ensuing encounter with The Firm was fast taking on the flavor of the Inquisition. They were once again all back in the Queen's Royal Closet, only this time, there wasn't any banquet awaiting any of them—unless, of course, you consider Sizzled Daisy to be a newfangled R.F. version of missionary stew. For, they had her submissively seated in a chair—albeit with comfy cushions—while they most politely took turns circling around her, like cannibals with good party manners. As she squidgeed around in her seat, Daisy realized that the balance of power had definitely shifted again.

"Did you really touch my son's person with those... cleaning lady's hands?" the Queen asked.

"You're a fine one to go around telling others how to act, when you yourself are no more than—" and here the Queen's little sister's cheeks filled up with air, like a balloon, while she strained to think up a scathing enough epithet to affix to her own accusation, "—no more than a product of imagination."

"I say, Aunt Margaret," Prince Andrew generously conceded, impressed, as he stood there with his hands in his pockets, "that was rather articulately put." Then he began to circle Daisy, thoughtfully, yet eager to ask the one question that had been burning in his mind for some time now, but which he had never had the chance to query her about before. For, while he had danced with Daisy before, had enjoyed ample opportunities for leering at her, he had never really felt that he'd had the right opening for asking his question. But now, thankfully, he could finally put it to her.

Bending down so that his face was level with hers, he asked his question with a patently admiring incredulity. "Did you really say that books on tape were the literary equivalent of the vibrator?"

Before he could achieve the fulfillment of an answer, however, his sister had to go and shove her big nose into things.

"Mummy, does this mean that I can't take Daisy to Africa with me?"

"Except for that one dance in Scotland, I never even got the chance to play with her," Edward added, petulantly, waging an internal debate on whether or not he should stalk off to phone Jodie to tell her that there was going to be a slight change in the script.

"What is *wrong* with you people?" Daisy cried in exasperation. She was having some trouble digesting the fact that while her own relationship with Charley lay shattered at her feet, the only thing that they seemed to be concerned with was their own petty problems.

"You people are like a bunch of caged animals," she continued. "Sometimes, I think that you spend too much time together, all cooped up in this place. In fact, I think that you all should *just get*—"

"DON'T YOU *DARE!*" roared the Duke, sighting along his extended arm with its accusatory finger, as though it were a fencing sword. "Don't even think about it! After all of the faith and trust I put into you... Now we shall probably have to all go back to watching Oprah."

"For goodness' sakes," Daisy objected, "don't do that. Most of you are already skinny enough as it is. Besides, when people watch those shows, they always end up feeling like they should change something, the only problem being that the things that they end up wanting to change are the wrong things. But you of all people should be able to appreciate how damaging it can be. A human being is not something to be molded like... like... oh!... like Jell-O and bananas!"

"Jell-O?" the Queen Mother asked, showing a sincerely caring interest. "What's that, dear?"

"Oh, Mother," her daughter—the Queen—cried, throwing up her arms in defeat. Circumstances had fast spun completely out of her control.

There was only one individual left in the room who had not as yet spoken. Approaching Daisy, he did so now.

Wearing an even more puzzled expression than his customary one, Charles, with the utmost of gentleness, took both of her hands into his own.

"Why, Daisy? Why did you lie about your name... your religion... your job? Why did you lie to *me*?"

She gave a tiny Max-like shrug of the shoulders—a gesture perfected from childhood years of watching the Grinch with her non-Jewish friends—and made an attempt at a winning half-smile.

"Because it seemed like a good idea at the time?" she wincingly responded, more as though she were asking than telling, really. "Besides, who could get a word in edgewise? I mean, I thought for sure that, with those ears and everything, you'd be a good listener. Turned out to be not much different than any other man. Given a wide enough opening, you just go on about yourselves forever. And I never really intended to lie; it was just that I coughed and you heard me wrong and by the time I went to fix it, it was too late. And you were the one who just automatically assumed that my father must have been some kind of homburg honcho, some kind of pharaoh of the fedoras or something. And I never lied about my religion, but the chain just got lost and besides, you never even asked. Sometimes, I honestly think that you people just think that everybody else thinks the way you do. And, as for my job... oh, yeah, right. Like I'm really going to go through life saying, 'Daisy Silverman, glad to know you. But, hey, don't shake the hand until I've told you where it's been.' I mean, come on! Give me some credit. And, anyway," she added, with a small sad sigh, finishing up on a listless note. Having peaked early, she'd plumb run out of steam. "Your life was always much more interesting than mine was."

"That does not answer the most important question!" The

Queen was attempting to wrest the control of events back again. "WHAT DO YOU INTEND TO DO ABOUT THIS?"

Daisy nearly wilted under the unforgiving glare of the Queen.

"CHARLES?" the Queen insisted, making it clear by the focusing of her attentions, that she had no longer any interest in the world in hearing anything Daisy might have to say about anything. Ever. "There are traditions, protocol, procedures to be followed. Attention must be paid… Of course, everything can probably still be fixed up, provided, that is, that she is willing to remain in the background, with her legs crossed and her mouth shut. NOT like…"

Triumph and disaster were both now very real concepts for Daisy. Having seen how she dealt with the one, it was anyone's guess how she would deal with the other.

Daisy Silverman bestowed one last wistfully longing look upon the face of the man whom she had come to adore.

Then she bolted.

28

Daisy was running through the palace again.

Only this time, she was fully conscious of the fact that she was running for her life.

How had she ever gotten herself into this mess in the first place?

If only she had been content to stay at home with her two hands wrapped safely around a good book, she thought to herself, instead of taking her chances with stupid lotto tickets. Herbert had always warned her that no good ever came from living off money that you didn't earn yourself. Unless, of course, your daddy gave it to you.

If only Charley really had been all ears, like he had promised. Okay, so maybe everybody wouldn't have lived happily ever after, with the first Archbishop/Rabbi ceremony for a Windsor ever taking place in Prague, but still, at least then everybody would have known where he or she had stood and could have acted like responsible adults accordingly. Yeah, right.

If only she had been genetically predisposed to be a seeing person, instead of a smelling person. If only the Queen had been possessed of any senses at all. If only...

Hey, wait a second here.

She pulled herself up short, looking at the thousands of images of Daisy through the doors of the Principal Corridor, as her reflection bounced back at her from out of the mirrors situated at the opposite ends of the hallway.

Was she beginning to go off on one of these co-dependent types of tangents, trying to pass herself off as a victim? Was she blaming any and all outside agents for her own circumstances? Was she, was her very life, becoming—heaven forfend—Oprah fodder?

She decided to take charge of her life and thus, began to run again. She sprinted towards the jasmine refuge of the Yellow Suite. She flew over the tiresome, tedious, infinite, endlessly ongoing red.

And as she flew, she found herself allowing for one last, teensy-tiny "if only" outward-agent responsibility type of question.

So, okay, even she knew all about her cruel stepsisters by now; how the press had exposed her; how Parliament had demanded her excisement, as though she were some sort of painful boil on the bum of the British Empire.

But who the *heck* was her cruel stepmother then? For it only stood to reason that there had to be one still lurking in there, somewhere in the woodpile. Who had tipped her hand, started the ball rolling, made it possible for the other two to really give it to her good?

Was it the nefarious Duke, him with all of his poisons? Or the Archbishop of Canterbury who, for God alone knew what reason, had failed to take to her in the way that others usually did? Could it be perhaps the Queen herself, Daisy wondered, her mind flashing on a memory of that gently uncompromising profile?

(It really was a good thing, that she didn't know about the Master of the Household's wife's little sis's burning need to rid herself of her virginity—*again*—back in August. Else, that might have set her off on a whole other string of "what ifs.")

Well, no matter, she finally shrugged. Very soon, she would be outta here.

29

Daisy had already begun packing, when Pacqui called.

"I told you so," were the very first words out of his mouth, after the palace switchboard had patched him through.

"Oh," she muttered in frustration, casting about for something equally searing to say. Somehow, "go put a sock in it" didn't seem sufficient to the occasion. And she really was at the end of her rope, otherwise she never would have spoken so witheringly to such a good friend, one who had really only ever held her best interests at heart.

"Why don't you just... ooh!... go to an embassy party or something!" she shouted. Then she slammed the phone into its cradle.

• • •

Bonita finally caught up with Daisy at Heathrow Airport.

"Lose something, dear?" she cried, tossing an object into the air, where it flew, shining over the heads of all of the others who were queuing to board the plane.

Daisy, dropping her carry-on and, relinquishing her place at the head of the line, leapt, snatching the luminously radiant thing out of the air just at the nick of time, right as the ephemerally shimmering object was about to make its exit, disappearing into the windy gap between the boarding tunnel and the terminal.

"What the heck...?" Daisy gazed, dumbfounded, at Rachel's Star of David, where it lay across her palm.

"Might need it later."

"Where did you...?"

"Where you're going."

"How did you...? You weren't even there today." Daisy's hand flew to her mouth. "Oh, my gosh... It was you! *You* turned me in. *You* snitched to the press. *You* sent the message in a box." Daisy stared at Bonita, her own eyes wide as double-latte saucers. When she spoke again, it was in a voice that was peculiarly reminiscent of Shecky Green. "*You're* my evil stepmother?"

"Only one you've got," said Bonita, who was ready to move on to another topic.

But Daisy was not yet ready to renounce her role as Inspector Javert. "*You* were the one who started them telling all of those lies about me—"

"No, Daisy, *I* was the one who finally told them the truth." Bonita was at long last throwing personal pronouns incautiously to the four winds.

"But why? I hadn't meant anybody any harm. And, besides, it wasn't as though I really did any of it on purpose."

To this, using the exact same words that had been passed down through the ages—from Eve to Medea to June Cleaver—coined for the all-purpose duty of verbally alibiing the compulsion to wipe baby's bottom or eat one's children or interfere with one's progeny's choice of prom date or otherwise engage in general meddling around in the growing child's affairs, Bonita responded, "Did it for your own good."

Daisy merely shook her head in childless mystification.

"Besides, somebody had to stop you. You'd gotten way out of control."

The public address system, overhead, announced last call for Daisy's flight.

Daisy looked at Bonita and thought about Charley.

Once upon a time, she had made a single pile of all of her

winnings. Now the time had come for her to risk it all on one last game of pitch-and-toss. Now it was time to return to her beginnings.

Daisy kissed Bonita on the cheek.

Then she hopped on the plane.

30

Meanwhile, back at the palace...

After years of dedicated service, Sturgess was finally giving his employer a piece of his mind. And, really, he only had his best interests at heart.

"Snap out of it, Sir. This is real life now, not a rehearsal! Ye canna sit on ye're thumbs for the rest of it, Sir, just a waitin' fer things ta happen ta ye. YE'RE NOT SOME BLOODY TWIG IN SOME BLOODY STREAM. Go after her, Charley!"

31

For the first time in a very long time, Daisy found herself giving thanks for the meal she was about to eat. And what food! Creamed chicken, six peas, four julienned carrots, and a square of plastic cake with pretentious delusions of chocolate that should have been embarrassed to even call itself by that noble name.

Still, it was a meal whose effect, in terms of lack of flavorful input and lack of conspicuous output, could be predicted with unerring accuracy. It would be both tasteless and constipation-provoking. There was something comforting about being back in the world, where causes could be depended upon to produce the expected effect. And was there actually an aroma coming off of that chicken? She whiffed. No, probably not. But, in her nose's mind's eye, she could distinctly smell the unique perfume of Kennedy Airport in her future, and the malodorous scents were downright intoxicating. The Nose was definitely back full force.

Safely buckled into her seat, on the Virgin Airways transatlantic flight back to New York, Daisy found herself once again among her Russian forebears.

But this time, rather than Fyodor, it was the more verbose Leo whose hands she was trusting herself to.

As she hefted the tome—which she had picked up on Charing Cross Road for an irresistible song thinking that, if all else failed, it would make one heck of a doorstopper someday—she began to idly turn the pages. She wondered, as she ate her pretend meal, what force had impelled her to select this book of all books. After all, she had read this one before. It wasn't as though the relentless march of history could be altered, could it? In capable Leo's world—where the course of things took on an Aristotelian flow, such that each successive event was at once surprising and inevitable—it wasn't likely that the expected ending was going to change, was it? Anna perhaps not throw herself under the train this time?

Highly doubtful.

But, before she knew what was happening to her, Daisy found herself turning the pages at a rapid rate, felt herself being sucked back into the fairy-tale world, a world in which a delicate foot might peek out from the bottom of a flowing gown, tapping out its impatience, a world where one might conceivably still be moved to dance the mazurka.

If only someone else were perceptive enough to ask.

32

Daisy was standing in the middle of Kennedy, hunting for an exit sign, when she felt the hand on her shoulder and heard the familiar voice.

"I doubt it, Daisy."

"What...?" She turned. "How did you...?"

"The Concorde, of course. But that is neither here nor there," Charles said, resisting the almost unconquerable urge to shoot his cuffs. Which was just as well, since he didn't really have a jacket to shoot them from. Following the advice of Sturgess, he was traveling incognito and thus, was clad in jeans, long-sleeved T-shirt—bearing the legend *Go, Metsies!*—and a backwards-turned baseball cap. It was rather cold without a jacket, but at least no one was bothering him.

He took her hands in both of his and, looking down, gazed fondly at her feet. Even among thousands of people, he'd have known those neon-pink-laced trainers anywhere.

"As I was saying," he said, "before I was so *rudely* interrupted, I highly doubt that my life was more interesting than yours; just different. This is, one would hope, an adequate response to a remark you passed earlier."

Then his playful smile vanished, his facial features assuming a more serious expression. He cocked The Ear in her direction. "I promise: I'll listen to your story now, Daisy."

• • •

"Ooh, I love this smell!" Daisy cried, her nose immersed in a bag of French fries.

They were sitting in the airport McDonald's a little while later.

"Here, let me try it," the Future King of England asked, holding out his hand for the bag and taking a whiff. "Nope, I cannot smell a thing." He tapped his own nose with his forefinger. "You know, considering the size of it, I hardly ever smell anything. But I can hear you, Daisy. And the sound is making me feel positively inebriated."

"I think I'll kidnap you," Daisy spoke with her mouth full. "Take you back to Danbury with me." She chomped away, merrily gazing into his eyes. "Oh my gosh!" she cried all of a sudden, French fry held aloft, mid-flight. "What about your boys? What about Gaston and Alonzo?"

He looked at her, puzzled for the moment. Then his brow cleared. "Ah, yes, you must mean Wills and Harry. Well, to tell you the truth, I think the move to Danbury might be too much for them." He paused, thoughtfully. "And, besides, Wills would make a much better King."

So that was that.

*   *   *

"Say, by the way, what will we be living on?" the Former Future King of England enquired, as he held open the door of the Connecticut Limousine station wagon for Daisy.

"Well, I've still got a few dollars left over from that paltry million or so that I won in another lifetime. Which should be fine for me, but for you will be kind of like trying to scrape by on Skid Row." She regarded his designer jeans fondly, if a trifle ruefully. Those things probably cost somebody a couple of hundred big ones. "Maybe one of us will have to get a job."

33

A few days later, in England, the Queen was delivering her annual Christmas message. Televised, the speech was traditionally more social than political.

"We look back upon this year with cement-mixer emotions..."

Christmastime at Windsor Castle was turning into a rather grim affair that year, the inhabitants all cast into a gloomy state of group depression. In fact, the whole of London appeared to be tired of itself, and even the Christmas Carol services, held at Trafalgar Square on evenings in December—great crowds gathering and singing beneath the giant tree that was presented each year by Norway—as well as elsewhere throughout the city, were not the rousing success that they usually were. Everybody's ho-ho, it would appear, had already hummed.

No point in beating a dead horse, the Monarch decided, opting to keep this year's message brief. One had to know when people were in no mood to be jollied and, besides, if one did not have anything nice to say...

"And in closing..." And, here, the Queen held aloft a seemingly simple milk carton, at the express suggestion of her newest best friend, the President of the United States. This, however, was no ordinary milk carton. For, on one side of it, rendered in blue and white, was a rather youthful picture of the Prince of Wales. The Queen dearly hoped that Bill's strategy would work.

"...if anybody has seen this man, please, please do not hesitate to phone the palace." The Queen paused, thoughtfully. "It is not so much a matter of wanting him back, per se, but we do sort of need him…"

Postscript

An Accident of Birth
Or
Its All Down the Drain, Part Duh

Cophetua sware a royal oath;
'This beggar maid shall be my Queen'

from *The Beggar Maid*
~ Alfred, Lord Tennyson

January

1

"I'm in the mood for love,
Simply because you're near me..."

Alfalfa had never sung it so well, but then, Alfalfa had never used a yarmulke to keep his cowlick under control either.

As Charles Silverman, nee Windsor, leaned over yet another toilet bowl—Daisy's Star of David depending down from the chain around his neck—he thought that perhaps American television wasn't as bad as he had previously thought. One could do far worse than to model one's love affair along the lines of Alfalfa and the beauteous Darla.

Charles had kept telling Daisy that he wanted to make himself useful, that all of his life he had been dying to know how the other half lived.

"Well, here's your golden opportunity," she had offered, turning over the reins to the cleaning bucket.

One week's passage of time then found the former Prince, the Former Future Defender of the Faith, emerging from Mrs. Reichert's toilet. In his left hand he carried the bucket. And on his right hand he wore a yellow rubber glove.

"Damn the Bottom Feeder," he muttered under his breath as he slammed the door, rather ungraciously, behind him. That little hoyden should have warned him that this Reichert lady was completely starkers. The woman had kept asking him if he was sexually involved with someone that she referred to as the "Double Banger," whatever the hell that meant.

Still and all, he figured, it was a funny old world and life could certainly be far worse. His ears twitched in delight. At least he had Daisy to go home to.

As he strolled down the street towards the waiting van, Charles whistled to himself, all the while thinking how Daisy had been right and how there was a certain Eastern-inspired religious quality to cleaning things, a kind of Zen and the Art of the Pristine Toilet Bowl. It was all so straightforward: you put a little elbow grease into it, and you came out the other end with a pleasant place to relieve one's bowels. Lovely, really. And not all that much different, when one thought about it, from running a small kingdom, neither in input nor output.

Now, if he could only get the Bottom Feeder off of his back, Charles Silverman would be all set, in Schaeffer City, as it were. The synagogue, after all, was the perfect ruse for a life to be lived incognito. And those jaunty little yarmulkes were just the ticket for camouflaging that nasty bald spot that had been growing in—or growing out—of late.

2

When Charley arrived home, later on that evening, Daisy was already in bed.

"I got a letter from Bonita today," she muttered, half asleep.

"Mm, what did she have to say?" he asked, nuzzling her neck.

"She's remaining in London. She and Sturgess are to be married in the spring."

"Mm... do you think we should go?"

"Are you crazy?" she laughed. Then she thought about it for a moment. "Well, I'll probably be pretty big by then. And if we were to sneak in and be real quiet about it... between that and your yarmulke and my size... Oh..." She yawned, rolling over. "We'll see."

Charles spooned behind her, gently caressing the slightly swollen abdomen. The Silverman Succession had been secured.

"You were wrong about one thing."

"What's that?"

"People can change."

"Turn out the light, Charley."

3

Once upon a time, in a not-very-faraway place, little Daisy Silverman's parents told her that it would be just as easy to fall in love with and marry a rich man as a poor one.

So, Nu? Do you think she listened?

Lauren Baratz-Logsted is the author of over 25 books for adults, teens and children, which have been published in 15 countries. She lives in Danbury, CT, with her husband, daughter and cat. You can read more about her life and work at **www.laurenbaratzlogsted.com** or follow her on Twitter **@LaurenBaratzL**.

THE SISTERS CLUB

Some families you are born into. Some you choose. And some choose you.

Four women have little in common other than where they live and the joyous complications of having sisters. Cindy waits for her own life to begin as she sees her sister going in and out of hospitals. Lise has made the boldest move of her life, even as her sister spends every day putting herself at risk to improve the lives of others. Diana is an ocean apart from her sister, but worries that her marriage is the relationship separated by the most distance. Sylvia has lost her twin sister to breast cancer, a disease that runs in the family, and fears that she will die without having ever really lived.

When Diana places an ad in the local newsletter, Cindy, Lise, and Sylvia show up thinking they are joining a book club, but what they discover is something far deeper and more profound than any of them ever imagined.

With wit, charm, and pathos, this mesmerizing tale of sisters, both born and built, enthralls on every page.

THE THIN PINK LINE: A JANE TAYLOR NOVEL

Jane Taylor is a slightly sociopathic Londoner who wants marriage and a baby in the worst way, and she's willing to go to over-the-top lengths to achieve her dream. When Jane thinks she's pregnant she tells everyone. When it turns out to be a false alarm, she assumes she'll just get pregnant, no one the wiser. But when that doesn't happen, well, of course she does what no one in her right mind would do: Jane decides to fake an entire pregnancy!

CROSSING THE LINE: A JANE TAYLOR NOVEL

In the madcap sequel to the international hit comedy THE THIN PINK LINE, London editor Jane Taylor is at it again, only this time, there's a baby involved. Having—SPOILER ALERT!—found a baby on a church doorstep at the end of the previous book, Jane is forced to come clean with all the people in her world when it turns out that the baby is a different skin color than everyone had expected Jane's baby to be. As Jane fights to keep the baby, battling Social Services and taking on anyone who seeks to get in her path, what kind of mother will Jane prove to be?

Only one thing's for certain: no matter how much kinder and gentler she is now, she is still and will always be crazy Jane.

THE BRO-MAGNET: A JOHNNY SMITH NOVEL

Poor Johnny Smith. At age 33, the house painter has been a best man a whopping eight times, when all he's ever really wanted is to be a groom. But despite being everyone's favorite dude, Johnny has yet to find The One. Or even anyone. So when he meets high-powered District Attorney Helen Troy, and falls for her hard, he follows the advice of family and friends. Since Helen seems to hate sports, Johnny pretends he does too. No more Jets. No more Mets. At least not in public. He redecorates his condo. He gets a cat. He takes up watching soap operas. Anything he thinks will earn him Helen, Johnny is willing to do. There's just one hitch: If he does finally win her heart, who will he be?

ISN'T IT BRO-MANTIC?: A JOHNNY SMITH NOVEL

What happens after Happily Ever After? That's what Johnny Smith is about to find out. Having wooed—and won!—the girl of his dreams in The Bro-Magnet, he is ready to take on married life. Finally, Johnny will be the groom. But right off the bat, during the honeymoon, things start to go wrong. And it only gets worse when the newlyweds return home to their new house in Connecticut. Different taste in pets, interior design, friends. Too much togetherness. Jealousy. Nothing is easy, given that neither Johnny nor his wife has ever even had a roommate since college. Can this couple, still so in love, share a home without driving each other crazy?

CPSIA information can be obtained at www.ICGtesting.com
Printed in the USA
LVOW12s1543110216

474713LV00007B/712/P